Hope Beyond All Hope:
New York Stories

Thomas Crockett

For information, please contact the author:
321 Dartmouth Road
San Mateo, CA 94402
wease54@gmail.com

ISBN-10: 069250625X
ISBN-13: 978-0692506257

*Dedicated to Ella and Joe, and all the people
who populated my world in New York*

TABLE OF CONTENTS

Introduction i

The Mystery of the Missing Leg 1

The Right Bus to Heaven 15

The Gang War Days 31

The Devil in my Pants 47

Joe Jack, in Search of Home 61

Friday Night Prowls 87

My Grandmother Got on the Train 103

Hope Beyond all Hope 119

The Dawning of a New Religion 143

Even Jesus Dies 163

Meeting with a Murderer 175

My Night with Doris 193

INTRODUCTION

Sometimes the line between art and reality is slim. In these stories, a collection of memoir and fiction writings, the line is even slimmer. Though not always factual in terms of dialogue and detail, the memoir stories contained here are, nonetheless, true. The same can be said for the fictional stories. That may sound contradictory since they are fictional stories. Nonetheless, they are shaped by something essential to my actual experiences, and in that sense, where they land and settle in my heart and brain, are as true as anything. In any case, these stories, taken as a whole, whether considered memoir or fiction, or—and this might be most accurate—a blend of the two, reflect the people and circumstances I remember growing up in the 1960s in New York, in a neighborhood on the dividing line between East New York, Brooklyn and Ozone Park, Queens.

Admittedly, I take the high road in these stories. I do not dig in the deep recesses for moral, psychological, and emotional clarity. To me, the world I come from—and I do not mean to simplify it—was poignantly funny. That's how I choose to view it now, and that's the mindset from which I wrote the stories. It was an amusing world, complete with colorful characters and personalities, in a culture that held few, if any, standards for behavior and achievement. To say there was much lacking in the development of one's mind— and one's eye towards the future—is to state the obvious.

And yet, when it's all said and done, I would not trade my experience for any other because it was a cultural phenomenon, and I am nothing but grateful for having lived it in the time and place that I did. I became, ironically, the person I am today because of that culture and its deficiencies. Because there were no music, writing, and acting lessons, I became a person drawn to those arts. Because there was little or no encouragement to read and appreciate literature, poetry and theater, I became a teacher in those very fields. Because there was nothing, in the way of opportunity, I created something through will and determination.

These stories aim to celebrate, not criticize, the world of my upbringing. I write with gratitude that I belonged to a culture, a family, a neighborhood, at a specific time and place. I wish to give voice to the voiceless people who populated it. I do not wish to—nor can I, even in my wildest dreams or imagination—elevate them to a heroic or mythic status. The opposite is true. I wish to honor their lack of status, the smallness of their lives, to say that even in that smallness, there was a great impact on those who received the communications and experiences.

In some stories, I use actual names; in others, I don't. I can't explain why I do or don't. I wrote on impulse and on the wings of creative license, and if I offended, it was not done with the intention to defame or degrade. I wrote with humor, affection and compassion. Therefore, the way I see it, it makes no difference what names I use, for there are no deep, hidden secrets, no skeletons in the closet. I pay homage to the dead and the living, in equal measure.

That is not to say the stories are without condemnation. It is there; I can't lie. The stories, to a degree, require it, though the writing tone is never vindictive or at least not intentionally so. This is, of course, a subjective area, I realize, and each reader will form his opinion based on moral and emotional experiences.

The stories mostly focus on a period between 1962 and 1969, though a few of them reach beyond that time. The stories are hardly new. They have been inside me all my life. In fact, the majority of them were included as anecdotes and vignettes in a novel I wrote many years ago. Written when I was much younger, the novel centered on characters and place, not plot lines. At the heart of the book were the people and their stories. Therefore, it made perfect sense to take the people and stories out of the novel and craft individual stories that can stand on their own. I believe they work better this way.

Several are Catholic school stories. Given that I attended Catholic schools for twelve years, the impressions from those experiences have remained indelible on my consciousness. The three stories, "The Right Bus to Heaven," "The Devil in My Pants," and "The Dawning of a New Religion" come close to being satirical pieces about my vulnerability—and subsequent struggle—upon being introduced to the magnitude of Catholicism, in all its fear-evoking glory. As exaggerated as the stories may seem, their emotional and imaginative truths are undeniable. Many of the stories—"Joe Jack, in Search of Home," "My Grandmother Got on the Train," "The Mystery of the Missing Leg," and "Hope Beyond all Hope"—have their basis in biographical sketches of people, namely family members (who are all deceased, by the way). These sketches, though painful, at times, in their revealing truths, honor the enduring beauty that is part of the human struggle, the history and timelessness of family blood, and life itself, in our continuous state of survival and release. A couple of neighborhood stories, "The Gang War Days" and "Friday Night Prowls" paint portraits of where and how I grew up. These are classic coming-of-age stories about hanging out in the streets, in search of early manhood, girls, and identity. The final three stories defy any classification. "Even Jesus Dies" is written from the point of view of a middle-aged woman. Though clearly a work of fiction, the story has its basis in something very real. The same can be said for "Meeting with a Murderer." The story has as its premise a middle-aged man returning to his New York neighborhood after many years of absence. It is the story of a murderer, a murder, and those who are afflicted by it. Again, though clearly fictional, it is based on an actual experience I vividly remember. The last story seems, admittedly, out of place. It is a hitchhiking story that takes place in the 1970s. Why I include it in this collection I'm not certain. It is, nonetheless, a memoir piece about my encounter with an outlaw woman named Doris, who gave me a ride one night in upstate New York. More than anything, it belongs in the category of biographical sketches, like many of the other stories.

Rather than arrange the stories by their classifications, I place them in an approximate time sequence, beginning with the earliest point of view, when I was eight years old in 1962. They, of course, do not need to be read sequentially, though some details in the later stories pre-suppose that earlier ones have already been read. Regardless of the order or the classifications, I hope these stories resonate in the hearts and consciousnesses of all who read them.

T. Crockett

THE MYSTERY OF THE MISSING LEG

Uncle Joey had one leg and half a mind, and each noon-time Wednesday he turned the corner on 75th Street, on his crutches, making like the Ancient Mariner, as one who had seen it, been there and done it, but the kids on the street hadn't seen it and been there and done it. They were flat out curious. They were stickballers, punchballers and Skelly gamers, and all they knew was that people had two legs, and when they saw Joey, thrusting his crutches forward on the sidewalk, they stopped their doings and yelled, "Hey, Tommy, your uncle with the one leg!" I wasn't proud. No one else's uncle had one leg. Some had been to jail or were drunks or hit their wives and kids or had dropped out of school before it was fashionable to do so, but they had two legs. And my uncle had one. That fact couldn't easily be dismissed. Lucky for Joey, the half part of his brain that was missing insulated him from a world he was better off not knowing. Like, for instance, the nature of kids. They followed Joey from the moment he turned the corner, all the way down the street, to the entrance of my gate, where inside it stood the front door that flashed 97-27, our address on 75th Street.

Joey smiled an unknowing smile, yet befitting for a one-legged Messiah. While the kids stood with mouth and eyes agape at the gate, I alone could follow him inside and see for myself what it was like to have an uncle with one leg. What the kids couldn't see, but I could, was the smile on Joey's face when he smelled my mother's peppered ham and eggs—his preferred dish on his weekly visit—frying with certainty in a pan, permeating the hallway and the

1

kitchen entrance. Or the chortle of boyish laughter escaping his lips, knowing his beloved Red Sox might be on the TV screen, if they happened to be playing the Yankees that day. Just the same, the kids on the street had no idea how hard it was having an uncle with one leg. It was up to me to find out the truth behind the nagging mystery:

Where was the missing leg?

It couldn't be true what my grandmother, Susie, one of Joey's sisters, told me: that he had been sitting in the backseat of his father's car, dangling his legs out the open window, when a truck passed close by in the next lane and knocked off one of his legs. Her story was suspicious for two reasons: First, she was born in 1899. She and her family were immigrants from Italy, having come over in 1905. They had to scrounge to find food, usually droppings of fruit and vegetables from train cargoes on the tracks in the lower east side of Manhattan. Where would their family have gotten a car? Besides, she didn't have a father, at least not one who was alive. He had been murdered by the Black Hand in Naples. And, second, just as suspicious, she had told me that story the day I was dangling my legs out the open window in the backseat of my father's '59 Hudson, while she sat beside me.

I heard a different, equally improbable, story from his brother Sal, who lived on the streets, homeless, most of his life, and visited each noontime Thursday, sitting on our stoop, drinking Italian red wine and eating leftover spinach and beans from a jar. He said a cop shot Joey's leg off; that Joey had been stealing morning newspapers for a long time, papers still freshly bundled and tied, in front of candy stores that weren't yet open.

"Why would he steal newspapers?" I inquired.

"To get results."

"What kind of results?"

"Gambling results: Horses, craps, numbers, you name it."

According to Sal, here's what happened: At six a.m. on a grey day in Brooklyn, in the year 1918, give or take a few years, Joey walked by Jerry's candy store on Fulton Street, the top of his coat covering his chin, a Lucky Strike hanging from his lips. Joey cocked his head to the right, and jerked it to the left, to see if the coast was clear. Somehow his dumb eyes hadn't seen the cop standing fifty feet away, behind him, tapping his fingers on a traffic light pole, watching the candy store, in particular, the way a mother hawk watches her nest. Joey, thinking he had scored yet another morning paper, chirped like a bird as he slipped the paper under his arm and walked in the direction opposite the cop.

"Hey," yelled the cop when he realized Joey was stupid enough to rob a paper in front of him. "Put that paper back."

"What paper?" said Joey, as he turned and held up his hands, revealing a right-off-the-press newspaper.

"The one you're holding, buster," said the cop.

Having failed to convince the cop with his half brain, Joey put his brawn to the test, running like the true bandit he was, leaping over hungry dogs and garbage pails, the paper flapping and tearing in his hands. The cop followed right on his heels, rumbling like a thoroughbred, beating himself on the side of his thigh with his policeman stick. He yelled "Stop" three times, and when Joey didn't obey, the cop did what he was paid by the citizens of New York City to do: he shot off Joey's leg.

Another of Joey's brothers, Sacco, told me not to believe anything Sal said because Sal made a habit of lying, stealing and cheating the system. "Here's a guy who was a draft dodger in World War I," he said during one of his noon-time Tuesday visits, ripping bread and dipping into a beef stew my mother made especially for him. "How do you trust someone like that?"

He told me Sal was a rotten American, to the core. While everyone else was enlisting to fight the Germans in 1917, Sal wanted nothing to do with war. He was such a lousy American, in fact, that he continued to put sauerkraut on his frankfurters, when it was common for everyone else to avoid sauerkraut and anything German. Sal didn't care. He knew he would be drafted if he didn't enlist, so he devised a scheme. One day he went to an Army recruitment center in South Brooklyn, along with everyone else, to enlist, even though he had no real interest in enlisting. But he had to make it seem like he really wanted to fight for his country.

Sal had a special talent. He possessed special powers in his lungs. He could swim and, according to legend, stay under water for an hour or more, by holding his breath. He was also able to wheeze and cough and make his lungs appear dysfunctional. When the military doctor gave him a physical, he held his breath the entire time, for more than twenty minutes. The doctor declared he had scarred lungs and was unfit for military service. Sal protested vehemently, grabbing the doctor, and saying, "I want to kill Germans, and if you prevent me from killing Germans, I'll kill you." Minutes later, the same doctor declared Sal mentally, as well as physically, unfit for the military. So while everyone else went off to fight the Germans, Sal stayed home, to—in his words—"watch the women." These very same women would apparently, when Sal was young, climb up the fire escape where he lived, only to be met by his mother wielding a broom, sweeping them away.

When he wasn't watching the women, Sacco said with disdain, Sal made a living throwing himself in front of construction sites, purposely getting injured so he could collect disability insurance from the companies who owned those sites.

"Forget what Sal told you," said Sacco. "If you want the true story about Joey's missing leg, you'll have to get it from me." Sacco told me Joey, as a young man, got venereal disease from a bad prostitute.

"What's the difference between a bad prostitute and a good prostitute?" I asked Sacco, not in the least trying to be facetious or clever. After all, I was eight years old.

"I can't tell you," he said, defiantly. "That's a conversation for a son and his mother, when you're of a certain age. It's not my business. I'm just your uncle."

Anyway, he told me that this venereal disease that Joey acquired eventually damaged his circulatory system. The doctor treating him said the situation had gotten so bad that Joey had to choose between his leg and his life. According to Sacco, Joey asked the doctor, "What happens if I choose my life instead of my leg?" Sacco, who claims to have been in the room when this conversation between Joey and the doctor took place, said the doctor just scratched his head and didn't respond to Joey, at which point Joey looked at Sacco beseechingly and gestured with his hands, as if to say, "Did I say something stupid?" Sacco said he leaned over and whispered to Joey, "Tell the doctor you choose your leg." And that's what he did. He chose to have his leg amputated.

Sal, of course, said Sacco was the liar, not him. "Just look at him," Sal said. "His face is all smashed in. Have you noticed?"

"Yeah, I've noticed."

"He fell in the street, as a kid, and you know what he did?"

"What?"

"Nothing."

"Nothing?"

"That's right. He just stayed there and let a car run over his face. That's why his mouth and lips and nose sit on the left side of his face. Have you ever noticed?"

"Yeah, I've noticed."

"So how you going to believe him about Joey getting venereal disease? It was my sister Maria who had the venereal disease."

"From a bad prostitute?"

"No, a bad soldier."

"And did she get her leg amputated?"

"She died, and this was long before Joey got shot by the cop and lost his leg."

Josie was yet another sister, and I had always thought she seemed the most sensible and clear headed in her family, the one least likely to hold a personal grudge against a sibling. Still, she disputed every story I'd heard about Joey's missing leg. She knew the truth, she said, but it was too horrible for my young ears. I persuaded her that I could handle the truth. I would soon turn nine years old.

"Oh, nine years old," she said. "I see. Yes, that makes a big difference."

She wanted me to know before she told the story that

5

she had never been prejudiced against black people, that she had always believed they had every right to equality and a peaceful life. But that was before they did what they did to Joey.

"It was the blacks," she said, seething with anger and tears, during one of her Monday noontime visits to our house, eating the cold cuts, bread and cole slaw my mother had laid out on a table, in anticipation of her arrival. "They did it."

"The blacks took Joey's leg?"

"Yes."

"Why would they do that?"

"Well, you know Joey only has half a brain, right?"

I assured her I was well aware of that fact.

She said he'd sometimes forget where he lived. He'd get off at the wrong subway station. She made it clear that in New York, in those days, you had to get off at the right subway station. One day, Joey wound up in Bedford Stuyvesant, wandering on Utica Avenue, in the heart of the ghetto, wondering where all the Italian bakeries were. Suddenly a group of black kids surrounded him.

"What are you doing here, wop?" One of them said to Joey. "You must be pretty stupid coming into our neighborhood."

Joey informed them he only had half a brain.

"And if you come here again," this black kid, presumably the leader, said, "You'll go home with half of your legs."

"They let him go?" I said to Josie.

"Yes, they let him go. That time."

"That time?"

"Yes, but not the next time."

"Why did he go back?"

"Well, if it was me or you, we wouldn't have gone back. Even Sacco and Sal, as dumb as they are, they wouldn't go back. But Joey had no sense; especially no sense of direction. Two weeks later, there he was standing on the same corner on Utica Avenue in Bedford Stuyvesant."

The group of black kids took it as an affront, she said. It challenged their manhood, their entire race, and that day

Joey lost his leg, just as they had promised.

"They took his leg? How?"

She said that was something she couldn't or wouldn't explain to me. She said I had to be eighteen years old, at the very least, before she'd give me the details of what the blacks did to take Joey's leg.

My grandmother said her sister Josie was an unreliable source of truth. She was the youngest in the family, and as the youngest, how could she possibly know anything? The truth was that the day Joey lost his leg—my grandmother kept to her story about a truck knocking it off—Josie was in a hospital, having a baby of her own, and it was common knowledge back then when a woman had a baby she sometimes confused reality and fantasy. My grandmother emphasized that her sister never learned to tell the truth after giving birth. Therefore, her story was even more unreliable and false than her brothers, and that was saying a lot, since Sacco and Sal were full of hot air. If you poked a hole in them, my grandmother would often say, they would deflate like balloons.

My mother, when she wasn't cooking noontime meals every day of the week for one of her uncles or aunts, was not one given to flight or fancy. She said she knew what really happened, and if I weren't so under the spell of the Troisi clan (my grandmother's family's surname), she would tell me the definitive truth.

"I'm not a Troisi; I'm a Ciampa," she said. "Ciampa's tell the truth."

"Well, if you're a Ciampa, then I'm a Ciampa," I said. "Therefore I must know the truth."

The story of Joey's missing leg started, she said, before Joey was even born. It was a story of poverty and ignorance, the story of the Troisi family, minus the not-yet-born Joey, taking a boat from Italy, living in the boat's steerage for three weeks, eating garlic and wood chips, before landing in Ellis Island three weeks later, only to learn that their father who was supposed to be there to meet them was no where to be seen. The government officials took them all by the scruffs of their dirty necks and sent them all back to Italy on the next boat. But they didn't get on the boat, according to my mother. They ran for their lives—Sal, Susie, Josie, Sacco and their mom—suitcases in tow and lived for a time in the streets, among the pigeons and the Irish. And that was the poverty and ignorance part, my mother said.

"What does any of that have to do with the missing leg?" I wanted to know.

"That was just bad medical care," she said. "Which is what you get when you come from poverty and ignorance."

She said it was the hospital's fault, the doctor, in particular. He had a Jewish name. He pulled Joey out of the womb the wrong way. He was supposed to come out head first, like most babies, but he came out leg first. The doctor pulled on the leg, and then he pulled some more, until he realized he was holding Joey's little left leg, but the rest of Joey was still in the womb. By the time the Jewish doctor got the rest of him out, Joey's head had been so twisted around that his brain was permanently damaged. And, that, according to my mother, was what happened to cause Joey to have one leg and half a mind.

Asking my older brothers didn't help either. My brother Davy, six years my senior, said Joey lost his leg in a bath-tub, taking a bath in water that was too hot. His ligaments and bones and skin melted. When his mother drained the water, his left leg dissolved in the water and went down the drain. Miraculously, his right leg was spared.

"Who told you that?" I asked, incredulously.

"Grandma," he said.

"What about the truck?"

"What truck?" he said.

My brother Bob, two years older, said Joey lost his leg in a washing machine. One of the kids in his neighborhood, of German origin, had dared him to stick his leg in it while the machine was spinning. Joey, with only half a brain, took on the challenge. He stood on the lid of a closed wash-ing machine and thrust his leg inside the moving one. His leg was chopped to pieces and swallowed up in no time.

"Who told you that?"

"Uncle Sal."

"But uncle Sal said Joey got his leg shot off by a cop."

"The cop shot his good leg, not the one that's missing."

"So when Joey stuck his leg in the washing machine he only had one leg?"

"No, first he got shot in the leg, but the doctor, with a Jewish last name, was able to take the bullet out without Joey suffering any damage. The washing machine incident came later."

I would have asked my father, but he wasn't around much, and even when he was I didn't talk to him. Why, I don't know. That's a different mystery; a different story that needs to be addressed in its own time and place. But this one is Joey's story.

Joey, with that half a mind of his, wasn't much help resolving the mystery. When I asked him what happened to his leg, he said, "What do you mean?"

"Your missing leg," I said.

"What missing leg?" he replied. He got defensive. "I have more legs than you, Tommy. You have two, but I have three."

"How so?" I was befuddled.

He held up his crutches and wanted to know if I could count. That's when I realized the missing part of his brain also insulated him from truth and reality. He was gifted, I suppose you could say.

"Three legs, Tommy. I have three. You only have two."

When I told Sal on a Thursday what Joey had said on a Wednesday, Sal said, "He would say that. When you're missing a leg and half your mind, you say things like that." When I told Sacco on a Tuesday what Sal said about Joey on a Thursday, Sacco said, "It's not like Sal had a full mind either. Just because he was a draft dodger doesn't mean he was smart. It just means he was a draft dodger." Josie didn't mince words. One Monday, she said of her brothers: "If you added up all their brains, you still wouldn't have a full brain." My grandmother didn't have to visit on Monday, Tuesday, Wednesday or Thursday. She lived in the upstairs flat. As always, she had the last word on her siblings. "Whatever brains they had were destroyed by either getting run over by cars, dodging the war, or having too many babies."

If there was anything more mysterious than Joey's missing leg it was that the Troisi family was never seen together. To my recollection, I never saw any two of them in the same room, let alone talking to each other. My mother explained that that's the way that family was: separate.

"But weren't they all squished together on a boat for three weeks?" Even there they were separate, she told me. I told her I didn't understand.

"They were born hating each other," she said. "When they ran from the government officials at Ellis Island, they were really running from each other, and they never stopped running." I still didn't understand.

How could people be born hating each other? Didn't you have to know the person first, and then you'd have good reasons to hate them later?

Joey was the exception in the family. He didn't hate anyone, and none of the others hated him. As Josie once explained, "How do you hate someone with one leg and half a mind?" Sal concurred. "I can't hate someone who doesn't have it as good as me." And this coming from someone who lived on the streets and depended on handouts! Sacco summed up all their feelings: "It would be indecent to hate Joey, just as much as it is very decent to hate the others."

When I told my mother I didn't hate my siblings (and I had, in addition to my older brothers, two younger brothers, plus a younger sister), my mother replied, "You're young still. Give it time."

At four o'clock on Wednesdays, Joey would leave our house, and the street kids would be waiting near the gate, as if they had never moved. In truth, they did move. While we were inside they played stickball, punchball, Skelly, Ringalevio and Mump Freeze, but they knew Joey's schedule as well as Joey and I did. Four o'clock sharp they were at the gate, and I knew what they wanted; what they demanded:

The truth about the missing leg.

"So what happened, Tommy? What really happened?" I couldn't tell them each and every version of what happened. I usually said, "That's something only a family can understand and discuss." They were never that disappointed because what came next was the highlight of their Wednesday afternoons, if not their entire lives: Joey's walk to the subway station, and his courageous flight up the twenty or so stairs to the token booth.

You had to be there to believe it, for it was very much a spectacle, equal to any Olympian feat. First there was the procession; the three block walk to the 77th Street station. The way the kids followed him, you would have thought Joey was the Pied Piper. It would start out with six or seven kids following, and then along the way kids would climb down fire escapes and run on to the sidewalk to join the throng. "It's the guy with one leg. Let's follow him." Jesus himself, if he visited our neighborhood, would have been hard pressed to get the kind of reception and attention Joey was receiving. And the best part was that Joey wasn't taken aback or offended, knowing that he was only popular because he had one leg. He came to expect the attention to his one leg. He gave the crowd what it wanted. As the kids whistled and cheered, Joey smiled. If in his half brain he possessed a characteristic such as pride, then this was his moment of pride. He walked like a man who was saying, "I have three legs. The rest of you have only two." And he would have been right thinking and feeling that way. We were the limited ones. His one leg and half a mind made him special in ways none of us could ever know.

I never climbed twenty steps on one leg and crutches. In my imagination, it seemed the most impossible thing to do. And that's what made Joey gifted, and all of us kids appreciated the feat. The crutches moved first. He'd plant the left, then the right, and then heave himself up, one step at a time. He kept his head down, his eyes on the steps, his breathing steady. He didn't rush. He couldn't. One bad move and he'd tumble backwards and probably kill himself. In all the years I watched him, though, he never missed a step. It was his moment to shine, and he never disappointed himself or the crowd of kids who cheered his every move. I always went ahead and stood at the top of the stairs. Some of the kids did this as well. Most stayed behind him. Each thrust of the crutches, each heave, each breath, brought genuine joy and laughter and bouts of clapping from his followers. Honest to goodness clapping, and, at that moment, I would feel proud to have an uncle with one leg and half a mind. The other kids had uncles so drunk they couldn't make it up the subway stairs with two legs, but Joey showed everyone what was possible in life. There's no other way to explain the phenomenon.

Each time, without exception, when he'd make it to the top of the stairs, he looked like a man who had discovered a new world. He'd stand there, breathing heavily, sweating, yet always smiling as he waved goodbye to the grateful kids below. And then he'd disappear, into the station, on his way home. At least that's what I always hoped, that he'd get off at the right station. I prayed he wouldn't accidentally get off in Bedford Stuyvesant again. He couldn't afford to lose the one leg he had left.

I would wait another week, till the following Wednesday, when he'd return for his scheduled visit, and the mystery of his missing leg would start again. And that got me, from time to time, thinking about other mysteries, such as: Why my father and I didn't talk. Why the Troisi family was never seen together. Why they were born hating each other. Why the kids in the street got their kicks chasing after Joey because he had one leg. How Joey could manage to be good spirited about having one leg. How he could climb the subway stairs, all twenty of them, and not fall or slip or curse under his breath. How Joey could take a train, with half a brain, and know how to get off at the right subway station. How, with one leg and half a brain, he could live by himself on the government money he received. Why I never saw him cry. Why he didn't scream and yell and say, Why me?

Joey continued his visits for at least ten more years. The reception and attention he received from the kids in the street waned, as, I suppose, was inevitable. They became teenagers and had other things on their minds besides people with one leg. Joey's spirit never waned, however. I could tell he was a little sad that he no longer had followers when he arrived and left, but his sadness could easily be appeased with a plate of peppered ham and eggs and a Red

Sox baseball game.

One Wednesday, when I was eighteen years old, he didn't come for his visit. My mother had been notified that he died. By that time his older brothers, Sal and Sacco, were gone as well. Only my grandmother, the oldest, and Josie, the youngest, remained. It was clear to my grandmother why she outlived her brothers.

She had worked for a living.

While I was sad about Joey's death, as I was when his brothers died, I was glad about one thing. There was no mystery about his death. He died in his sleep, from an apparent heart attack. That was the official report that no one —not my mother, my grandmother or my brothers—could deny.

As for his missing leg, I never found out definitively the truth. While the unknowing caused me much perplexity when I was young, I began to embrace the fantastic and varied stories as I grew older. I am glad now that the mystery of Joey's missing leg can still be called a mystery, because mystery feeds my ever-evolving imagination and the widened lens through which I see my life and the lives of my predecessors. The storytellers took their stories with them, to their graves, all of them, including finally my grandmother, her sister, Josie, at 102 years old, and mother. Only my brothers remain with their versions, but we don't talk about the mystery of the missing leg. In fact, we don't talk at all because we live in different time zones, and perhaps, because we have the Troisi blood running in our cursed veins. Why we have chosen to live separately is a mystery unto itself, a story that must be addressed in its own time and place, but, as I said before, this one is Joey's story, and it must remain so in closing.

I no longer live in New York. I haven't in over thirty years, but if there's one image I hold to as much as any other it is the sight of Joey turning the corner on 75th Street, walking with the aid of his crutches, being cheered and followed. Not many people can say they've experienced what he did, with such grace and good spirit, and not many people leave the world, and the people behind, with such mystery to ponder. Still, when I close my eyes and see him

13

standing on the top of the subway steps, with one leg and half a mind, waving and smiling, I no longer think of his missing leg. I just feel good.

THE RIGHT BUS TO HEAVEN

Sister Frances Carmela told the fifth grade class if we were good and free of sin a bus would pick us up on Judgment Day and take us right to heaven. From where I sat, exiled in the unholy corner, she appeared as a giant crow, flailing its wings above an uncertain sea. Up front sat sixty arched students, the boys with buzzcut hair, the girls with lolly-popped cheeks, their eyes, like mine, reflecting the nun's muddy black robe. A halo of words stenciled the chalkboard in white calligraphic paste:

Guard Well Thy Thoughts
For Thoughts Are Heard Above.

As Sister Carmela began walking the aisles, I signaled to Donna DeGregorio, another unholy hostage, sitting adjacent to me. As always, she didn't acknowledge me when I talked. Instead, she chewed her pencil with squirrel teeth, her small hand moving the eraser end adroitly.

"Do you pray?" I asked her.

She clamped her teeth on the pencil and closed her mouth, creating the illusion of a stick being driven through her lips. A primordial grunt escaped her throat, something akin to "Huh?" as her eyes swirled into a mix of vanilla fudge beneath the thick lenses she wore. As I repeated the question, she removed the pencil, allowing her tongue to slide out from between her lips like a thin slice of meat. Her clothing emitted a smell of pine-sol, and from her mouth came waves of Listerine and soap.

When Sister Carmela walked near us, with raised arms,

my eyes went black. She shuffled student-name cards and spoke of the 1963 World Series, Dodgers vs. Yankees, scheduled to begin later that day.

"Who would win?" she asked me, calling me by my first name, Thomas, proudly showing me the student-name card with my name on it. Every time she shuffled the cards and selected one, it seemed my card, my name, was chosen. I imagined she held sixty cards, each with the name "Thomas" written on it.

My balled hands and feet turned cold, and even the spittle in my mouth formed like ice. Head down, I unclenched a knuckle-white hand to wipe the chill from my face. While my nerves jumped and jittered, I managed to say the word "Dodgers." That warmed her Brooklyn heart, she said, shuffling the cards faster, only inches from my face, her bleached hands smelling of Mercurochrome. I sniffed the residue of blood inside my nose, tasted it on my lips, and saw in the periphery Donna's pencil disappearing into her mouth.

Sister Carmela temporarily put her student-name cards away in a pocket of her robe, and with it her regard for something as trivial as baseball. She walked to the front of the room, where she lifted her yardstick from her desk, and, while tapping her open hand with it, spoke of something more relevant and revered for a nun teaching students in 1963. She spoke of Life and Death, of sin and redemption, and other delicacies embodied in the Baltimore Catechism, Lesson 30. She asked if someone could tell her the meaning of Contrition, and how many kinds there were. She laid her yardstick on her desk, and once again removed the student-name cards from her robe pocket. She shuffled and lifted a card. She smiled a hateful smile and said, "Thomas." Her voice, sounding my name yet again, pinpricked the skin inside my ears. I sat mute. Others around me dropped their heads. They were lucky, and they knew it. Their names never got called. Only mine. Even in my dreams I would see her shuffling the cards, holding one aloft, saying my name, smiling as she did.

I, too, like the others dropped my head, hoping it was just another bad dream—and like a dream it would go away when I lifted my head and opened my eyes. But it was not a dream. I felt the yardstick under my chin and the heat of her hostility towards me, as she stood gigantic and crow-like above me.

"I'm talking to you, young man," she said. I opened my eyes enough to see her hand squeezing the yardstick, her fingers turning the color of candy canes. I noticed, as well, the crucifixion hung by beads from her waist; an encapsulated view of Christ's nailed feet and thorn-bloodied head, his eyes dying again and again.

"Answer the question I asked," she commanded.

I watched the stick in her hand, the front end snapping like a snake's head, speaking curtly to my knuckles, mimicking the nun's voice that held it.

There you are, in hell, your tongue a flame of straw, tasting of worms that feed on your ears and nest in your eyes...

"I'm talking to you, young man. Did you read Lesson 30?"

Her robe smelled of chalk and dust. I sniffed. The silence of the room was filled with my breath. Again I dropped my head, in shame, in fear, in embarrassment.

"When I ask you a question, I expect you to look at me."

Her stick tapped the underside of my chin, continuing to speak snake-like, personifying Sister Carmela in all her serpent glory.

...while you lay in wicked laughter, knowing you can do nothing else because you were a fool to have chosen wrongly...

"I ask you again—for the final time!—did you read Lesson 30?"

"Yes, I read it," I said, lying, in a voice that squeaked from my throat. "But I don't remember it."

She lifted my chin with the stick and forced me to look at her. Her eyes were baby chick black, and in the folds of her face, above a stitched upper lip, grew two silver-grey hairs, rooted like thorns.

"You don't remember it? Perhaps you didn't read it at all, and would like to stand and read it to the class now."

I felt the needle-sharp prick of sixty sets of eyes upon

me, all with snake eyes, all with voices.

...laughing a wicked-devil laugh, as you pick worms from the corners of your eyes, and scrape them from between your toes with the sharp edge of a burning rod.

"Bring your Catechism up to the front of the room and read for the class."

"I can't," I said, closing my eyes, imagining the hot lick of the stick on my knuckles.

"You can't?"

The stick snapped, like an attacking snakehead, slapping my desk, burning my throat and eyes in a fire of fear.

"Why can't you?"

This time the stick stung my knuckles. I felt the breath of hell coming from her mouth. "I don't know...I just can't."

"I bet I know why you can't get up."

The stick relaxed on top of my hand, as she teased me with affection, stroking a few hairs from my eyes, which had broken their capsules in a spasm of tears. She bent down low, and, in an act of compassion, whispered to my ear, out of earshot of the other students.

"Is it because you wet yourself again? Is that why you can't get up?"

I nodded, dropping my head further into my chest.

I must explain the unholy corner. It was the area in the back of the classroom where Sister Carmela sat the sinners, who had either uncontrollable bodily functions or uncontrollable behavioral functions. Donna DeGregorio and I belonged to the former group. A few days after the previous episode, Donna removed her reticence, and, at least for a day, she and I became soul mates.

Once again, this time, shortly after lunch, before class started, I asked her if she prayed. The poor girl must have eaten all her pencils. She was fast at work, chewing the flesh around her fingernails. When she heard my question, she stopped and looked at me with those vanilla-fudge eyes, and said, "Why do you keep asking me if I pray?" Don't you pray?"

Did I pray? I could have told her how many syllables were in each line of each prayer.

"I asked you first," I said.

"So?"

"So? What do you mean, so?

"So, I asked you second."

My eyes became awash in a sea of blue and white uniforms, a swirling mix of boys and girls sitting straight as blocks as Sister Carmela rapped her yardstick against the dark chalkboard. "Attention," she shouted.

Father Blaney's voice came over the intercom, as it did every day. First he cleared his throat and coughed, and, in his Irish brogue, thick as fog, wished us a good afternoon. He spoke for minutes about how each student had a responsibility to his parish and school, St. Sylvester, for caring, protecting, and teaching us. Then he came right to the point and said it was mandatory for each student to sell five books of raffle tickets for an upcoming event.

As soon as Father Blaney's voice left the intercom, I quickly turned to Donna. I knew by talking I was risking my life and my after-life, with the possibility of eternal damnation if I got caught, but my need superseded the potential danger.

"Well, do you pray or not?"

She adjusted her lenses, sat up straight, and coughed. "Of course I pray," she said.

"You do?"

"I already said *of course.*"

"But why?"

"Because I'm sick, and I want to get better."

We stood for the "Pledge of Allegiance," yet my heart raced so fast I couldn't speak along with the rest of the class. I clung to Donna's words as I stared at her face. Even the fat lenses she wore could not conceal the torment of her physical malady. As she attempted to pledge allegiance to the flag, she kept stopping because the more she opened her mouth to speak, the more likely she was to begin burping and then throwing up her morning breakfast. This was the foul, incessant habit that doomed her to the unholy corner, adjacent to me, the incessant seat wetter.

When we sat back down, she scowled at me and said, "Why do you keep staring at me?"

"I'm sorry."

"You should be. It's not polite."

"I know. I said I'm sorry."

"Okay, I forgive you."

Specks of sunlight pooled along the walls like a constellation of spherical stars. Sister Carmela moved swiftly to pull the shades. The moment she turned away, I once again tested Donna's indomitable stubbornness.

"I pray all the time," I said.

She rolled her eyes up into her head and pursed her cracked lips.

"Of course you do."

"Why would you say that?"

"You want to get better, don't you?"

"But it doesn't seem to work."

"It takes time," she said.

I wanted to kiss her cheek, but who knew what kind of revulsion that would stir in her stomach. Sister Carmela asked the class to open our Catechisms to Lesson 33, and I complied along with everyone else, though I had a greater urgency to discover more in my conversation with Donna. When Sister Carmela asked a girl up front to explain the meaning of indulgences, I continued to interrogate Donna. "Are you getting any better because of praying?"

She held her catechism over her face, to shield herself from the watchful eye of Sister Carmela. "I'm not better yet, but someday, maybe, I'll be." I leaned across, towards her so far, I nearly fell from my seat.

"What makes you think you'll get better?"

"God keeps people waiting sometime to test their beliefs. If I give up on Him, He'll give up on me."

"Who told you that?"

"Sister Carmela."

"What else did she tell you?"

"That we should be grateful when God sends us sorrow; that if we're pleased with God, He'll be pleased with us."

"Is that all?"

"She said you and I are different and must pray extra hard."

"How often?"

"Very often."

"Will God ever forgive us?"

"Yes."

"When?"

"He will decide."

The girl up front knew how to get to heaven. She answered Catechism questions as if the grace of her soul depended on it. She explained the meaning of indulgences, how many kinds there were, and what we had to do to gain them for ourselves. She kept smacking her lips the whole time, and Sister Carmela loved every moment, smiling like a grandmother. Everyone else up front appeared to be smiling as well, as if they had no greater worry than what they were going to wear, and what lunch to pack, on their bus ride to heaven. They already had their tickets; even Joseph Corollo and Louis Petrosini. Joseph always stuck pencils up girls' dresses, and Louis tried to make out with them in the coat room, yet Sister Carmela didn't seat them in the unholy corner.

I looked at Donna. Her open mouth appeared to be swallowing the Catechism in her hands.

"You know," I said, "I bet the others in the class don't have to pray like we do."

The moment she dropped the book from her face, I realized I wasn't speaking with a child. Those eyes, blind as they were, behind the bifocals, had seen a hundred years and reflected the soul of someone who had lived and learned by life's hard knocks.

"They don't have to," she said. "They're not sick."

"Isn't that a bitch."

The voice came from behind us. Donna and I turned to observe Johnny Germanso, another member of the unholy corner. He scratched a scab from his forearm, rolled it into a microscopic ball, and flicked it toward the window.

"She can't keep you from riding the bus," he said, his eyes askance, continuing to navigate his arms with a fingernail.

"She can't?" I said.

I turned back around and saw the holy rollers up front raise their supplicant eyes to the nun who gyrated her hands as she spoke of Sacraments and Holy Orders. She had told me to stay away from Johnny, who was a year older and had been left back a grade.

"She's not the bus driver," he said. "Just a ticket agent."

Again, I turned to him and watched as he picked another scab, until a droplet of blood appeared. He sucked the blood from his arm.

Sister Carmela rapped her yardstick against the chalkboard, calling attention to Lesson 36, question 205: What are the Sacramentals? She told everyone to read the answer with her. As I buried my face in my book, listening to the chanting students in the class, I heard Johnny's voice whisper from behind me.

"Meet me after school. I'll help you."

I looked across at Donna. Clearly, she wanted nothing more to do with either Johnny or me. She stared unblinkingly at her book and began chewing a pencil which had appeared, as if on cue. It had already been scissored by her teeth.

Shielding my face with my book, I twisted my neck and whispered behind me.

"Where?"

"The Grotto."

"The Grotto?"

"That's what I said."

I listened to the maddening tick of the classroom clock, and to the boy behind me who cleared his throat and coughed and wiped his runny nose. Earlier that day, in the morning, I sat in my seat, soaked to the bone. I did what I did nearly every day for two or three years. During lunch, I walked home, where my mother had a change of clothes waiting for me. She knew well the expectations and patterns of my school mornings, ending invariably with my wetting myself. Why she never went to school and talked to the nuns about my problem, to seek out a solution, is a mystery better left alone. She dealt with the problem the best way she knew how; making sure I was dry in the afternoon. I didn't want to wet myself. It just happened. I wouldn't have been able to explain if someone had asked me the cause. (Even today I don't believe I can.) All I knew is that when it happened there was enough urine flowing to flood the streets of Galilee and bring a curse from the King of Virtue, or, even worse, from Sister Carmela, who made it clear my actions held no sacred authorization.

God doesn't like little boys who wet their pants in school.

I turned completely around, to face Johnny.

"I'll be there," I said.

Enclosed by a spiked iron gate on a corner lot of the church grounds, the Grotto, from a distance, appeared as a cave, a hallowed out area of staggered rock, where ancient men might have carved hieroglyphics under a yellow moon. What distinguished it from the primitive was its occupants, the Blessed Mary statue, ensconced in a flower bed of roses, and an altar, clothed in a white tapestry, over which hung a white-marbled crucifixion. No one, particularly sinful school kids, was allowed on the grounds unless it was for a special service commemorating Mary. Rules, however, meant little to Johnny.

Shortly after the bell rang, ending school, we huddled beneath the Mary statue, shielded from the street by lush trees heavy with leaves. Hordes of schoolchildren passed on the street, oblivious that two of their peers violated a holy space. Johnny sat cross-legged on the asphalt beneath the Mary statue, his eyes deep brown as the earth and eleven years wise, flashing beneath a head of dark, anarchic curls that obeyed no brush or comb. He told me his plan, giving it a name:

How to get to heaven.

It stood clear to him that Sister Carmela would never forgive us our sins. If we wanted forgiveness, we would have to seek it in a more sacred place; a place where priests and nuns and omnipotent creators did not tread. He suggested we use our imaginations and pretend to be God and the Blessed Mary. We could forgive each other our sins and ride the bus to heaven together.

"That's the plan," he said.

The scene recalled for me the Garden of Eden. Here was Johnny, the serpent, telling me I didn't need priests, nuns or omnipotent creators. We could, with the will of our imaginations, decide for ourselves what was right and wrong. I was about to eat fruit from the forbidden tree, the tree of knowledge, of good and evil, and I would suffer worse than I had already suffered. It was a crazy plan, for sure, and if I had sense I would have run into the safety of the church, knelt at the altar beneath the crucifixion and asked to be forgiven, the traditional way, through prayer and sacrifice, with the aid of priests, nuns and omnipotent creators. I should have trusted my faith to Sister Carmela and God, not betrayed them with the will of my imagination.

Like Adam, I was too weak to resist the serpent's temptation. Johnny knew something, and I knew nothing. I would only learn by taking his bait and eating from this tree of knowledge. Yes, the Garden of Eden was about to be played out all over again, only this time at the St. Sylvester Grotto, in Brooklyn, New York. The fall of man was now embodied in a ten-year-old boy named Thomas.

"I'll be God, and you can be Mary," he said. "I'll forgive you first."

The Blessed Mary's mouth drew inward. Beneath her foot she killed the serpent snake, an image fixed and forever; the serpent spitting gouts of blood from between its teeth, its eyes a purple haze of repentance. In her eyes, the grassy knoll of heaven grew.

Johnny rose and stood upon the altar, one hand held in a perpendicular position, pretending to be God. In his school uniform—blue slacks, white short sleeve shirt and attachable crossbow tie—he looked more like a cartoon caricature, someone irreverent and satirical from "Mad" magazine. I restrained a laugh. He was eleven years old. I assumed he knew what he was doing.

"I am your God," he said, in a low, Biblical pitch.

I looked at Jesus on the crucifixion, above the altar. His sad eyes opened momentarily. He jerked his head forward, toward me.

I died for your sins once. I won't do it again.

"Confess to me."

Even the Blessed Mary's eyes moved, blinking rapidly,

in warning.

Don't do it. You will be crushed like the snake beneath my foot.

Blood seeped from the snake's eyes, its tongue a soul in flames.

"What should I confess?" I said.

"Kneel down and tell me your sins."

I knelt down, my knees burning against the asphalt, and looked up at his face. His eyes spun, like large brown worlds, without restraint. Inside them I saw my life unfold before me. I saw myself side by side with this boy in the fires of hell, taking turns picking worms from each other's eyes.

"I wet my pants in school."

"Do you do it on purpose?"

"Of course not."

"Do you do it to spite God and the church?"

Jesus opened an inquisitive eye, before dying again on the cross. Mary crushed the snake's head further, smiling as she did. I imagined Johnny wearing a nun's habit and robe, gripping a yardstick in his tight-fisted hand.

"I would never do anything to spite God or the church," I said.

"Then why do you do it?"

"I have no control," I practically shouted.

"Why don't you ask to be excused?"

"We're not allowed."

"But you have special circumstances, I would think."

"I still wouldn't ask. Sister Carmela frightens me."

A squirrel ran up a nearby tree, scrambling in the intricate weave of branches. I imagined my nervous system to be like that, jittery, scrambly, squirrely. The tolling church bells jangled them even more. I noticed Johnny hadn't moved his raised, perpendicular hand. He was a hell of an actor.

"Listen to me," he said, in a soft, grandfatherly tone. "I am your God. Do you trust me?"

I closed my eyes (the statues around me were moving way to much for my liking) and told him I trusted him.

"Take my hand," he said.

My eyes still closed, I reached and took his hand in mine.

"Do you try your best to follow my ways and be good?"

I clasped him with both hands, rocking forward and back as I spoke. I did more than speak. I beseeched; I pleaded; I spilled my soul.

"I try to be good, God. I don't mean to wet my pants and turn the classroom seat purple from pee. I have no control, as I said. I've prayed every day, for the past two years, hoping my prayers would end this problem, but the prayers have failed me."

He freed his hand and laid it on my shoulder, then guided my crestfallen stature, raising me to my feet. He told me to open my eyes. I did.

"You have not sinned my son."

Though he was a hell of an actor, he was, nonetheless, eleven years old and looked more like a cherubim, drunk on happy air, than the Almighty creator of Heaven and Earth. Still I desperately needed to believe he was God. I was too far immersed in this cathartic game to quit.

"I haven't?"

"No. Sister Carmela is wrong to make you feel you have. As your God, I say you are free of sin. Go home and pack a lunch and clothes. You have a reservation on the bus to heaven."

I smiled. The Blessed Mary smiled, as well, her blue veil moving like pieces of sky. Jesus didn't move. I wanted to tell him he didn't die in vain.

I felt my pants. Shockingly, I had remained dry through my confession and subsequent redemption. Johnny sat cross-legged beneath the Mary statue, picking at the dried blood droplets along his arm, becoming, once again, the kid who sat behind me in the unholy corner.

"Damn, I'm tired," he said. "It's hard work being God."

He spit into a nearby bush, scratched a few flakes of dandruff from his unruly head of hair and said, matter-of-factly, "Are you ready to be Mary?"

I studied her stoic expression, trying to get a read on whether she'd be flattered or upset at my mimicking her.

"How do I play Mary?" I said. "She's a woman."

"That makes it all the more fun," he said. "Watch me."

He stood up, held his outstretched arms, palms turned out, tilting his head so that his eyes projected downward. He pursed his lips, and held this pose for many seconds.

"See, it's easy," he said. "Now let's switch places. You stand in the same pose, and I'll kneel before you."

The eyes on the Mary statue glared. She moved her pursed lips enough to emit a few words of warning.

Don't you dare.

The snake beneath her choked one last time on its fireball tongue, spitting out a prophecy born of first-hand experience.

You're a fool if you mess with her.

At that point, unnerved and possibly hallucinating, I noticed Father Clarke's shape across the street, making his way to the Rectory, where he lived. I had confessed myself to him many times, had literally put my soul in his care, and now I would have yet another sin to tell; how I had violated sacred grounds and the most sacred deities of all, God and Mary. I could only hope he'd go easy on me, and maybe he would since he was a compassionate priest, aware that his job was to hear and absolve the sins of boys, not gods. I rather liked his ripe, fruity smell and the way his nose tapered to a friendly point, his nostrils always clean, his nose hairs trimmed. Best of all was the way his cheeks lit up like stars whenever he doled out penance in a heartfelt, Irish accent.

Penance is your best friend.

I would need penance, plenty of it, after this experience, as I ascended the altar, trading places with Johnny, opening my arms and hands like the all-forgiving Mary.

As Johnny knelt down and clasped his hands before me, I began. "I am here to console you, if I can," I started. "Tell me your needs."

He rocked backward and forward, lamenting like an old washerwoman, playing the role of repentant sinner with exaggerated drama.

"Oh, please, Mother of God, hear my prayers and cleanse my blackened soul!"

I did my best to restrain my laugh, to keep my lips

pursed, my pose controlled and dignified. After all, I was portraying the Immaculate Blessed Virgin Mary, not some Saturday morning cartoon figure. Besides, Johnny had played God with believability. I had to do the same as Mary. I sucked in a breath as he continued.

"I know I haven't always been good. I know my attitude sometimes sucks. But from this point forward, I will do my best to change. Please don't send me to hell with the Protestants and public school kids. I want to go to heaven, on the bus, with all the kids in the front of the class who suck up to Sister Carmela."

He contorted his face into a mask of tragedy, his eyes stained with tears. I needed to help him, as he had helped me. I kept my pose, pursed lips and all, and felt the power of Mary's undulating veil, like the wind of heaven on my back.

"Do not despair. You shall sit in glory with God."

"You mean I don't have to go to Purgatory first, to sit among ashen, grey-faced people as they stand nude and sweating, waiting for someone to hear their case?"

"You may skip Purgatory."

Tears ran from his cheeks. I touched his shoulder and patted it.

"Sister Carmela mistakes your originality for a bad attitude. The sin is hers, not yours. Go home and pack your belongings. You are heaven bound."

He looked at me, wiped the tears away, and said, "You're easy."

"Not so fast." I shot an outstretched hand in front of him. "For penance, I want you to recite ten *Hail Marys* and ten *Our Fathers*."

"You can't do that," he protested, standing up. "You're not a priest, you're Mary. She doesn't give penance. She just forgives."

"I didn't tell you how to be God," I said. "Don't tell me how to be Mary. Be careful, or I'll throw in an *Act of Contrition*."

He threw up his arms to protest again. I cut him off.

"No one said the road to heaven would be easy."

He shook my hand and said, "Thank you, Mary."

"And thank you, God," I responded.

Before we left for our respective homes, we made a pact for our afterlife. We would sip lemonade all day and lick like lambs our cherubed lips, like a couple of flush-faced angels drunk from too much sun and song. To seal the deal, he brought out of his pocket a small switchblade and began scraping our names into the asphalt below Mary's altar. When he finished, he stood up, draped his arm on my shoulder and said, "What do you think?" Together, we admired his knife work.

Johnny & Tommy
Heaven Bound, 1963

Johnny was a magician. By the end of fifth grade, I had stopped wetting my pants. The following year, in Sister Teresa Margaret's class, I sat up front with the heaven bound kids, including Donna DeGregorio, who had solved her former regurgitation problem and, along with that, her pencil-chewing fixation.

Johnny and I never returned to the Grotto. In fact, he never returned to school. For several days, after our redemption in the garden, his seat behind me remained empty. I found out, from Sister Carmela of all people, his family had moved. When I inquired where, she said only "Out of state."

I never saw him again and often wondered about his whereabouts and whether he still had inclinations to use his imagination to save his soul. I visited the Grotto many times in my youth and early adulthood to relive the episode and see our names carved in stone. The last time I visited, as a middle-aged man—our names no longer visible in the time-worn stone—I came to this conclusion: It wouldn't surprise me someday, in another time and place, in another realm, to see him sitting next to me, as we ride the bus to heaven together.

THE GANG WAR DAYS

Leaving the anonymity of 75th Street, I dodged quickly in and among and along the shadows on Liberty Avenue. I had to be careful at all times, for a war raged nightly. The year was 1966, and while Vietnam had become a TV and newspaper war, seemingly millions of miles away, made real only because several neighbors on my street fought there, the war on Liberty Avenue, though not as noteworthy, seized my immediate attention.

75th Street, where I lived, bordered two rival gangs. On one side lay East New York, Brooklyn, home of the notorious F&P gang. The initials mystified me, though I knew they didn't stand for Friendly and Personal or anything associated with goodwill to mankind. On the other side lay Ozone Park, Queens, home of the infamous OZ gang. Their initials bore no resemblance to the Wizard of OZ. Born as demons in a dark land, they would die as such.

Each gang declared a pride that its members could spit better than talk; and write their names better with a knife than a pen. I retain memories of standing in Max's candy store—on F&P turf—chewing on a black licorice stick, mesmerized by a gang war outside, on the sidewalk or street, watching guys hit each other with belts and trash cans, slash each other with knives, and whip each other with car antennas. A kid didn't need to go to the movie theater. He had all the action he would ever need, right there on the avenue, on any particular day or night.

I learned to enjoy the passive role of bystander, though I hadn't always felt that way. For three days in that same year, 1966, when I was twelve years old, the pull of gangland swept me into its violent vortex. Living on 75th Street was like living in Switzerland. It was a neutral zone, meaning no gangs roamed there. But it also meant it had no identity; that those of us who lived on the street held no significance. Sure, we played all the street games: stickball, Ringalevio, Skelly, to name just a few. But the truth is we were a group of nobody kids, doing nobody things, while the tough guys in the gangs got to have all the fun. That's the way it seemed, at least for those three days when the temptation to be like the F&P and OZ took hold in my brain. I wanted to be a somebody, and the only way, where I lived, to be a somebody was to be tough and beat kids up. So that's what I set out to do during those three days, even though I had the muscles of an altar boy.

This decision did not materialize out of thin air. It had its basis in the reality of the streets. Living outside the parameters of gangland invited harassment, which became as frustrating as learning decimal points in school. If you were a nobody, you got targeted, picked on, abused, and sometimes beat up and made to feel small and diminished.

The turning point came one balmy night, when driven by stupidity more than courage, I walked alone, along the avenue, smack into F&P territory, on my way to Max's for a few nuggets of chocolate. Gang members were assembled in front of Flora's Pizzeria, complete with leather jackets on their backs and hickies on their necks. They never played stickball or punchball or any games that didn't involve intimidation, violence, and stupidity. When they weren't harassing kids or fighting, they laid blocks of dried ice on their arms. That's what I saw one of them do one day, long before the night and episode I will describe. His name was Jiggles. The day I saw it happen I was sitting in the safety of Rico's Barber Shop, getting my semi-annual regular haircut, while outside the shop a mob of guys huddled around Jiggles. Apparently, he had stopped a kid who sold Eskimo Pie ice cream in one of those portable wagons that could be wheeled around the streets. Story has it he told the kid he wanted to borrow a block of dried ice for a while. That request, alone, is pretty astounding when you think about it. After all, how do you borrow ice for a while? In any case, as I was getting my curls cut, Jiggles held an enormous square block of dried ice on his arm, while his gang members grunted and cheered. It turns out Jiggles was attempting to break the record for how long someone could hold a block of dried ice on his arm. He not only broke the record; he shattered it.

Rico, while cutting my hair, said, "That kid doesn't have a brain in his head."

It was the only thing Rico said during the entire haircut. I didn't mind. I didn't like to talk while getting a haircut. Besides, I had all the entertainment I needed outside the barber shop window. It didn't take long to realize that what Rico said was true. While there was no denying that Jiggles was a tough guy (one of the toughest by neighborhood accounts), it was also clear that between the ears he was putty soft. He could have slept nude on a frozen lake and won an Olympic medal, and it still would have been a dumb thing to do. Talk about not being aware of consequences. A couple of days later, I went into Gallo's Meat Market and saw Jiggles buying a pack of cigarettes. He had a blister on his arm the size of an inflated balloon.

I mention Jiggles because on that balmy night, that turning point night, it was he who occupied center stage again, among his gang, as I tried to pass on my way to Max's for that chocolate I mentioned. He stood among his friends who drank and cursed, covered by umbrellas of cigarette smoke, laughing and whirling their heads in frenzied movements. Consumed by their extra-curricular work, it appeared unlikely they would notice me walking by, stepping innocently on the sidewalk. But, then, that's what they were best at, observing, noticing, and, ultimately, destroying innocence.

It was their profession.

Jiggles stepped from the circle, spit near my shoe and grabbed the collar of my shirt, his face resembling a mountainous region on a globe, his mouth dark enough to house an army of bats. He wanted to know who I was and where I came from. When I told him I lived on 75th Street, he slapped my head.

"75th Street! That's OZ turf! You're one of the enemy!"

I understood then the reason for his name Jiggles. His bulging eyes hung loose from their sockets and seemed to spring in a forward trajectory as he spoke.

"I don't belong to a gang," I said, my neck convulsed from the grainy touch of his hand. "75th Street is neutral."

"Then why are you on F&P turf," he said, squeezing my arm.

I told him I was on my way to Max's.

"You're going to Max's? For what?"

Dirt blew from his face as he got excited.

I told him I planned on buying some chocolate.

"Chocolate! Hey, man, I love chocolate!" he said.

His teeth gave credence to his words.

Soon enough I would learn the not-so-subtle art of lying, of telling gang members I was going to a Laundromat to fold clothes, but first I had to learn the hard way. Jiggles escorted me to Max's and squeezed my arm until my twenty-eight cents fell from my hand, into his waiting hand. After buying himself twenty-five cents worth of chocolate, he handed me the change and said, "Get whatever you want." (In those days, believe it or not, you could still buy yourself some candy for three cents.)

Outside the store, he shook my hand. Then he unwrapped chocolates and stuffed them in his demon mouth. "You're a good sport," he said, his teeth blackened with chocolate. "Now run along home to your mother before you get hurt."

That was the night, bemoaning the loss of my twelve-year-old honor, I made the fatal decision to become a somebody. The next day, my friends and I, having finished a game of stickball, hung loosely on 75th Street, talking senselessly, saying things that only nobody kids said.

"Hey, what do you guys feel like doing now?" asked Louie.

"You guys feel like going up the avenue for a soda?" said Danny.

"Nah, I don't want to go up the avenue," said Vinny. "I'm not in the mood."

"I'm not in the mood either," added Louie.

"How about we play another game?" said Bobby, swinging a stickball bat.

"I can't play no more," Danny said. "I'm too thirsty."

"I'm not in the mood for another stickball game," Vinny whined.

"I'm not in the mood, either," added Louie.

"What about you, Tommy boy?" said Danny. "What do you feel like doing?"

During their inane conversation, I tried to imagine gang members talking like they did. It wasn't possible. No one talked like they did. Something had to change, and it had to happen now.

I took the bat from Bobby's hands and tapped it against the asphalt, my eyes askance. Inside, I steamed. It wasn't hard to read their subtext. They didn't want to go up the avenue because it risked humiliation, at the hands of the F&P. They didn't want to get slapped, have to say they were neutral and didn't belong to a gang, which was the same as saying they were nobodies. Well, I was tired of being a nobody, tired of being pushed around, having to worry about where and when I was going to buy a piece of candy and possibly have my money taken from me. The harassment had to stop. Even a twelve year old needed honor.

When I didn't answer Danny's question, the group became impatient.

"Well, what about it, Tommy boy," they said, seemingly in unison. "What do you want to do?"

I flipped the bat in the air and snagged it at the handle. I looked at their goofy, vapid eyes.

"I say we start a gang," I said.

Their faces appeared expressionless, and for several seconds no one spoke. Then, finally, they turned their heads to one another, perhaps to confirm, through a silent signal, that they all heard correctly.

Danny, nearly thirteen years old, the oldest of the group, stepped forward.

"It's okay with me, Tommy boy," he said.

Though he was the oldest, his voice was the highest pitched.

The floodgates had opened. If Danny and I wanted to do it, it was a done deal. The rest of them were pathetic followers. I could have grabbed a flute and, like the pied piper, I could have gotten them to follow me off a cliff, to their deaths.

"I'm into it if everyone else is." Bobby reached for the bat in my hands. For a moment, both our hands held it. I looked into his eyes and saw a warrior's heart. I let go and let him have it.

"What about you guys?" I looked at Vinny and Louie. "You guys in the mood to start a gang?"

Vinny shrugged. "I guess so."

Louie mimicked Vinny's shrug. "Yeah, I guess."

"I appreciate your enthusiasm," I said to them, my voice dripping with sarcasm.

"What about Tony over here?" Danny said, indicating Tony Fontanino, who sat on the curb, absentmindedly, killing ants with a stick. He was practically a mute and hadn't said a word in days. He surprised us all when he stood up, fists clenched.

"Yeah, let's start a gang!" he screamed.

We all laughed. Anytime he spoke, we laughed, because it was always unexpected. He had two ways of communicating: silently, which was most of the time; and loudly, like a scream. There was no in between with him.

"Okay, it's settled," I said. "From now on we're called ARCHIE COOCARUMBA."

To this day, I don't know why I said that. I had never heard that name before. Where it came from remains a mystery. In any case, none of the others questioned it.

What happened next—power must have been surging in my brain—was even stranger, and I'm sure did not conform to the how-to-start-a-gang guidelines. I gave each member a title, a shared ownership in the name. I bestowed upon Bobby, perhaps the most gifted warrior in the group, the letters COO. Vinny received CA, Louie RUM, and Tony, having newly discovered his voice, BA. I showed respect to Danny, the oldest, giving him the very first letters of our name, AR. That left me with the letters CHIE. Everyone knew what that meant. It wasn't necessary to add the letter "f" to the end of it. CHIE was clear enough. It meant I was a somebody.

The next day we pooled together our piggy bank money and whatever we were able to abscond from our mothers' purses and headed to the discount stores that lined the avenue. We accessorized ourselves with pocket knives, garrison belts, packs of cigarettes and, of course, black leather jackets. First on the agenda, we needed to practice how to spit, curse and smoke. That done, we used our knives to carve our names in the street to seal the deal, to give us identity, purpose and meaning.

For two days we were a gang in training and name only. To solidify our place in the history book that would some day be written, I was certain, we had to prove ourselves in action. We had to prove ourselves tough.

On the third day we were ready to do just that. All the preparations were in place. We had the look, the sound, the motions, the gyrations. We were ready to be born. We planned to walk on Liberty Avenue in broad daylight, dressed in our tough-fitting outfits, to show the neighborhood world our new identities, to stake out a territory, and announce to all who saw us that we were ARCHIE COOCARUMBA.

The six of us stepped urgently along Liberty Avenue. Still early morning, we were the only group in sight, since the real tough guys didn't go to bed until the sun rose. They were late afternoon and night creatures. It would have been a great time to go to Max's, though today I held no inclination for chocolate. The leather jacket felt heavy on my back and shoulders, but I didn't care. I was more interested in its symbolism. Inside one of its pockets, I fingered a switchblade. Though I was the shortest of the group, I felt like King Kong, like I could devour the street and its occupants.

Bobby walked alongside me. He stepped big, and from his breath I smelled the fury of his motivation. He had the look of a marine, fresh out of boot camp. He was ready to kill, if necessary. Tony Fontanino went mute again. But he had in the previous two days discovered how to spit, and this past time occupied him as he walked. Vinny and Louie did their best to walk the walk and talk the talk, though I was sure if I'd asked them, they would have said they weren't in the mood to be tough that day. Danny was not only the oldest, but also the tallest. He pranced on spindly legs, looking more like a zoo animal, escaped from its cage, than a tough guy. Nonetheless, there we were, the ARCHIE COOCARUMBA, passing Forbell Sreet, walking by Max's and Flora's Pizzeria and Kuck's Deli and Rico's Barber Shop. Mostly what I sought was the reflections in the windows, which helped verify our existence.

Mothers and small children wandered the early morning sidewalks. They averted their eyes when they passed us. I couldn't understand, unless they were shopping, why mothers took their children for walks along Liberty Avenue. A mile away stood Forest Park, a place with trees and a pond with ducks. It was unlikely the ducks were alive, but, nonetheless, they were there. Even looking at dead ducks would be a better option than walking along Liberty Avenue, populated by tough guys day and night. Tough guys like us. Of course, we weren't going to hurt them. Unlike other gangs, we had morals.

At the corner of Eldert's Lane, in front of John's Pharmacy, I spotted a blond-headed kid, no more than ten years old, standing by himself. I noticed, right away, the dozens of freckles on his face. Everyone knew freckled kids weren't tough. It was common knowledge. He peered about, jerking his head left to right, as if he were lost. The time of reckoning had come for me to destroy his innocence.

Recalling the legacy of Leo Gorcey, he of *East Side Kids* and *The Bowery Boys* fame, as well as every tough punk who roamed the streets of this neighborhood, I walked up to the boy—the COOCARUMBAS at my side—and stared him down.

"What are you doing here, freckle face?" I said.

His freckles swelled, and his adam's apple moved in a rapid line, up and down.

"I'm waiting for my sister," he said, gulping. "She's in the drug store."

"The drug store!" I gave my best Jiggles impersonation. "I don't care if Sister Superior's in the drug store. You're standing on ARCHIE COOCARUMBA turf. Do you know that?"

Other than gulping the lump in his throat, he didn't move. Even his eyes were frozen. He could have been a discount store mannequin.

"Have you ever heard of the ARCHIE COOCARUM-BAS?" I said.

The frightened boy shook his head. Behind me, Tony Fontanino continued to spit, and Bobby grinned and grunted. Danny mostly laughed. Vinny and Louie weren't in the mood to pick on freckle-faced kids, I was sure of that.

"We're a new gang from 75th Street," I said. "Don't you forget that."

"Yeah, we're a new gang from 75th Street!" Tony Fontanino screamed.

That made us all laugh. But the boy didn't laugh, not in the slightest.

"I don't want to see you around here anymore," I said. "Do you understand what I'm saying to you?"

"What if I have to go to the drug store?" the boy said, seriously.

"Don't talk back to me!" I slapped him—I thought playfully—on his head.

"Good one, Tommy boy," Danny said.

"Yeah, don't talk back to him," Tony Fontanino screamed.

That made us all laugh again. The boy stood there, rubbing his head. He was close to crying. I could see his eyes begin to water.

"Maybe that's enough for today." I heard Vinny say. Or it could have been Louie. The two of them mimicked each other all the time.

I turned in their direction and said, "It's enough when I say it's enough."

"That's right, Tommy boy," Danny said. "When you say it's enough."

"Why don't you ask him if he has money," Bobby said. "I can go for some chocolates."

"Do you have money?" I said to the boy.

The boy scratched a freckle. He shook his head.

"I bet he has money," Bobby said.

"I don't have money," the boy said, and now the tears began to form. It brought out a sudden compassion in me.

"Okay, that's enough for today," I said, turning to my gang members.

I looked at the boy one last time and issued a final warning. "Next time I won't be so easy with you." As a demonstration of my compassion, I shook the boy's hand, and then we turned and left him standing there, dazed and confused no doubt.

We walked back down the avenue, toward 75th Street. We lit cigarettes, inhaled and coughed ourselves silly. Passing Forbell Street, I tried to pat a small child on the head, but his mother pulled him away before I could, holding on to him like a precious glass sculpture. Bobby whistled like a bird at my side. I liked the sound.

We had arrived as a gang.

We celebrated on our way home, back to 75th Street, chanting, "We are Archie Coocarumba," in a sing-song way American Indians did in movies, when they wanted rain, rejoicing in the kind of success that only comes from victory in warfare.

"Damn, Tommy boy, you really slapped that kid good," Danny said, as we approached 75th Street.

"The kid's lucky I was in a good mood," I said, cheerfully.

I had finally gained admiration and respect, and I was ready to settle in and enjoy my new life. For a couple of hours I did, as we hung around in the street and plotted and planned further tough guy exploits. We even considered going up the avenue in the late afternoon or early evening, when the other gangs were out, to see what kind of reaction we'd get from them.

As fate would have it, however, we didn't need to go up the avenue to find out their reaction. I had begun carving the name of our gang in the street and made the letters ARCH, but that's as far as I got. Vinny yelled "Holy shit!" Louie, keeping in character, mimicked Vinny, repeating "Holy shit!" I was about to tell them to shut up because they were ruining my reverie. Then I heard a chorus of

"Holy shits" coming from Bobby and Danny, as well. Finally, just as I heard Tony Fontanino scream "Holy shit!" I looked up and noticed what all the "Holy shits" were about.

A dozen kids had turned the corner at 75th Street, and they were walking—or, I should say, storm trooping—toward where we huddled in the street. The lead storm troopers were none other than the infamous gang leaders of the OZ, Benny-the-Blister and his colleague, Catman. Benny, at fourteen years old, had already written the book on evil. The tough crowd revered him, lavished him with the name "Blisterman" in honor of the prodigious blister he wore like an Olympic medal on his cheek. I'd grown up hearing legends about the immeasurable depths of his hate, and each tale involved his blister: how he savored a fetish for pinning kids to the ground, taking out his pocket knife, and poking a hole in his blister to let it leak on his victim's face. The scars on his blister made everyone who met him a believer. I had always wondered where the blister came from, but having witnessed Jiggles, of F&P fame, that day I was getting my haircut, I had no doubt that Benny's blister came from a block of dried ice.

As awful a demon as he was, he appeared as Snow White compared to his partner in evil, Catman. His parents had named him Joseph Cattatano, but it never suited him the way Catman did. He had been in my fourth grade class at St. Sylvester, though he was two years older than everyone else. Even back then, it was obvious he would lead a mean life. One day Sister Maria Joseph found out just how mean. She'd been warning him to stop interrupting class with obscene comments and incessant laughter. He didn't respond well to the *Please-be-quiet* type of language. She knew that, so she stood over his desk, raised her yardstick, and said, "I'm going to hit you, Joseph, if you don't behave." He wasn't the type to say, *Please don't hit me, I'm sorry*. With a style all his own, he got up out of his seat, grabbed the yardstick from her and shoved her to the floor. Standing over her, he yelled, "You ain't no different than my mother. She tries to hit me, I kick her ass. You try to hit me, I kick your ass."

After the nuns kicked Catman's ass out of St. Sylvester, he attended P.S. 64, but he had trouble with the curriculum there as well. He lasted less than a year and a half—and that includes skipping school most of the time—before finally quitting school for good in the seventh grade. That's right, he didn't wait until high school to be a high school dropout, like half the people in my neighborhood. He was a seventh grade dropout, giving him plenty of time to hone his evil skills.

He didn't wear a blister like Benny. What he wore was knives everywhere: in his sleeves, in his shoes, in his hair, down his pants. If you touched him, you would cut yourself, and everyone knew he didn't waste his blades carving his name on the asphalt.

Catman, Benny, and their traveling troupe of trolls came quickly. The way they spit and growled, the way steam emitted from their clothing, it was clear they weren't interested in challenging us to a game of stickball. I'd never seen a gang break up so fast. I don't mean the OZ gang. I mean my gang, ARCHIE COOCARUMBA. One right after the other, they fled to the metaphoric hills, fleeing in the name of innocence.

COO...CA...RUM...BA...!

They would not be confused with Anglo-Saxon warriors from a different time and age. They had no interest in maintaining loyalty, dying with their chief. Gone were the days of honor and bravery. Long live the preservation of the self, they cried in their hearts. The gang had been reduced to ARCHIE, just the loyal Danny Neltino and me, Tommy boy. To this day, I don't know why we didn't follow the cowardly—yet intelligent—steps of our friends. I'm sure we didn't hold our ground due to some code of street honor. More likely, we were so wrapped up in our new identities that we confused reality and fantasy. The real world, though, would soon come into focus, especially when I recognized the face. Not Benny's or Catman's face.

The blond-headed, freckled face I had slapped earlier.

Only now his face bore an altogether different look than it had that morning. His freckles were as big as fists, his adam's apple tight as a pipe.

The OZ encircled us. Catman stepped forward.

"We hear there's a gang on his street called the Archie Cockroaches," he said, rubbing his knuckles. His trolls laughed, as if on cue; except Benny. He massaged his blister, while chomping on a toothpick, as if he was going to swallow it. It wouldn't have surprised me. I was sure he had swallowed worse things, like door knobs and belt buckles. Catman waited for the laughter to abate.

"I also hear that one of you creeps slapped my girl-friend's little brother this morning in front of John's Pharmacy."

I wanted to say, *Hey, Catman, don't you remember me? I used to sit next to you in the fourth grade.* I couldn't, though. He had said only one thing to me all year. One day he wanted me to hand him my Geography quiz when I was finished. But I didn't do it; I couldn't. Sister Maria Joseph was walking the aisles, tapping her yardstick on her palm. I couldn't say to Catman, at that moment, *Hey, Catman don't you remember me? I was the kid in fourth grade who betrayed you one day. I didn't let you cheat off me. I was the Judas to your Christ.* How could I say that? I would have been better off jumping from the Brooklyn Bridge.

I kept my head down, hoping the freckle-faced kid wouldn't recognize me.

Boy, was that a pipe dream.

I heard him say, "He's the one who slapped me. The little guy."

I cursed my Southern Italian pygmy genes.

At that moment, I didn't understand why Danny didn't run. He probably could have gotten away. After all, they wanted me. I was the perpetrator, the instigator. It had been my idea from the start. I was the one who wanted to start a gang and, in doing so, make a name for myself, to become a somebody.

And, now, it would spell my doom and bring about my destruction. I would never have another birthday and see 1967. I would never be a teenager and experience all the drugs, sex and rock 'n roll awaiting me. I would be dead, in the ground, and my epitaph would read, as follows:

The idiot, Tommy boy, he of Archie Coocarumba fame,
who slapped an innocent, freckle-faced boy, and, in doing
so, brought upon himself dreadful punishment and subse-
quent death. May he rot in hell, where all gang members
belong.

It's difficult to chronicle what happened next. I don't remember much. Maybe I don't want to remember much. What I do remember is one or two trolls grabbing my arms and holding them behind my back. Poor Danny, though innocent of the actual crime, received the same treatment as me. Both of us were being held by trolls, and that's when Benny stepped forward, swallowing the toothpick he had been chewing. I saw him take out his switchblade and touch his blister with it. The rest of the details are a blur. They happened so fast, all hurly-burly, motion and commotion, and sound and fury. I recall the taste of Catman's breath in my mouth, and felt Benny's volcanic blister erupting in a river of hatred.

At some point, I lay on the ground, next to Danny, also on the ground, and the OZ gang was gone. For two days I couldn't talk or open my mouth and ate only aspirins for my swollen head. It would take much longer than that for me to eat real food again, to erase the taste of Catman's breath and the foul stench of Benny's blister.

Danny Neltino would never again call me Tommy boy. In fact, he didn't want to be my friend anymore. Soon after the incident—which apparently traumatized him even more than it did me—he began to find solace in smoking marijuana instead of trying to be tough. The others stayed away from me for a long time, and not because they resented my decision to start a gang. They were too guilt-ridden to face me. Vinny and Louie remained as indecisive as ever. They were never sure whether they were in the mood or not to be my friend. Bobby struggled the most. Every time he looked at me, he saw himself running, losing the warrior image he had believed defined him. In the end, it became too painful for him. He ran away for good, his parents having moved to Long Island, where gangs didn't roam, where kids went to good schools, to learn and evolve as human beings. Tony Fontanino, as far as I know, never spoke again. I, for sure, never heard him speak again, though I often saw him roaming the streets, looking for ants to kill with a stick.

Most of the gang members from F&P and OZ became junkies sometime during 1967. If they were to take your money, it wasn't chocolate they were interested in buying. They desired something much sweeter, called heroin. Gang wars occurred less frequently or not at all. It became hard for them to hit each other with trash cans or endure blows to the head when they were stoned senselessly, when their bodies drooped, as if their spines had become soft and brittle. Their eyes, barely open, became dead end streets, and their lips and mouths were useless in forming words. It was pretty sad seeing the tough guys become the stoned guys.

My gang war days lasted three days, though the lessons learned lasted a lifetime. I never again wore a leather jacket or owned a knife or belt or smoked another cigarette. After I survived my ordeal, I learned to live in peace, in shadows and shade, if necessary, understanding there were better ways to become a somebody. Most important of all, I got to see 1967 and experience all the wonders of my ensuing teen years during the Age of Aquarius.

THE DEVIL IN MY PANTS

The realization of attending an all-boys high school run by Christian brothers made more active my already active imagination. I had heard from older kids in the neighborhood that the Christian brothers didn't use yardsticks for disciplinary purposes; their fists worked just as well.

The year was 1967. I was thirteen years old, about to attend Bishop Loughlin Memorial High School in the Fort Greene section of Brooklyn. Though I was born in 1954, my mother—bless her soul—for reasons that go against all common theory (not to mention common sense), enrolled me in first grade, in 1959, a year earlier than planned. At St. Sylvester, I attended school with the children born in 1953. I was the only one in my class born in 1954. Consequently, throughout my elementary and secondary education, I was always a year behind, and I was very conscious of that fact. To say it didn't influence my inability to learn would be a blatant refusal to accept what's true. I always felt behind others and, as a result, more than a little reserved and fearful.

At thirteen years old, I was introduced not only to the Christian brothers, but to the A train; the underground, pitch dark tunnels, and the purgatorial stench of its riders. To get to school, I rode twenty five minutes through East New York, Brownsville and Bedford Stuyvesant, arguably some of the worst areas in New York City, on my way to Fort Greene, Brooklyn. There I was, a diminutive Anglo-Italian-American boy, wearing a sport jacket and tie, riding through the ghettoes. No school experience in the world could prepare me for the true-to-life sociology lessons I

47

learned on a daily basis as war between the races raged. The train, in particular, was a main battlefield. It was there I learned everything I needed to know about staying awake and aware.

The truth is school taught me little in comparison, and I remember next to nothing, since most of it was forgettable. Some of it, though, was impossible to forget.

I am referring to the religion classes. I can't say the religion I learned was more fearful and authoritative than what I had received at St. Sylvester. That's not possible. While the brothers may have used their fists, they had nothing on the nuns, who, from my experiences, were more frightening. Maybe it was because I was literally a child when I attended grade school. Nonetheless, I suffered more embarrassment and humiliation at the hands of the nuns, wetting my pants and living in terror of going to hell. In any case, I survived my ordeal with the nuns. I had paid my dues and had struggled to keep my faith, to believe that I would one day ride the bus to heaven. There was no reason, as I entered high school, to believe I wouldn't continue to hold and value the same beliefs.

My first day shattered my hopes. I waited in Room 101, along with thirty-plus adolescent males, everyone spic and span, with new shoes, socks, sport coats and ties; no one's hair much longer than a marine's, and everyone's shirts white like a magazine model's teeth. The room smelled of shaving cream, deodorant and Vitalis. In silence, we observed each other with dread, confirming a truth: nary a girl would pass these halls in four long years.

Brother Ambrose walked hurriedly in the room like a nun in drag, his black gown flapping, making a mockery of the miniature Christ crucified and chained to his waist. Moving his nippy-lipped mouth, he announced that he would be our religion instructor and, more importantly, our physical and spiritual advisor.

"Welcome to Bishop Loughlin Memorial High School, boys ... or, I should say, MEN!" He smiled, revealing not only his teeth, but the gums above them.

From the neck down, he resembled, in physique, a keg of beer. He barreled around, smacking his nippy lips and lifting his lashes, his eyes, blinking fast, a touch of rouge highlighting the fat on his cheeks. A bullet of spit escaped his mouth, along with an affected laugh, as he zig-zagged among the students, shaking hands with an ostentatious flair. I could see his hands were pink and fatty and probably sweaty. They were definitely not the type of hands that would make a fist to hit someone. I was glad about that.

Fortunately he didn't come far enough down my aisle to shake my hand. I sat in the back, where I had hoped to go unnoticed not only on this day, but for my entire four years of school. Most of the students around me cleared their throats or squirmed in their seats, wondering, like me, I was certain, what plans this flamboyant Christian brother had for us.

He came to a stop in front of the room. His smile was larger than life, as were his teeth and gums, and his lips smacked repeatedly, as if they had been programmed to do just that. He was funny in an unintended way. I could never say that about any nun I had had as a teacher. Funny, whether intentional or not, was never a part of their constitutional framework.

"I called you men a minute ago, for good reason."

His voice was pitchy and more womanly than manly. In fact, his entire appearance reflected less masculinity than any nun I had ever had.

"You may have been boys on your way to school this morning, but once you stepped foot in this school, your boyhood ended."

His dark eyes darted excitedly, and his pink tongue loosed itself between his smacking lips. It was clear he enjoyed his job; enjoyed terrifying young adolescents with his enthusiasm.

"You are no longer children in the eyes of God. He fully expects you to become adults, which means you should be responsible, caring Christians. Therefore, consider today the beginning of your adult life. This school has been producing responsible men since 1851. That's right, 1851; meaning this school is even older than me."

He laughed, and as he did, his cheeks puffed and his teeth rattled. No one laughed with him. The students just stared, mostly expressionless, probably bemoaning, like me, the loss of their boyhoods, and looking, with fear and dread, upon what lay ahead in the world of adulthood Ambrose talked about.

"Let's see, if the school began in 1851, and it's now 1967, that means we've been producing responsible men for ... well, you tell me? Who's good in math?"

My heart stopped for a moment. It had always stopped when nuns asked questions because they had a knack for calling on me. I was relieved that Brother Ambrose didn't pull student-name cards from his gown pocket. Nonetheless, his dark eyes darted around, looking for someone who might answer his question. I dropped my head, avoiding his eager eyes.

"Oh, come on, don't be shy. If we began in 1851, and it's now 1967, it means we've been teaching young men for how long?"

"One hundred and sixteen years," a voice up front squeaked.

I was temporarily relieved. But that response didn't suffice for Ambrose. He wanted the class to say it in unison.

"Come on, don't be shy," he squealed. "Everyone together."

"A hundred and sixteen years," a chorus of voices, excluding mine, responded.

"A hundred and sixteen years! Yes, that's wonderful!" He clasped his hands and clapped them numerous times. "This is, indeed, a smart group of boys ... excuse me, did I say boys?" He laughed again, full-throated and loud. "I mean men; a smart group of men ... because you are men ... aren't you?"

Something about the way he said, "aren't you?" made me squirm. I knew it wasn't an incidental remark. He wasn't smiling when he said it, and his pitch lowered, as if he were exercising a masculine impulse. For certain, the remark had an agenda behind it. That agenda would soon become clear.

"This is the time of life when changes occur, physical changes, in particular. You go through puberty, you grow facial and bodily hair, you grow taller. Even though you're sitting, I can tell some of you are very tall."

He obviously wasn't looking at me. While everyone in my eighth grade class grew taller, I stayed short, and it wasn't because I hadn't yet gone through puberty. I experienced physical changes at ten years old. That critical time in life to grow taller had come and passed me by.

"Some of the physical changes can seem confusing. A lot of things grow on us, unexpectedly, if you know what I mean."

I knew exactly what he meant, and so did everyone else. It was clear by the way many wiped their brows and cleared their throats and twisted and turned in their seats. His quivering tongue freed itself from his tight, nippy lips, moving snakelike, in an obscene trajectory. He was enjoying himself a little too much now, and the more he did, the more anxious I became. I was not amused by any lecture that addressed male body parts. I had sat in pools of sin at St. Sylvester and wanted to leave those sins behind.

The bell ending class curbed his appetite for a day; however, I learned, to my dismay, beginning the next day, that male body parts and sin consumed Brother Ambrose's consciousness. He returned with a hunger to devour my young brain, and he did more than a fair job of succeeding.

"Good morning, MEN," he said, wheeling in an overhead projector. He smacked his hands together and made a series of pop sounds with his puckered lips. "I realize some of you may have gone home yesterday perplexed over what I said about you becoming men and your bodies changing so let me follow up and clarify." His eyebrows alternated moving up and down as he spoke.

He pulled down a screen near the board, plugged in the overhead and placed on it a picture divided into two parts, each showing the male reproductive organ. One side showed a limp penis; the other side an erect one. Now, understand, the year was 1967, long before children received sex education in a healthy and proper way, taught by people trained to do so. Brother Ambrose's training was self-appointed, sanctioned, in part, by the Brooklyn Diocese, the same organization that allowed nuns to whack kids with yardsticks whenever they got an itch under their habits.

I looked at the kid across from me to check the validity of my eyes. It was clear he saw what I did and was equally aghast. His face turned the color of ground beef. Others around me laughed quietly or coughed or sighed. I loosed my tie and slouched low in my chair.

"Some of you look embarrassed, but you shouldn't be," he said. "After all, we're just looking at ourselves. We are, all of us, the same, aren't we?" His dark, beady eyes searched the room, running like light from face to face.

I sank lower.

"Always remember, when your reproductive part grows into maturity, it is a gift from God. Be grateful, and don't abuse the gift He's given you. The erect penis—that's right, laugh if you must—should be reserved for love and marriage, for creating children. All other uses are vile and against His wishes."

At that moment I missed Sister Virginia Carmel and Sister Maria Joseph and Sister Brian Elizabeth, and all the other crazy nuns who had abused me and others psychologically, emotionally and physically. At least they didn't show us any pictures of the male penis or—God forbid!—the female vagina. I was grateful to them for that.

I wasn't prepared for Brother Ambrose's lecture. Because he taught in Catholic school, in 1967, no one, especially not working class parents, would have ever questioned it. If the nuns and brothers said or did something, it was for our own good. They knew best, and that's the way it was. Therefore, Brother Ambrose and his twisted tales about the male penis could not be stopped. He had license to do and say what he pleased, and he took full advantage of this opportunity.

"If you feel your lower instincts instigating you, tempting you, bothering your conscience, renounce yourself, give your passions notice to quit. When such time occurs, you need to exercise self-control, gentlemen."

His eyes became darker, more penetrating; his face more sweaty and red; his voice less pitchy, less friendly, more commanding and authoritative.

"To sit at his side is reserved only for those courageous

enough to earn it. Ask yourselves this question: Is it worth sacrificing everlasting happiness by His side for the sake of passing pleasure? Pleasure is deceitful, gentlemen; just as the apple presented to Adam in the garden was deceitful."

I was beginning to think I had entered a different level of Catholic school. St. Sylvester, all of a sudden, seemed like the minor leagues. Brother Ambrose was a major leaguer, and he swung for the fences and was not going to stop until he hit a homeroom and cleared the bases. The more he talked, the more his eyes began to spin, producing spit from his mouth and venom upon all those who disobeyed God's laws pertaining to what one could or couldn't do with his penis.

"When your lower instincts tempt you, cast your thoughts aside, for they will lead you to sin." His hands trembled as he lifted a black book from his desk and opened it to a marked section. He read lustily. "As Matthew tells us in the Bible, 'If thy right eye scandalize thee, pluck it out and cast it from thee … and if thy right hand scandalize thee, cut it off and cast it from thee: for it is expedient for thee that one of thy members should perish, rather than thy whole body go into hell.'"

I nearly gagged from the smell of perspiration in the room. I tried to decipher Ambrose's message. In my adolescent confusion—I was thirteen years old, for heaven's sake—I understood that if I stayed limp, I wouldn't need to cut anything off from me, to secure my seat on the bus to heaven. The problem was that the erect part of me had already been practicing its primordial scream for more than three years (remember, I had "matured" before the age of ten). And it happened in the unlikeliest of places; on trains and buses, in classrooms and libraries, even at the nine o'clock mass on Sunday.

When I had stopped wetting my pants in the fifth grade, I thought God had finally forgiven me. He had tested me, given me the heavy cross to bear, and I had borne it. I had paid my dues in piss and prayer; yet, now, after two classes in high school, Ambrose had convinced me that the devil lived in my groin, and I had in my mental possession little evidence to think otherwise. Later that night, I was lying in bed innocently, thinking of baseball, of all things, when it suddenly rose from the fires of hell. I tried my best to renounce it, but it didn't work. Like Lucifer, it committed the worst sin of all; the sin of pride, serving no master other than itself.

As much as he tried talking about other subjects, Ambrose always found his way back to the male reproductive part. He couldn't keep away. He would start a discussion about St. Augustine or St. Francis or John, Luke and Paul, or about one of the many miracles Jesus performed, when out of nowhere he would say, "Speaking of St. Francis; now, here was a man who had no concern for his body at all. In fact, he called his body Brother Ass because he knew his body would lead him into waters moving swiftly away from God. He knew, come Judgment Day, he would not be measured by his body's accomplishments; rather by his courage and self-control in the face of bodily temptation."

More than a few students wanted to know why God had given us bodies—specifically erect penises—if they were going to distract us from His Holy Laws.

"God wants you to enjoy the fruits of life," Ambrose said, "in given time, under the proper circumstances. But be patient. Let nature—the nature given to you by God—run its proper course. Someday you will be rewarded and know the pleasure of uniting with a woman, but only when you are married."

He told us about a saint who had sinned night after night, indulging in the demands of his lower bodily instincts, until he became blind and crazy, at which point he took up the life of the spirit, repelling his body's demands, thereby strengthening his case before he met his God.

One day in class, out of nowhere, with no provocation, my penis began to sin, arising in my pants like the devil himself in the hot river of temptation. I mumbled the word *shit*. The student in front of me twisted his body around and looked at me as if I were a complex algebraic formula. I felt self-consciously stupid, but I couldn't tell him I was responding to the devil between my legs. He wouldn't have understood, unless, of course, he was wired in the same complex psycho-sexual-religious fashion as me.

I wasn't certain what Ambrose meant by indulging in the demands of your lower bodily instincts, or, what, for that matter, the demands were. All I knew was that the devil stretched its muscle at a most inopportune time.

I didn't indulge him, did I?

I did the only thing I could. I wiped the perspiration from my brow, bowed my head, and whispered an *Our Father*. It didn't work, though. When the bell rang, I couldn't even get out of my seat. The devil ruled.

That night, as I was getting ready for bed, putting away the baseball cards I had been reading (I enjoyed reading the short biographies of the players on the back of the cards), the devil arose again. I had to wonder if there was a perverse connection between baseball and night-time erections, but it made absolutely no sense at all. Nonetheless, I did what any Catholic, God-fearing kid would do. I fired some religious bullets; first an *Act of Contrition*, then a *Glory Be to the Father*. Still, the devil wavered not. As I stared at it with utter dread and disgust, I thought of Matthew: Cut it off and cast it from thee.

You don't have the guts, the devil-penis boasted.

Don't mock me, I cried.

I am the master of the universe, he retorted.

I hate you! I replied.

Yes, but you shall worship me forever.

At that moment, I heard only laughs coming from hell.

Go away, you son of a bitch!

I became so enraged I tried to strangle it.

Nature never got a chance to run its proper course. My innocence erupted into a million senseless fragments. I had done—albeit by accident, the victim of deception—what Brother Ambrose had warned us against doing.

I had indulged the demands of my lower instincts. It mattered not that I had been tricked by the devil. The act stood as a testament to my weakness and from thereafter I would wait in sordidness and sin; wait to go blind and crazy like the sinners before me; wait for the only bus that would come for me: *The Devil Express to Hell*.

Whatever hope remained for me rested in the compassionate folds of Father Clarke's soft eyes. The following day, returning from school, I walked to St. Sylvester, knowing he heard confession every afternoon at four o'clock. First, I stopped near the Grotto and stood before the Blessed Mary, whose cape turned a phosphorescent blue in the afternoon sun, her arms appearing to hold the sky, and all of heaven, on her back. I came to her as a supplicant, seeking, through prayer, her consolation and advice, but she must have known what I had done because as soon as I approached, her marble hands came unglued, clutching angrily for my throat. I skipped the prayer and ran into church.

I dipped my hand in holy water, made the sign of the cross, and genuflected before the crucifixion high above the altar. I proceeded down the center aisle, gawking at the sunlit, stained glass, revealing the Stations of the Cross, each one conveying the pain Christ suffered to bring me salvation. My eyes dodged the windows and fell into the flames of burning candles, novena devotions to those who worshipped in this hallowed hall; those whose eyes burned with fervor as their voices spoke from the building's domed top and gilded frame.

Here comes that boy who indulged the demands of his lower instincts.

I turned to Jesus, the blood on his feet fresh as guilt, and traded places with him; saw myself nailed like a scarecrow, allowing the Christian saints of ancient lore to pick my brain with their sharp, incisive words.

Cut it off and cast it from thee.

My eyes spun a montage of glass and yellow flame as my bone-limp body became wrapped in cerements of sin, lost in a chapel of silence, waiting for my final judgment.

"Hello?"

I was born at your behest, O God, and tried my best to be good.

"Excuse me?"

Redeem me, O God. I am not your fallen angel. I am just a boy, thirteen years old, for crying out loud!

"May I help you?"

Please, O God, do not cast me in the closet of your hate.

"Have you come to stare, or are you deep in prayer?"

Father Clarke stood outside the confessional booth, breathing hard, his hand reaching in a pocket for a hand-kerchief. He blew his nose and asked again, a bit more irritably, if I needed assistance or help. I wanted to fall at his knees and say, *Kyrie Eleison*, but he may have locked me away in a far-away bell tower with nothing to eat and drink but bread and water if I had, so, instead, I said, "Good afternoon, Father, I'm in need of confession."

He motioned for me to follow him into the divided booth. As each of us settled in our places, he sitting and me kneeling, I stared across at his barely perceptible face, shrouded and shaded by the grill that separated us. I began instinctively.

"Bless me, father, for I have sinned. It's been three weeks since my last confession." I cleared my throat re-peatedly.

"What would you like to confess?" he asked.

"I've committed sins."

"Yes? Why don't you tell me."

I couldn't just come out with what I wanted to say. I needed to preface it with other, less shameful, sins. I told him I stole money from my mother's purse, cursed at my brothers, and had hateful feelings towards my father and did something awful to him. He pestered me with questions about my father, asking me to explain in more developed detail. So I concocted a story which was part true and part false. I told him the day I stole money from my mother's purse she asked me if I took money and I said, 'No,' only she didn't believe me, so she told my father. When he asked me about it, I lied again and, of course, he didn't believe me either. He commanded me to tell the truth, and I remained steadfast in my lie. I had only taken thirty-five cents from her purse, but for some reason I didn't want to own up to it. Finally, he took off his belt and slapped my head with it, believing the beating would force the truth out of me. I took the blows and vowed vengeance on him. After receiving my beating, I went into the back-yard and filled up a plastic bag with dirt and rocks. Then I went back inside and spread the dirt and rocks under his bed sheet, hoping he'd sleep like a sinner in hell that night. I even watched as he went to sleep. But I got no satisfaction, for he was snoring the minute his head hit the pillow. Next time I vowed to put needles under his sheet.

As Father Clarke listened to my story, he kept saying "I see ... I see ..." over and over, as if he knew the story was made up, as if he was really thinking to himself, *This boy is lying to me, and that could mean only one thing. He must have indulged the demands of his lower instincts*. Finally, when I was finished he said, "Hostility towards your father is a sin. Recite your *Act of Contrition*, and I will give you penance."

"Excuse me, Father," I said, "I'm not finished yet."

"What else have you done?" he asked.

I didn't like the way he asked the question; more like a cop than a priest. He didn't seem like the Father Clarke who had heard my confessions since an early age. His ripe, fruity smell had been replaced by an odor of ash, the kind burned at funerals. The confessional became hotter, and Father Clarke's shrouded, nearly silhouetted face began to grow horns on his forehead. Surely, if I told him the truth, told him what I had done in my room the night before, he would tell me only one thing could save me.

Cut it off and cast it from thee.

"What else have you done?" he repeated.

"I...I ate two hamburgers instead of fish last Friday."

"I see...I see," he said. "Very well, now say your *Act of Contrition*."

My mind went blank. I hadn't confessed what I came there to confess.

"Have you forgotten the *Act of Contrition*?" he said.

I shook my head, clasped my hands and tried to pray.

"Oh my God, I am heartily sorry for having offended thee, and I..."

I had recited that prayer hundreds of times, but, for some reason, at that moment, the stress I felt consumed me, and along with it my memory of the words. I expected Father Clarke to become angry, maybe even take off his belt and hit me, for forgetting such an important prayer. Even worse, he might say to me:

I know why you have forgotten it. It's because you indulged the demands of your lower instincts, and your mind is already becoming diseased, like a vestibule of stink and sin, losing its ability to remember anything sacred, holy or divine.

To my surprise, he didn't berate me or cast me into a never-ending night of suffering. He said it was understandable that I had forgotten it; that memory loss happened to everyone once in a while. Then he helped me along, slowly reciting with me.

"And I detest all my sins because of Thy just punishments, but most of all because they offend thee, my God, who art all-good and deserving of all my love. I firmly resolve with the help of Thy grace, to sin no more and to avoid the near occasions of sin. Amen."

After he granted me penance, he sighed like a man in need of a cigarette or a drink, or probably both. By the time I stood up and exited the confessional booth, he had already disappeared through a door near the altar. He had given me ten *Hail Marys* and ten *Our Fathers* to recite. Usually I would kneel at the altar and offer my penance there, but I couldn't kneel or pray in the church. When I looked above the altar, Jesus had broken the nails that held him bound and came from the cross dripping blood and walking dispassionately in my direction.

Forget the Hail Marys. I want you to lick the blood from my feet.

I ran towards the exit, feeling his thorns prick my head, and the devil's whip peel my skin. I stood on the church steps outside, with the taste of blood pasting my tongue, checking for holes on my hands and feet.

I could not—and would not—go home without being forgiven. I would once again, like I had years earlier, find solace in my imagination. I climbed the Grotto fence and knelt near the altar of the Mary statue. This time I would not play Mary, and there was no friend to play God. I would play Father Clarke, the absolver of sins, as he listened to me, the confessor, with compassion and absolution in his heart.

Father, I called you here to tell you my terrible sin. I

thought my you-know-what was the devil whenever it popped up. Last night I tried to stop it and accidentally indulged its demands.

Has your father talked to you about such things?

My father has never talked to me, period.

Your mother?

You're joking, aren't you?

Anyone else?

Just Brother Ambrose.

Is he still teaching young men to be responsible, caring Christians?

I'm afraid he is.

Relieve your troubled conscience, young man. You committed no terrible sin. What you did was part of your nature. You had to discover it sooner or later.

But Brother Ambrose said ...

Brother Ambrose is a hundred and sixteen years old. Forget about him.

But he said it was a sin.

It is a sin.

It is?

Of course it is, but you committed it by accident, so we'll call it a sin of omission. It's easily resolved.

Will I be forgiven?

Of course, as long as ...

I do my penance, right?

That's right, because penance is...

My best friend.

That's right.

Believe me, Father, I know that.

Rest your conscience, my son. You are heaven bound.

From that day forward, I dismissed Brother Ambrose and his teachings. After all, he was a hundred and sixteen years old. The world had changed since he was born, and it kept changing every day, in ways that rendered him obsolete.

He was still funny in his unintended way. But he was no longer a threat to my world. I was indeed becoming the young man he had promised I would become, only on my terms, not his.

JOE JACK, IN SEARCH OF HOME

My father sat at the parlor table and removed his soiled work shirt, revealing a tattoo on his left bicep, an emblem from having been in the Navy during World War II, of a naked woman sitting seductively in a martini glass, her legs draped, beginning to wilt with wrinkles and age. He lit a Camel cigarette, which he balanced expertly between his lips, leaving his hands free to arrange the objects near him; a can of Planter's peanuts, a faded deck of cards, a glass ashtray and a silver lighter. No one sat at that spot but him, and no one, ever, touched the objects. If a peanut was missing, he knew. If someone shuffled his cards, he knew.

As usual, he came home looking like a coal miner, his face, neck and fingers smeared and dark, like soot. He worked in a dye factory in the Bronx, where he stuck his hands and face in machines, repairing them, in between drinking a few beers. He reached for his deck of cards and began shuffling them, using long sweeping strokes, meanwhile steadying the cigarette between his lips, sucking the smoke and shooting it from his nostrils, creating, at the top of his head, the illusion of a halo. Though not an Olympian feat, it was, nonetheless, a skill. After cutting the deck enough to his satisfaction, he began turning and laying the cards, smooth and even, forming seven perfect piles. Solitaire was his game, and he put himself in a trance each time he played. His eyes, the color of lead, winced from the smoke, but he continued to lay the cards in rhythm and precision. The ash hung, an inch and a half by now. Still, it didn't fall. No one could say he didn't know how to handle a cigarette.

My mother entered the parlor, holding a plate of fried chicken wings, layered with steamed corn. He continued to turn and flip cards, to place them in neat piles, as the smoke billowed from him, as if he had become one of the machines on which he worked. She asked him if he was hungry. He didn't reply or look at her. She asked again. After a sustained silence, she laid the plate on the table, said, "Go to hell" in a voice more weary than bitter, and left the room. At last, after a final drag, he guided the cigarette from his mouth with his hand, flicked the ash in the tray and crushed the butt. He lifted a chicken wing, handling it like a pair of pliers. He spit a bone into the plate, and, in what was seemingly the same motion, he lifted another wing, eating it as if he were mad at it. He looked at the corn with an equality of surprise and disdain. He burped, shoved the plate away, lit another cigarette and returned to his solitaire game.

I sat on the couch and watched him, and unless I was mistaken he didn't look once in my direction or show any indication that he noticed my presence. I wasn't offended. After all, we had never talked. I don't mean "Hi" and "Goodbye" and "Pass me that, will you?" I mean, talk.

Tell me about the nature of life and love, dad.

I was hoping you'd ask me that question, son, since I've been contemplating it from the moment I woke up this morning.

He played solitaire and, in doing so, practiced solitude and silence; a silence so loud it was deafening. He was, to me, a stranger, and I was an occupant in his strange land. Of course, he was a stranger in a strange land, as well, and maybe that had something to do with why he didn't talk or often acted mechanically and detached.

He lived and worked and raised kids in New York City, married into an Italian-Catholic family, only recently removed from the Mother country, but he wasn't a New Yorker, nor was he Catholic, may God and the angels forgive him. He was Anglo-Saxon Protestant, a mix of Irish-English-French ancestry, born and raised in Nebo, Illinois, population 85, a stone's throw from Hannibal, Missouri and Mark Twain's Mississippi River hillbilly world. I visited there in the summer of 1965, when I was eleven years old. The entire week or so passed like a bad dream. Kids there—all five or six of them—held shotguns, not stickball bats, and no one played street games such as Ringalevio and Skelly, the way normal New York kids did. The only game in town was hunting squirrels, and if you couldn't shoot a rifle and kill squirrels, you were little more than a pile of manure. Suffice it to say, I was a pile of manure because the day I was given a shotgun to hold and fire —to test my eleven-year old manhood, I assume—I fell backwards, causing black and blues and soreness for days. That didn't exempt me from going squirrel hunting with everyone else, though. Since I couldn't shoot without killing myself or someone else, I became the designated dead squirrel holder, and let me say, growing up in the streets of New York didn't prepare me for this job.

I remember with a fondness born of terror walking through some wood, on the tail end of a group that included fifteen or so men and boys—my father's people— dressed in torn overalls, dilapidated hats and time-worn shoes, looking very much, I'm sure, like the McCoys looking for the Hatfields, and each and every one of them, including my older brothers Davy and Bob, were blasting away at anything that moved. They didn't just kill squirrels that day. I'm certain they destroyed entire species of insects, birds, plant life, and all creatures that happened, with a misfortune worse than bad luck, to live in the hills surrounding Nebo. It was my job to hold blood-dripping dead squirrels by their tails. What I didn't understand at the time but would learn later was that these men and boys were not sportsmen. They were hungry people, and squirrel meat was the easiest, cheapest meat around. Where these people lived Italian delis did not rise from the sidewalks, as they did in New York. No one was going to slice ham and salami for them and wrap them in paper. If they wanted to eat, they had to hunt their food. That day they returned home to my grandfather's house, situated ten feet from a railroad track, where cargo trains, at least a hundred cars long, would pass several times a day and always once in the middle of the night. They brought with them at least fifty dead squirrels and a dozen or so birds, not to mention a bullet wound or two, because when they weren't shooting squirrels they were accidentally shooting each other. I watched my father's people, including the women, tear open the squirrels like they were unwrapping paper. In my naïve eleven-year-old world, it still hadn't dawned on me what they were going to do with the squirrels.

"We're gonna eat 'em, yum yum," my father's step-mother Hazel Brown, a gap-toothed, raw-boned, gun-touting pioneer of a woman, said, when I finally asked aloud. I remember looking at little cut off squirrel heads lying in the grass, and, even worse, mounds of guts everywhere. No way would I eat squirrel meat. I looked at my Italian, Brooklyn-bred mother, looking for assurance that I would not be fed squirrel meat. But she was evasive. Besides she had her hands full with my three younger siblings. The youngest one, Danny, three years old, kept walking on the railroad tracks, saying, "Trains, trains."

I did eat squirrel meat that day and for several days afterwards, as well. It was breaded and fried and tasted very much like chicken. Nonetheless, once I left that godforsaken place of my father's birth and returned to the civilized world of New York, I never ate it again.

As I watched my father studying his cards that day in the parlor, I wondered if he even knew the difference between chicken and squirrel and whether it made any difference to him. He was not discriminate. Food was food. He had been raised to feel grateful to eat anything.

"Get me a beer, will you?" I heard him say, as he kept his eyes on the cards he turned and flipped. Since there was no one else in the room but me, I assumed he was talking to me, but like I said before this kind of talk didn't classify as real talk. It was simply in the category of "Pass me that, you will?" talk. I got up, found a Schlitz in the refrigerator, and brought it over to him. He didn't look up. I put it on the table and returned to the couch to resume staring at this man who would forever go down in the annals of time as someone I would with equal measure affection and angst call my father. I watched him snap the lid open and finish the beer in one refreshing gulp.

I was impressed. At my young age, it was incomprehensible to me how someone could do that. While I could have just as easily been embarrassed by his behaviors, I had learned to celebrate quietly his small victories: beer drinking, cigarette smoking and card playing at the very top of the list.

On the wall, above his head, were pictures of children, six altogether, five boys and one girl. He had been the creator of each and every one of them, though at that time, on that day, he showed no interest in their whereabouts. I could have told him that my younger siblings—Linda, Dennis and Danny—were in the upstairs apartment, eating with my mother's parents, and that Bob was somewhere in the streets, wreaking havoc on the world, but I didn't say anything because we didn't talk, and he didn't ask.

I didn't have to tell him where my oldest brother, Davy, was. He knew, whether he wanted to or not, because my mother reminded him every day and night. He was in Vietnam, lost, captured, or dead somewhere in the jungle, apparently, since we hadn't heard from him in nearly five months. The picture directly over my father's head showed Davy in his marine uniform, fresh out of boot camp, smiling for some unforeseeable reason, most likely to show my father he had the resolve and mettle to serve his country and fight, whether it was just or not, because that's what men historically did. Men like my father who I once heard say in a drunken bout, to no one in particular, "I fought in a real war, and we won, damn it."

If my father was upset about Davy's unknown whereabouts he didn't show it. Then again, by not showing it, perhaps he was showing it, in his own way. My mother came in again and lifted the plate of uneaten food. "Why do I even cook?" she said. When my father didn't respond or look at her, she turned and looked at me. She seemed surprised that I was in the room, just staring. I shrugged.

"Why?" she repeated.

I heard him emit a grunt.

"God damn it, talk!" she yelled. Her voice struck a bad nerve in him. His lips twitched and buckled under, and his eyes spit a little fire. I could see that angry Nebo twang about to come out. He was about to say "Stop the bullshit, Ella" because that's what he always said when he was angry with my mother. I'm not certain "Stop the bullshit, Ella" constituted real talk. Nonetheless, it belonged somewhere in the category of communication.

This time, however, his stubbornness prevailed. He continued his silence, lighting another cigarette, turning and flipping more cards, doing his best to conceal whatever annoyance he felt toward the woman with whom he had had the six children. She, on the other hand, was not easily defeated by his silence. It did not deter her from saying what needed to be said.

"I wrote another letter to Colonel Plotskey in Washington, D.C.," she said.

Deciphering what my father would say if he talked was perhaps my finest skill in my young, undeveloped life. It was a skill I no doubt received from my mother who had had a lot more practice than me in reading his silence. That's how she was able to have communication and conversation. She would speak to him, pause for his response, which she received through his actions. Once she understood their meaning and the words behind them, she would then continue as if they were a normal couple conversing. Thus she learned, as I did, to make the dysfunctional functional. I'm not saying it was a happy-ever-after situation, just that she made a bad situation manageable.

He shot smoke from his teeth and nostrils, at the same time. Both my mother and I understood the words hidden in the action.

You just wrote a goddamn letter last week. Give the man a chance to reply.

"And I'll keep writing letters to him until he responds to me. That's his job. Why doesn't he do his job?"

My father turned his cards with even more snap. He no longer laid them gently in piles. He stamped them on top of each other. It was clear to us what he was saying.

The man's a Colonel in the Marine Corps. He's got a bigger job than responding to your letters. There's a war going on, Ella, in case you haven't heard.

"He's supposed to help families locate their sons," she continued.

The smoke came out faster, in bigger puffs, revealing a specific message.

He's not missing. He's fighting a war. Maybe he doesn't have time to write.

My mother said something really interesting. She said it was my father's fault why Davy was in Vietnam in the first place. When explored further that statement becomes a statement of many truths. First of all there's his name, Davy Crockett, which he, of course, inherited from my father. How does someone live up to a name like that? The legendary Davy Crockett wrestled bears, wore a coonskin hat and was played by Fess Parker in a 1950s Disney movie which made famous the annoying "Davy, Davy Crockett, King of the Wild Frontier" song which every school kid in the 1960s sang every time they heard the name "Crockett" called in attendance. The legendary Davy Crockett was an American folk hero, who shot down Santa Anna's men at the Alamo, left and right, before dying like a Spartan, for the sake and welfare of American imperialism.

The only way my brother could match an image like that, to do justice to the name he received at birth, was to fight in the war in Vietnam. Unfortunately, he had not received at birth, along with the mythic name, the hero's brawn or height. In his marine boots, my brother stood 5 feet 4 inches. No one's going to make a movie about you or sing your song when you're short. I know that for a fact because I inherited the same pygmy genes as my brother had. I'm just grateful I wasn't the first born, that my parents had enough mercy in them to name me Thomas, not David.

The Davy Crockett who stands out most—not the folk hero who was well documented and popularized, not my brother or uncle or numerous cousins bestowed with that name—is my grandfather. Born on a farm in Norborne, Missouri in 1893, this Davy Crockett created his own mythic legacy, albeit a very dark one. To understand my brother's motives—why he went to Vietnam and didn't write for five months, and my father's silent, detached behavior—my grandfather's story must be told, in brief.

One thing about my grandfather, Davy Crockett, is certain. Disney would never have sanctioned a movie about him. Fess Parker's career would have derailed had he played him on screen. My grandfather, you see, was not a hero, unless you consider racism and cold-blooded murder attributes for a hero. He wore overalls and a train conductor's cap and was unusually tall—six feet in his prime—for my family. His French-Irish father, Albert, and his Irish mother, Luella Stevens, did their best to raise their eldest son. A kind husband, father and sweet old granddaddy he did not become, however. Just ask his petite wife, Ola Mae Smith, my father's birth mother, whom he beat so much with his fists she had no natural teeth left, or the black man he killed in 1923, or the man he sliced with a carving knife in 1925.

Killing the black man was a simple act of social protocol, according to Grandpa Crockett law in the early 1920s. Legend has it he was in a town sitting astride the Mississippi River, where he traveled and worked as a dredger. For some reason he felt it was his duty as an American to shoot and kill this black man who was walking towards him, without provocation, because he passed him on the street. Black men did not pass white men where my grandfather was from. He did what any man in his situation would have done; any man who was indeed a man, that is. He shot the black man in the back. He did it, most assuredly, to save his own self-respect and pride and to preserve social order. In other words, he did what was best for America at that time, and anyone who would question his motives or authority might find a similar punishment.

Like my father, my grandfather didn't talk. He didn't need to: weapons such as fists, guns and knives communicated clearly. Wherever he traveled he designated himself sheriff of that time and space, and as sheriff he could shoot and kill whomever he pleased, especially a black man who had no business walking down the same street as a white man, and who had the added audacity to pass him in broad daylight. It couldn't have been good karma for my father to be born the same year his father was killing a black man in cold blood.

My grandfather's other murder was more personal and could have, to some degree, been called an act of violent passion, except my grandfather wasn't a passionate man. He was cold-blooded and matter-of-fact when it came to murdering someone, and this episode I'm about to tell is testament to his cruelty. I already mentioned he beat Ola Mae Smith. What I didn't mention was that she wanted to leave him, by way of divorce. He would not hear of a woman leaving him. If they were to separate it would have to be on his terms. Still, a bigger, more significant complication existed. Whenever he was away, which was often (purportedly he had women in every town along the Mississippi) he was convinced his wife was cheating on him. When she became pregnant with their fifth child, he did not believe it was his. One day he saw for himself that his suspicions were true. He walked in his house, saw his children sprawled about, unattended, then saw Ola Mae Smith scurrying out of the kitchen, into a bedroom. When he walked in the kitchen, he saw a man he'd never seen before sitting at the table, eating a sandwich. My grandfather grabbed a large carving knife, generally used for cutting open the animals he hunted. The man stood up, probably said, "Let's be civil." My grandfather surely would have said, "I'm Davy Crockett, king of the wild frontier" because his name afforded him certain unalienable rights, such as murder, if necessary. Once again, as he had with the black man walking down the street, my grandfather acted on protocol, this time marital protocol. A stranger has no business in a man's house, enjoying the pleasures of his wife, especially with his kids present. In a rage more ironic than tempestuous, he systematically sliced the man from the nave to the neck, leaving the man squealing like a pig on the kitchen floor, until the last of his blood drained from his body. Ola Mae Smith heard everything. She had locked herself in the bedroom, but Davy Crockett could not, and would not, be deterred by locked doors. He banged on the door with his large arms until it broke open. He could have killed his wife, as well as the man. It was within his rights—those unalienable rights—to do so. But there were children nearby, so he settled for beating her the way he always did, with his fists, until nearly all the wind had been taken out of her sails, leaving her a heap of sagging flesh and crushed bones.

It's more than possible that my father, two years old at the time, witnessed this crime; for where else would a two year old be but with his mother? That is, when she wasn't with her lover, of course. But whether little Joe Jack saw and heard everything has never been validated by anyone currently alive or long dead. What is a certainty is that on the same day, at the same time as Ola Mae Smith lay crumpled on the bedroom floor, my grandfather packed her clothes and threw his pregnant wife out of the house, ordering her, under sheriff's decree, to leave Nebo, the joint states of Illinois and Missouri, and, most importantly, her children. If she ever dared return, he would kill her as he had the black man and her lover. She could keep the baby in her womb, if it was still alive after the beating. It wasn't his anyway. The other four children, including the youngest, my father, she'd never see again.

True to his father's words, my father never saw his real mother again, until 50 years later, in 1975, after his father died, when he found the old, dying woman in a shack in the Arkansas Ozarks. When he told her his name, Joe Jack, she said she never heard of anyone named Joe Jack. When my father tried to explain that he was one of four children she had had years earlier, she insisted she had no other children, other than the one who was standing by her bedside, her son Glenn. It was the first time my father saw the brother he never knew. He had always been told that the boy had been fathered by another man, but, as fate would have it, this man Glenn looked eerily similar to Joe Jack, his full brothers Charlie and Tom, and, not coincidentally, my grandfather. But Glenn, like his mother, had no knowledge of kin in the town of Nebo, Illinois. (It is interesting to note that in family records, as recently as 1998, Glenn is, of course, omitted from having had any association with my grandfather's lineage.) My father left the Arkansas Ozark shack and his brief encounter with his mother and younger brother. He never returned there.

The following year after my grandmother's forced exile from Nebo and the children she bore and raised, my grandfather married a woman named Hazel Brown, and they would eventually have seven more children. She had little in her heart for the two-year-old Joe Jack, who, even in infancy, had a hankering to leave. She'd find him hugging the train tracks, looking longingly at how far they stretched. She showed her concern by tying him to a clothesline each day, to keep an eye on him. If he yelled or screamed, she tied him tighter and kept him there longer. He learned to silence himself, and, if possible, unknot the rope on his own, or if it were his lucky day someone would walk by and do it for him. In time, as Joe Jack grew to be three, four and five years old, she herself untied him, but he would always feel the knots of the rope. He would forever be engaged in trying to untie himself, even, when as a young man, 14 years old, he discovered just how far the trains could take him from Nebo, Illinois.

That day in the parlor, he was 45 years old. At that point in my young life there was no way I could see with foresight or wisdom or in any way understand why he was silent and distant. I didn't understand—as I now know better, though not completely—what wounds do to a man and how they dig deep into the roots of the soul, cutting off circulation to healthy, sustainable behavior. All I knew then was that though he was my father, he exhibited little that one might call fatherly. I expected that what I saw and heard was as good as it was going to get; simply existing in the same room, at the same time, sharing the same space.

He wanted another beer. He didn't ask for it in words. He held up the empty one and rattled it, in my direction. I could only imagine how many he had had that day. I couldn't help but think he'd have to go to the bathroom at night, more than once. Getting up to pee would, for most people, not be unordinary. For my father, because of how he grew up (his family didn't have a bathroom in the house) peeing at night could possibly become something extraordinary and categorically mythic.

I refer to a nightmarish night when I was eight years old, in a bedroom that also included my mother and father, and not far from my brothers and only sister who were in the adjoining rooms. (We lived in a railroad flat, with three consecutive bedrooms and no doors separating them; eight people in a space that nowadays might, if a family had the money and means, be occupied by a single couple or an only child, perhaps.)

It was the middle of a wind-howling, winter's night, and I couldn't sleep. Through the blinds I saw the moving shadows of tree branches and heard them scraping the outside wall. In other words, it was already pretty frightening for me. What happened next elevated frightening to the status of horrifying, turning it into something I could not easily dismiss at eight, ten or twelve years old, or for that matter even now, at 59 years old.

As lightning cracked in the sky, the shadows of tree branches became the shadow of a large form—surely a monster—on the wall. It turned out the monstrous form belonged to my father. He had gotten out of bed, and for a few minutes he didn't move. There I was, my eyes propped open, shaking in bed, the unmoving shadow of my father (a shadow of man to me) above my bed, the wind blowing the blinds open, whistling through the foundation below, as cats and birds screeched in the street. I remember thinking if I see the shadow of a knife appear high above his head coming towards me, I'm getting out of bed and running. But the knife shadow didn't appear. Something more horrifying happened. My father began to move, but for some reason his shadow remained in place on the wall. To say I was experiencing a Freudian mind fuck would be a statement true as blue.

I turned from the shadow and watched my actual father walk, in slow motion no less. He seemed as confused as yours truly, his third son, terrified and wet to the bone in his bed. He walked without making a sound, if that's even possible. He walked in the direction of the window, as if the wind were calling him, to return him to his true nature, the world of mystery, from whence he came.

A year or so before this episode, my mother had told me something revelatory. Perhaps I was seven or six years old, and should have known better, but I distinctly remember the following conversation:

"Who is that man who sometimes appears in the parlor and sometimes sleeps in the same room as you and me?" I asked. "You know, the man who doesn't speak and smells like beer and smoke."

"That's your father, silly," my mother said.

"Tell me you're joking," I said.

"I am not joking," she replied. "He's as much your father as I am your mother."

I received that knowledge with resistance. It couldn't be true because I didn't want it to be true. Nonetheless, he kept hanging around. Eventually, like it or not, I had to accept my fate, though I continued to hold out for a much different reality.

Well, here, finally, on that windy winter's night, the truth—the dark secret of his existence and presence in my life—would emerge. He would disappear through the blinds, evaporate like mist, and I would later find out the truth from my mother; that he was no more my father than the shadow of a figure in a dream.

He didn't disappear, however. He stopped at the dresser. What happened next shook my young fragile foundation even further, fixing me forever to the mystery of life and death and made the writing of stories such as this one my only salvation, because I was about to learn just how true it was that fact was stranger than fiction. With two hands, unusually controlled and calm, my father opened the third dresser drawer, approximately waist high. If my mother had never told me that this man was my father, I would have suspected a stranger—albeit one in his boxers— was robbing the house, looking for the family jewels in the dresser drawer. It would have been an altogether more pleasing scenario that the one that actually took place.

I have occasionally thought that perhaps my imagination was over active that windy winter's night, that what I saw only took place inside my mind. But I've always come to the same conclusion: I was wishing upon a star, because it really did happen. My father really did fish his penis out of his boxers, and he really did begin to pee inside the dresser drawer. The sound of his pee hitting the clothes in the drawer was deafening, like a waterfall had rushed in through the blinds and enveloped the room, drowning me in detail I could never forget. What made it worse is that it lasted for a minute, at least.

How my mother or the rest of my family didn't wake up is a mystery I will always ponder, but the room and its occupants remained still. Finally, the waterfall spent itself, becoming a trickle, before running dry. At the end, a sound escaped my father's lips: "Aaah." He returned his penis to its rightful place and walked slowly back to his bed. Within seconds, he was once again snoring. But that wasn't the end of the nightmare. It was far from over. It would, in fact, never be over because for some cosmic reason (perhaps the gods in heaven were playing) his shadow stayed on the wall, and not just that night, but for many nights and weeks and years. I can still see it now, if I dare so much to look at walls on shadowy, windy winter nights, but I've trained myself not to look. That, my friends, is what the masters refer to as acquired wisdom, I suppose.

That's where my mind traveled as I watched my father drink another beer at the parlor table. This time he savored the beer. He even—I'm not kidding—said, "Aaah" once or twice after sipping from the can. I was thankful that I no longer slept in the same room with him. I believe I put in for a transfer sometime after that nightmare incident.

Years later when I thought about the incident I realized he was sleepwalking. At the time I thought he was just too lazy to go to the bathroom down the hall. Or maybe that was the way people did it back in Nebo. After all, they didn't have bathrooms in their houses, and if you have to go, you have to go, right? But that made little sense in our house since we had a bathroom. One small bathroom for eight people was not ideal, I realize. Nonetheless we had an indoor bathroom.

For many nights, I would lie awake, just his shadow on the wall and me. I would wait for him to wake up and walk to the dresser, to open it and pee. But he never did it again. At least I never saw it again. One thought did occur to me, morning, noon and night: What did my mother think the following day when she opened the dresser drawer, looking for something to wear? Had she known my father had peed on her clothes, and if she had, had she wondered about the unexpectedness of matrimony.

Actually, their union was never consciously declared or imagined by either of them. Fate had intervened in their lives, in ways both comical and tragic. Cupid was surely drunk on folly, laughing in the heavens, the day they met in 1942. Years after my father ran away from home at 14 years old, after working on farms in Kansas and Colorado, he joined the Navy, and that's how this boy from the land of murderous fathers met my mother, first generation Italian, from the biggest of cities.

While his ship was stationed in the Brooklyn Navy Yard, he went out one afternoon with a sailor buddy of his named Pierce. They drank in a bar, and then rented bicycles to tour the sights and sounds of South Brooklyn, my mother's home. At the same time, my mother and her girlfriend Mary were out walking, stepping into the crosswalk at the 34th Street intersection. That's when fate intervened (those damn laughing gods!), bringing together these two unlikely pairs—and, in particular, my parents. Either the girls walked into the bicycles, or the bicycles rode into the girls (it wouldn't be hard to guess which was true based on who had been drinking and who hadn't been), but, in any case, in no time at all, the four of them were sprawled in the street; two out-of-town sailors, who talked as if their mouths were full of sticks and stones, and two Brooklyn girls, dressed fashionably, for the time, in low cut dresses and high-heeled pumps.

Little did Joe Jack Crockett or Priscilla Ciampa know that this innocuous, chance encounter would, in the near, post-war future, produce a family of six children. My mother, in her early 20s, though still naïve to dating or romance of any kind, may have believed, unfortunately, that collisions of this sort were part and parcel for everyday courtships, that a man, at some absurdly designated time and place, came crashing into one's life, forever altering it, till only the mercy of death brought relief.

However ridiculous their meeting, when the dust cleared, and my mother opened her eyes, she saw a very handsome—albeit drunk—young sailor, staring down at her. He saw an exotic Italian girl, dark and mysterious, blinking rapidly and uncontrollably. Surely he had never seen anything like her in Nebo or in the many brothels he visited in the South Pacific or wherever he was when he wasn't looking for Japanese to kill. Legend has it she saw Gary Cooper in his smile. It was a fatal vision, for he was no more like Gary Cooper than she was like Gene Tierney. They were two innocents, dazed and confused from their crash, and in a sane world (where the gods act with reason, not folly) they would have gotten up, brushed themselves off, said, "Excuse me" and walked and rode into different futures. But that's not the way life works, as we all know. It feeds on the absurd, the ridiculous, and does its best to make fools of us all.

Their connection had been made; their fates sealed and, with it, mine as well. They became Joe and Ella, beginning a courtship that would last five years, until the war, and his time in the Navy, ended. He never returned to Nebo, to his memory of rope and clotheslines. He went straight to New York and tied a tighter knot than any he could have ever imagined as a child, a knot that would, this time, hold him in place forever. He married Priscilla, in the month of December, the year 1947.

Twenty-two years had passed between their marriage and the night in the parlor. Their youthful expressions on their wedding day pictures had long vanished. Still, four extraordinary things happened in the parlor that night before it was over. One, my father, suddenly, and without warning, got up to get another beer. He snapped the lid in the kitchen, and as he carried the beer back to his seat, and before he sat back down, he—this is the second extraordinary thing—straightened the picture of Davy on the wall. It was as if a light switch had been turned on in the dark world he normally inhabited. The third extraordinary thing was much more amazing. He talked.

It happened when my mother re-entered the room and said, in a tone that was eerily affectionate, "You're a selfish son of a bitch, Joe."

"Stop the bullshit, Ella," he said.

His words had been long overdue, and I believe my mother was relieved to hear them. I know I was. She laughed an honest-to-goodness laugh, and I laughed as well. Joe Jack could have gotten mad at both of us, but he didn't. He, instead, did the fourth extraordinary thing. He smiled. He sipped his beer, tilted his head back and smiled just enough to show his small, yellowed teeth. It may not have been a *Robert-Young-Father-Knows-Best* moment. Nonetheless, it was as close to joy as I could remember.

"The boy is fine," he said.

"Then why doesn't he write?" She sat across from him.

"He's fighting a war, Ella. I know what that's like. You don't."

"Oh, yeah, well I gave birth to him. I know what that's like, and you don't."

One thing about my parents; on that rare occasion when they did talk, they never agreed on anything. If she said hot, he'd say cold. If she said yes, he'd say no. Still, there was something affectionate about this conversation. Maybe it was the fact that they were having a conversation.

"I was in the Navy for eight years. I know about war."

"You were on a ship, not in a jungle."

"I was on a destroyer, not a ship."

"Makes no difference to me. A ship of fools, that's what it was."

I caught the reference immediately, since I'd heard it many times. The "ship of fools" referred to my father's sailor buddy, Pierce. "Any ship that he's on is a ship of fools," she once said. She liked the sound of it and its pinpoint accuracy so much, she made it part of her staple of expressions.

Pierce was from Tennessee and, like my father, when the war ended he didn't want to go home. He stayed in New York because he liked the bars and the "Eye-talian" girls, as he liked to call them. The girls didn't care much for him, though. My mother, in fact, didn't like him from the start. While she saw Gary Cooper in my father's smile, she saw a James Cagney crookedness in Pierce's. Her friend Mary noticed it as well. The moment she dusted herself off in the street after the crash, she saw in Pierce who he really was; just a drunk, making a mockery of the sailor outfit he wore. While Joe and Ella were making a connection, Mary was looking over her shoulder, in a direction where Pierce didn't exist.

My mother had far better reasons to dislike Pierce. He had stayed with them many times after they were first married, and he was always drunk. More often than not, he took Joe away from her and made him drunk, as well. Every six months or so for more than ten years, he'd appear at our house. "I just happen to be in town," he'd say. My mother only tolerated him because she held to an old-fashioned belief that it was a wife's job to be hospitable towards her husband's wartime buddies. This obligatory belief wore thin, however, as the years passed, and it was apparent that Pierce was never going to leave their lives. The breaking point came for my mother one night in the parlor when I was five years old. What happened is, in fact, one of my earliest lifetime memories.

Pierce and my father were drinking heavily, and my mother, with much consternation, was serving them food. All of the children, minus my brother Danny who was not yet born, were in the room, as well. Davy was eleven at the time, and as the eldest he wanted to sit close to the men as they recounted their wartime stories. The stories they told, however, had little to do with war and more to do with booze and sex with hired women. Pierce was not a smart guy. Maybe he went to school past the sixth grade. In that respect he would have had more schooling than my father. But even if he had gone to school till the eighth grade, which was doubtful, he wasn't very smart, as was evident in his limited conversation. That night he put his arm around Davy and shoved his beer toward him and said, "Have a go." My mother protested vehemently. Pierce said, "He's going to have to learn sooner or later." He looked at Joe Jack for approval. My father didn't disappoint him. "You're right about that," he said. My mother fumed. "The two of you are worthless bums, that's what you are."

Pierce and my father laughed. Davy, thinking he should do whatever the men did, laughed as well. When my mother left the room, cursing under her breath, Pierce and my father talked about their brothel experiences during the war. That's all they talked about, as if the Navy and the war had been secondary experiences. (Here's a little side note worth mentioning: my parents' marriage had to be postponed, apparently, because Joe Jack had contracted syphilis in one of those friendly brothels.) Pierce said repeatedly that fat women were his favorite. Davy nodded his head and laughed. The rest of us children stared incomprehensibly at the blabbering, juvenile men at the table. The real trouble started when my mother walked back in the room just as Pierce said, "There's something about a fat woman. When she's on top of you, you know it."

My mother held a steak knife in her hand, though there wasn't any meat on the table. Pierce slapped Joe Jack on the back and said, "You know what I mean, Joe, don't you?" My father's eyes lighted on my mother's hand, which held the knife. She mumbled, first to herself, then aloud, "Shut your damn mouth, I don't want you in my house anymore." Pierce didn't hear her. He was too drunk to hear anything but the nonsense in his head. He turned to Davy and said, "How about you, Davy? I bet you like fat women, too?"

My mother threw the knife at Pierce. The handle struck his chest and bounced off him. "Get out, get out of my house," she screamed. "I don't want you here anymore. You're a bum, that's what you are. I don't want you near my children." She looked at Joe Jack. "Get him out of here, I swear." My mother banged her fists on the table.

"Stop the bullshit, Ella," Joe Jack said.

"What did I do?" Pierce said.

My mother gathered her children, even Davy, who, at eleven years old, enjoyed Pierce's vulgarity. "I'm leaving," she said, looking at Joe Jack. "When I come back I don't want to see him in this house. Ever again! And if you don't like it you can stay out with him, as well, with your fat whores."

"Stop the bullshit, Ella," Joe Jack said again. Then she marched us children up to her parents' apartment, upstairs.

Pierce never returned after that night. As far as I know,

my father never saw him again. If life were a dream world, then it's certain Pierce went back home to Tennessee and married himself a fat woman and lived happily ever after. But the more likely scenarios are that he got struck on the head with a broken beer bottle in a barroom fight and died from the injuries, or, if he somehow managed to survive the bar fights, he more than likely wound up in a hospital and died from cirrhosis of the liver.

My father understood clearly the "ship of fools" reference as well. Nearly ten years had passed since my mother threw Pierce out of the house for good. Joe Jack was not interested in revisiting the experience. In fact, he began to regret starting this conversation in the first place. He shook some peanuts from the can and shoveled them in his mouth. This was a sign, to both my mother and me, that he was finished with talking for the night, perhaps for the week, even. But my mother had a steam full of energy and feelings. She needed to express herself in words.

"This war's not as friendly as yours was," she said.

Joe Jack, as much as he didn't want to continue talking, found it impossible to refrain from commenting on what she had just said.

"Friendly? How can a war be friendly, Ella? Think about it."

"You know what I mean."

"No, I don't know what you mean."

"Go to hell, Joe, you know what I mean. He's over there in Ch—"

"China? Is that what you were going to say? It's not China, Ella. How many times do I have to tell you, it's Vietnam where he is. Not China. We're fighting the Vietcong, and they're nasty sons of bitches, nastier than any Jap I ever saw."

"I don't care if it's Vietnam or China. He has to write, that's all I care about."

"He will."

"When?"

"When he feels like it?"

"For five months he hasn't felt like it? Is that what you're telling me?"

He sighed. I could tell by the way he finished his beer and gathered his cards into one pile that he was finished with talking, for real. He had reached his quota of words not just for the week, but for an entire month. He tried. I had to give him that. Even my mother would have had to be pleased, though she appeared agitated.

All my father had to say was, "I bet he'll write tomorrow." And my mother would have said, "I hope so," and all would have been well. She just wanted a simple acknowledgement of how she was feeling. He didn't want to acknowledge, however. He preferred stabbing her in the heart. It was a game they played, give and take. She gave him her feelings, and he took and crushed them.

Most amazing of all was how I sat there, unnoticed by either of them. I was a witness and little more. Now that I think about it, I must have been placed there intentionally, so that I could someday chronicle their lives. What other purpose I had remained unclear.

Though the details of my father's behavior might indicate otherwise, these were days of great inspiration for me. I would—albeit indirectly—learn a great deal about fatherhood and parenting children. I recall thinking, on more than one occasion: I have all the tools to be a very good father some day, not in spite of my father, but because of my father. Why he didn't experience a similar epiphany in relation to the details and behavior of his own father, I don't know. Maybe it's the dissimilarity of where and how we grew up. Maybe it's a mystery of genetics and happenstance and all the confoundedness of life.

Two weeks later, my mother received a letter from Colonel Plotskey, informing her that my brother had been located and told to write home. He wasn't lost in a jungle, or wounded, physically at least, and he wasn't dead. The Colonel assured my mother that she would be receiving a letter soon. The letter was good news, of course, but also troubling. If he wasn't lost or taken prisoner, why would he purposely choose not to write. Then again, one only needed to meet my father to explain that one. Like father, like son. Silence begets silence.

Whether it was a coincidence or not, Joe Jack left Davy

when he was two years old. He didn't kill his wife's assumed lover and then kick his wife out of the house. After serving for eight years during World War II, he volunteered to go to Korea. Therefore, when Davy was two years old, Joe Jack wasn't home. It's a good thing Davy didn't have his own son. Otherwise he probably would have left him at two years old.

I never did have that heart to heart with Joe Jack. And I mean never. Not at seventeen or twenty-eight or even at forty-four, when my mother lay dying in a hospital in South Carolina, and I was alone with him in a dark apartment, watching him smoke Camel cigarettes and play solitaire and occasionally stare off forlornly. I tried, though I admit not as much as I should have. At one point I said, "We didn't talk much, did we?" He looked at me with his steely grey eyes. They looked mad, hurt, as if the shortcomings of his life were my fault; my fault that he lived a stranger all his life, to himself and others, in whatever time and space he occupied; my fault that my mother lay dying of cancer; my fault that he was living cut off from everyone, except for Davy, in a small apartment in South Carolina. I was living in California, three thousand miles away, even more if you factor in emotional distance. The truth is it wasn't anyone's fault, not mine, not his. Our lives and roles, as father and son, our relationship to each other, were too deep and complex to be explained or understood.

The question was too hurtful for him and, eventually, for both of us. I didn't push for a response. His eyes, staring forlornly, were impenetrable, as was his heart, which had long stopped beating in a way that made him care to try. In the silence of that room, as darkness descended, both outside and inside, where nary a lamp was lit, I took solace in what we shared mutually; our hurt, our pain, our discomfort and confoundedness for what it meant to be joined in genetics. If nothing else, we were there, in the same place, at the same time, breathing together, like a couple of rabbits. It wasn't much. Humans could do much better. But it would have to suffice.

My mother died August 19, 1998. My father, in a twist of irony, dreaded the silence he had always seemed to desire.

It wasn't until the end of his own life, when he suffered from dementia and required more intensive care, that what he really desired became clear. He was living in a state-run nursing home, still in South Carolina, where my brother Davy lived and assumed the role of caretaker. I knew little of his life other than what I was told by Davy; that Joe Jack kept trying to escape from the institution. I wasn't surprised. The room in the nursing home was the equivalent of a box or, more fittingly, a tomb. It was for all intents and purposes another clothesline holding him in place. Another knot he had to untie.

What the attendants at the nursing home didn't know was that Joe Jack knew how to untie knots. Most days he stood near the door, waiting for the swinging door that brought people inside and out, hoping he could camouflage himself as normal, and slip out unnoticed. A few times he succeeded but only for a block or two before he was intercepted by security. But he would not be denied. He would not stop until he found an open road and stood upon its stretch and limitlessness.

And that day came. He walked out wearing pajamas and slippers on his feet. He walked as a man who knew his whereabouts and the lucidity of his own thoughts. He was not, unlike when he was a boy, escaping from home. In a final, ironic turn of the screw, he was returning home, to continue his life, which had stopped long ago in Nebo at two years old. He used whatever instinct it is that animals, such as cats and dogs, use to return home after being lost. He found a highway and walked on its shoulder. He walked without need of water or food or without any sense of the cool air upon his skin or the dangerous rush of passing cars. His life had suddenly become the road upon which he walked. More than any other time in his life, he knew where he was and where he wanted to go. According to Davy, who later received a complete account of what in actuality happened, Joe Jack walked nearly twenty miles that day. How a man wearing only pajamas and slippers on his feet can do that seems impossible. But is it any more impossible than a man living his entire life shut down, emotionally, verbally, unable or unwilling to make contact with those closest to him?

After he walked twenty miles, undeterred, a police car finally pulled over on the shoulder of the road ahead of him. The policeman, a South Carolina State Trooper, got out of his car and approached Joe Jack, who was forced for the first time in hours to stop his movement and once again address a reality he had walked miles to forget.

"Where are you going?" The trooper asked.

"To see my mother," Joe Jack replied.

I always wondered how the trooper really reacted to seeing my father, and hearing him say what he said, dressed as he was, in pajamas and slippers, his once proud tattoo now shrunken like the skin that housed it. I imagine the policeman, other than upholding the laws of public safety, must have experienced a kinship with Joe Jack, knowing he was witnessing the universe and spectrum of man, not in his glorious rise through the levels and stages of consciousness, but in his final descent into a world of delusion and fantasy.

"Where does she live?" The trooper asked.

"Nebo, Illinois," was my father's certain response.

More than likely, the trooper looked askance, to where the highway stretched unseen. I imagined him whistling through his teeth.

"You're a long way away."

"I don't mind walking," Joe Jack most assuredly said, because it was the truth.

"What's your name, if you don't mind my asking?" The trooper continued.

"Joe Jack," my father said.

"And how old are you, Joe Jack?"

"Seven or nine," my father said.

He was, in fact, at the time, seventy-nine years old.

The policeman said, "I'll take you home." My father would have hesitated at those words, and his mind would have recoiled when the policeman took him by the arm and escorted him into the police car. He must have known, by instinct, the way an animal would, that he would never make it home.

And he was right.

The trooper drove Joe Jack to a hospital, where it was soon discovered that my father was a runaway from a state-run nursing home. The hospital transported him back to the nursing home that same day, and this time the attendants strapped him to his bed, in a tighter, more secure room, tying the knot tighter.

He died weeks later on January 24, 2003. The twenty-mile walk in the chill had damaged further his already scarred lungs. He came down with pneumonia and never recovered. He must have known, on that road, more than ever where he was headed and what he was doing. He was untying the knot, for good. The best way he knew how.

His ashes lay in an urn, beside my mother's in Brooklyn, at the Greenwood Cemetery, a stone's throw from where my mother grew up. Placing them side-by-side in the same urn wasn't my idea. But in time it made sense. My mother's home had become his only real home, excepting his first two years in Nebo. The engraving on the urn says, Joe Jack Crockett, 1923-2003; yet it tells only a partial story. The story I told is more complete because anyone who knows him knows that "the better part of man" in him —if you believe in Wordsworthian philosophy, that "the child is father of the man"—knows that he died a significant death in 1926, the day his mother—in tragic circumstances—left his life, and his childhood heart stopped. He waited 77 years, walking in pajamas and slippers, to retrieve it. Perhaps if he hadn't been stopped by the policeman, he would have made it home, where in a twilight-zone realm he would have walked in his house and resumed his life where it had stopped at two and a half years old. Still, if there is an afterlife, my father might read this brief portrait of him. He'd probably be upset and look at me with his leaden, smoke-filled eyes and say, "Stop the bullshit, Tommy." If nothing else, he would have to agree it's the best communication we've ever had.

FRIDAY NIGHT PROWLS

Mario Parmenti leaned against the front door, hands in pockets, toothpick in mouth, three top buttons opened on his white shirt, revealing tufts of black hairs on his chest. At fifteen years old, he stood as a living embodiment that we had indeed evolved from apes.

"It's Friday night," he said, declaratively.

"I know," I said.

"We're going to go look for girls. You coming?"

Parmenti moved with the aplomb of a would-be gangster, not a trace of friendliness in his voice or manner. He had moved to 75th Street a year earlier, living with an aunt and uncle in a bug-infested flat above Gallo's Meat Market, a setting most appropriate for someone who had seemingly metamorphosed from a cockroach. Seen only at night, his facial features could best be described as dark and glossy. On a sticky, summer night, if I wanted to, I could see my reflection in his face, only I never dared look long enough. He had a nickname, chosen especially for his complexion and his propensity to be seen at night: Oily Owl Puss.

If I were serious about finding girls, I would have avoided his company. As ugly as he was, his personality was even worse. The two guys behind him, leaning against the stoop banisters, opposite each other, were no better. I watched Phillip Harris and Tony Martinelli eat pistachio nuts like a couple of oversized squirrels, dropping the shells all over my stoop. Harris' height had spanned six feet by the time he turned twelve. His head alone came close to two feet, contributing mightily to his nickname, Mr. Potato Head. Martinelli, famous for having been left back in the first grade two years in a row, had a brain the size of the green nut in his mouth. He didn't even qualify for a nickname.

"You know we're not going to find girls," I said to Mario.

"Doesn't hurt to try," he said, smoothing a blemish under his nose.

The year was 1968. I was fourteen years old. Meeting girls for me did not hold the same priority as talking about and playing baseball. Nonetheless, I realized, intuitively, that seeking out the opposite sex was a rite of passage. I had to start somewhere, and that usually involved making an idiot of myself.

I had suffered many humiliating nights in the company of this bumbling trio; each night starting the same, with a plan, or, as Parmenti would call it, a "prowl," an evening of perusing streets in search of sexy girls, with Parmenti, our leader, teaching us how to move and think like bugs. Always alert, always shouting instructions, if he saw girls walking in our direction from as much as a block away (he even had the eyesight of an owl), he'd yell, "Be careful; don't let them see our faces." He made it clear to us we could only meet girls by hiding our faces in shadows. "Never step into the light," he'd say, "always hold conversations in the dark."

A week earlier our Friday night prowl had taken us several blocks away, to Forbell Street, on 97th Avenue, where a group of socially—and I'm sure sexually—advanced teenagers congregated. The girls moved like sprites in the night, under fluorescent lamps, while the young men, with smooth faces and muscular forearms, drank and laughed and smoked.

Parmenti had instructed us to hide behind trees—in the shadows, of course—from fifty yards away to watch the girls dance and listen to them laugh. He told us, as well, to keep an eye and ear on the guys. Maybe we'd pick up a clue or two about how to be like guys that girls liked. Parmenti stood behind the lead tree, grinding his thighs against the trunk, Harris next to him, hugging a branch, gawking like a parakeet, saying with a mouthful of nuts, "Wow, get a load of those girls, will you?"

"Watch yourself," Parmenti said to him, "you're swinging into the light. Be careful; otherwise you'll blow a good thing for the rest of us."

Martinelli crouched beside me, behind a tree adjacent to the others. He repeated whatever Parmenti or Harris said, obeying every one of their instructions to the tee.

"Yeah, those girls; look at them, wow!"

His words rang false, since from his position, covered completely in shade and darkness, he couldn't even see the girls. He only said what he did to appease Parmenti's perverted pursuit of manhood. He didn't want to spoil Parmenti's plan and give any indication that the prowl, and the execution of it, wasn't a success. He knew if he upset his instructor in any way, Parmenti would exclude him from future Friday night prowls.

While the three of them unabashedly enjoyed themselves, in a way that only pathetic teenage boys could enjoy themselves, I hoped and prayed I wouldn't be seen by any of the people in the street. I recognized one of the girls right away. It wasn't possible to miss her. Her name was Diane Castone. We were in the same class at St. Sylvester for eight years, and she was so hot my pencil melted every time she walked by my desk. Even in the early grades it was clear she was a woman in a classroom full of boys and girls. To say she was socially and sexually advanced would be an understatement. When she was in the sixth grade, she was dating a guy who was a senior in high school. Clearly she was light years ahead of me and the other buffoons hiding behind the trees. I definitely did not want her to see me. Not that she knew I existed in a real way. Nonetheless, she would have wondered how I, or any of us, ever graduated from eighth grade.

The four of us had earlier shared a six-pack of Rheingold Beer. Parmenti, he of the hairy chest, and Harris, all six feet of him, had no trouble passing for eighteen to buy the beer. Afterwards, taking our places behind the trees, each of us swore we had drunk three cans. No one dared question the awkward mathematics, for we knew that claiming a state of inebriation was our only excuse for behaving like the insipid juveniles we were. We stayed behind the trees for nearly an hour, until the gang in the street got in cars and drove away, leaving we tree huggers alone in the silence of the night.

"At least we got to see some girls," Parmenti said.

Harris and Martinelli concurred. I stayed quiet.

I was ashamed to be alive.

Satisfied that the prowl had brought a measure of success, Parmenti suggested something more easily attained than finding girls.

We went for pizza.

On this Friday night, as Parmenti stood at my front door and Harris and Marinelli ate pistachio nuts like men who hadn't eaten in weeks, he discussed the plan for the night. It wouldn't be a petty neighborhood prowl, he said. He stepped on to the stoop, cracked his knuckles and motioned for everyone to circle him.

"Here's the plan," he said, wrapping his arms around our shoulders, looking from face to face "We take the train to Rockaway Beach and do our prowling there. I hear there's chicks all over the beach."

What Parmenti failed to mention was that there were plenty of guys, as well, at the beach; guys with normal heads, brains and faces. I should have suggested we go to a ballgame or movie, where most of the non-lovers belonged, but the others, suffering from illusions of grandeur, liked the Rockaway Beach idea.

"It might be easier to pick up girls where no one knows our faces," Harris said, in between taking slurps from his bottle of Pepsi.

"Are we going to get some beer?" Martinelli asked, throwing a handful of pistachio shells on the stoop.

"The drunker the better," Parmenti said, wiping some oil from his face.

"Yeah," I said, "it'll be easier for us to make fools of ourselves."

We departed my stoop; four guys, one more blind and deluded than the other, on a summer night, in search of girls on another Friday night prowl. After Parmenti and Harris went into Gallo's Meat Market and came out with a two six-packs of Ballantine Beer and large bags of potato chips and pretzels, we headed for the A train, the 77th Street station, our destination Rockaway Beach, the end of the Queens line.

During the rocky ride, Parmenti dislcosed the first part of his plan. We would sit under the boardwalk, as dark as any den of sin, and drink lustily from our cans of beer, all the while keeping our lascivious eyes open for the big catch that was sure to come.

The first part of his plan wasn't a problem. We arrived at the beach, when it was approaching darkness, and staked out an area for ourselves under the boardwalk. We drank our beers as we crouched in obscurity, left alone by the winos and dope peddlers crawling like vermin along the soapy sand. We had finished one of the six packs and were ready to begin the second when Parmenti called for a huddle to reveal the rest of his plan. "All right, Tommy boy," he said, grabbing my arm, "since you're the least ugliest one among us, this is what I want you to do." He handed me a full can of beer. "Go out and stand in the middle of the beach, and when girls walk by offer them a sip of beer and tell them your friends are having a party under the boardwalk, with plenty of beer."

"Tell them we even have potato chips and pretzels," Martinelli added urgently.

"Uh-uh," said Harris, munching and crunching, holding up the now empty bag of Lays potato chips. "Forget about the chips." He crumpled the bag and threw it into the sand. "But we still have pretzels. Tell them that."

Parmenti looked crossly at Harris. "We didn't come here to eat pretzels," he said.

Then he turned to me again, still holding my arm. "You know what to do, Tommy boy?"

"Just be yourself, Tommy," Harris said.

"Why do I have to do it?" I asked.

"Because your face is the only face they won't be scared to look at," Parmenti said, in a tone that was both serious and truthful.

"Girls actually like you," said Harris.

"You're the only one here who had a girlfriend before," said Martinelli.

Yes, I had a girlfriend, but more in name than in reality. Her name was Josephine Ferrara. She and her family had moved into the apartment building at the corner of the street two years earlier. She and her sister, Annie, would hang out their bedroom window and watch us play stick-ball and other street games. One day, shortly after my eighth grade graduation, when I was thirteen years old, I learned from another girl on the street, Donna Palladino, that Josephine liked me. She, not Josephine, wanted to know if I wanted to go out with her. I said "Sure," not understanding what that entailed. So we became a couple, she sealing the deal by buying me a wrist bracelet with my name Tommy engraved on it. On the back it says *Love, Josephine, June 16, 1967.* Incredibly, I still have the bracelet, one of the oldest objects I own.

We went swimming at a public pool once and maybe to a movie, as well. Other than that, I don't remember ever having consummated our relationship with either a kiss or a conversation. We once held hands in silence for an hour. It was painfully awkward. She was shy, and I was shy. It did not make for fireworks. One day, after my 14th birth-day, Donna Palladino and Annie Ferrara came to my door and told me Josephine, whom I hadn't seen in four months, was breaking up with me. Did I mind? No, I didn't mind. I was single again and free to concentrate on awk-ward adolescence.

So, yes, girls liked me, and I had a girlfriend in name a year earlier, but it was no use to me that night on the beach.

"I don't even want to meet girls," I said.

"Everyone wants to meet girls," Parmenti persisted. "Do you want to hang out with us for the rest of your life?"

I observed the slickness of his face and the hollowness of his eyes. Behind him, I saw Martinelli's vapid smile. Harris was fast at work, eating the pretzels.

True, I did not want to hang out with them for the rest of my life.

"There must be a better way to meet girls," I said.

"Not when you look like we do," Parmenti said.

Martinelli nodded agreeably.

"Forget about the pretzels," Harris said, the last of the pretzels hanging from his chapped lips. He crumpled the bag and threw it in the sand next to the other bags and empty cans of beer.

"Let's say I do it, and the girls agree to join the party," I said. "Then what?"

"We talk for a while." Parmenti's face gleamed with oil. He smoothed it. "Maybe get their phone numbers."

"Then what?" I persisted.

"What do you mean, then what?" He hooted like an owl. "You know, the usual stuff."

"Yeah, the usual stuff," canary-brain Martinelli added.

"The girls will have to see your faces at some point," I said. "Then what?"

"One step at a time." Parmenti caressed his nose. "I'll worry about that later."

"Just do it." Harris slapped my back. "What do you have to lose? Here." He guided the can of beer to my mouth. "Take a good gulp. It'll help you."

"Come on, Tommy, be a sport." Martinelli kicked his feet in the sand. "I would do it."

"Would you?" I asked. "Then why don't you?"

"Mario wants you to do it."

"Why doesn't he do it?" I asked Parmenti.

"Would you go to a party if he asked you?" Parmenti reasoned.

"I wouldn't." Harris burped and wiped his sloppy lips.

"Well, the girls sure the hell won't either." Parmenti sipped a beer, carelessly allowing suds to dribble down his chin. Once again he grabbed hold of my arm.

"Listen, Tommy boy, this is ridiculous, it really is. I ask you to do a simple thing, so simple a kid could do it. Are you afraid? Because if you're afraid, then just forget about it; we'll go home."

His last idea was the only sensible one he had made all night. I told him I needed to urinate before I decided. I put my beer down, walked about twenty feet away, and began urinating. As I did, I looked over my shoulder and saw the three of them huddled close together. Parmenti was right. The way they looked, they had no choice but to go about meeting girls the improbable way.

But why did I have to do it the improbable way? Girls liked me. I didn't need to prowl on streets and beaches. I just needed to wait my time, till a girl, a third party, would approach me and say, so and so likes you, do you want to go out with her?

In my beer-beaten brain, I imagined myself going through life as either Oily Owl Puss or Mr. Potato Head or, even worse, Martinelli. I saw myself going to school each day with a brown paper bag over my face, with holes cut out for my eyes, nose and mouth. I would let people imagine how ugly I was. I wouldn't give them the satisfaction of seeing for themselves. Either way, though, I'd be miserable and worship darkness like a bride. No wonder Parmenti loved his shadows.

I listened to their whispers, saw their feet kicking stupidly in the sand. I decided I didn't need to suffer with them. If I did what they wanted it was because I chose to, for reasons my fourteen-year-old brain didn't fully comprehend.

The waves rolled mightily in my head, making me feel stronger and braver. I would be their hero, their savior, and teach them to accept themselves, to have the confidence to hold their heads up to any street lamp. I zipped my pants and walked back to them. "I'll do it," I said.

Parmenti hugged me.

Harris patted my head, saying, "Good luck."

Marintelli shook my hand. "Safe journey," he said.

I grabbed my beer and stepped out of the darkness of the cavernous boardwalk, on to the fluorescent-lighted beach; my eyes fixed on the rising waves, the smell of salt filling my nostrils. I stepped over and through the sand, feeling the engine of my brain, idling. To help it along I lifted the beer can to my lips and pumped more gasoline down my throat, at which point the waves crashed and boomed under a sloggy moon. I looked back at the three receding figures beneath the boardwalk, disappearing in the shadows of the dark. I raised my beer can to them and gulped some more. They cheered, and as the sand began to rumble, as my feet began to rise, I felt like Napoleon at the shores of Italy. The ocean, the sand, and the land, and all its inhabitants, belonged to me, as did the flickering star above, signaling my deliverance to a brave new world, past the pettiness of adolescence and inferior-minded friends.

A spirit rose from the waters, a giant ego serpent, chewing dice and tattooed women between its teeth. I lifted the beer and drank until the can was empty. I crushed the aluminum and threw it on the sand. "I can do it," I said to the serpent.

A wave rose, swallowing the serpent, and, along with it, my illusion. In its place I heard a primordial shout, coming from the sands of an ancient civilization, from a cavern deep and dark, where cowards cowered in the shadows of shame.

Parmenti's voice, critical in its urgency, echoed along the shores of time.

"GIRLS ARE COMING! GET READY."

Sure enough, headed my way were three girls with rather large outlines. In an instant, I lost whatever Napoleon bravado I had possessed and became Tommy boy, fourteen years old, shy and scared and needing to urinate again. The beach and my ears reverberated with Parmenti's passionate cry for recognition, to become an approved member of the male race.

"GIRLS ARE COMING!"

As the girls came closer, as their frames grew larger, my stomach mimicked the rise and fall of the ocean waves. When the girls were thirty yards away, I could see clearly they smoked cigarettes and looked pregnant, probably twenty years old or more and married, their husbands, no doubt, hiding in sand castles, waiting to attack like monster crabs. Finally, they stood adjacent to me. I smelled their aroma; a mix of hot dogs, salt and tobacco. I turned my head just in time to avoid their faces, the part not covered with cigarette exhaust. They passed in a puff of smoke, at which time Parmenti shouted from afar, like a commander, separated from his troops, in a battlefield, faced in a dire life and death situation.

"DON'T LET THEM GET AWAY! ASK THEM!"

I watched helplessly as the girls moved forward on the

beach, leaving their scent where I stood. Parmenti left the safety of the boardwalk shadows, running desperately along the sand, with Harris and Martinelli following. I expected Parmenti to rush me and tackle me, but he wasn't interested in me. He ran in the direction of the girls.

"Hey, are you girls looking for some guys?" He yelled. His face, exposed to the light for all to see, appeared reddish-purple, moist and slick; his eyes egg white. If I didn't know him, I would have thought the Creature from the Black Lagoon had come from the sea. The girls, twenty yards away, stopped and turned.

"We're having a party," Harris screamed, running up next to Parmenti.

The girls shrieked; part laughter, part horror-struck.

Parmenti walked several steps towards them. "We just want to talk to you for a while," he pleaded.

The girls ran like a pack of coyote and didn't look back.

Parmenti darted a step, as if he were going to chase them. Then he stopped and turned to Harris and Martinelli.

"I told you guys to stay under the boardwalk, didn't I?" he screamed.

"Don't blame us," Harris yelled back. "It was you they ran from."

"Oh yeah, I didn't hear them asking you for a piggy-back ride." Parmenti pushed Harris. Harris pushed back.

"There's one more beer," Martinelli said. "Anyone want it?"

Parmenti grabbed the beer and threw it in the water. Then, as I expected he would earlier, he rushed at me, grabbing my arm aggressively.

"What happened? Why didn't you ask them like we had planned it?"

I pulled away from him and began walking away. He persistently followed. "You didn't have the balls for it, did you?"

"Do your own goddamn work next time, you ugly bastard."

He took a swing at me, but I ducked and retreated. Harris and Martinelli held him back, but they couldn't stop his words.

"As far as Friday nights are concerned, you're finished, Tommy boy."

His words were music to my ears. I walked, without looking back, all the way to the train station. On the ride home, Parmenti and I sat at opposite ends of the train, while Harris and Martinelli walked up and down the car in senseless repetition. Not a word was exchanged between any of us during the duration of the trip. When we got off the train, Harris said, "Anyone want to get pizza?"

No one answered.

For several weeks Parmenti was true to his words. I didn't see him, and I wasn't sorry for his absence. Then, one early evening, on a Friday night, he reappeared in my life, and, as always, wanted to take me on another prowl.

I was sitting on my stoop, watching some of the younger kids on the street fill the summer night with pre-pubescent fun. Rosemarie Costelli and Roseyanne Marino, my neighbors, played "Two-Feet-Off," hopping like bunnies across the broken asphalt. Ten-year old Dominic Scalia and his friends were running for freedom, engaged in a game of "RINGALEVIO," an adventurous version of hide and seek, with limitless boundaries. In this game, one team, any-where from three to five guys, hid themselves in the street, while another team, equal in number, set out like a posse to find them. The object in capturing someone was to hold him and say "Ringalevio, one two three, one two three." At that point the guy was captured and went to jail, guarded by someone on the other team, so that one of the opposing teams' players couldn't free him, by tagging him. When each player was captured the game was over. The game was far from simple, though. It could last for hours and some-times more than a day. For instance, a guy could hide on a rooftop and stay there for twenty-four hours. Billy Higgins, a neighborhood Ringalevio legend, did just that. That's how much he wanted to win the game.

It could be especially difficult to find someone as wiry and ingenious as Dominic Scalia. As I stood on my stoop, resting my back against the banister, Dominic stopped in the street near my gate, crouched near my father's Ford Fairlane, and, in a moment, disappeared beneath it. He got under the car with the oil stains and the melted gum and the smell of gasoline. I understood. He was ten years old; the summer night was young, and Ringalevio offered escape and the possibility of legendhood.

"We're playing 76th Street," he whispered to me from under the car, his eyes shining like a cat's. "Don't say anything, if someone comes around asking."

Dominic, you have my trust. I played the game during my pre-pubescent prime. I know what it's like to rub my nose against a muffler and hide from the world on a summer night.

As I was leaning on the gate, whispering to Dominic that his secret was safe with me, I saw their shapes coming down the street, towards me. The trinity without hope; three misbegotten souls doomed to wander forever the purgatorial sidewalks of Brooklyn and Queens. The Lord and centerpiece of the trinity appeared most prominently, his moon face slicked with acne cream as he led his followers to my gate.

"How are you doing, Tommy boy?" Parmenti said. "Quite a coincidence, huh? We were just coming to get you."

"Yeah, quite a coincidence, huh, Tommy boy?" Martinelli parroted.

"Goddamn!" Harris punctuated the coincidence with eloquence.

"Listen, Tommy boy, I'm glad we ran into you like this." Parmenti slapped my shoulder and turned to his followers. "We're all glad, aren't we?"

Harris spit out a nut and nodded.

"I know I'm speaking for all of us," Parmenti continued, "when I say that we feel lousy about that night at the beach. Ain't that right, guys?"

"I feel terrible about it," Martinelli said, his head hung in shame.

"Hell, we were a little drunk that night, weren't we?" Parmenti slapped my shoulder again. "Shit, I know I was."

"Shit, I had four or five beers, at least," said Martinelli.

"Four or five?" Harris tossed an empty pistachio shell at Martinelli's head. "Shit, I poured down four or five in the first hour."

"Who cares how many we had?" Parmenti stuck his elbow in Harris' rib. "The point is we were drunk and got a little stupid, and I think I speak for everyone, Tommy boy, when I say we're willing to forget if you are."

Patty Quinn, a large-bodied boy from 76th Street, nicknamed Red—Dominic's adversary in Ringalevio—came by, sniffing like a hound dog. His copper hair flared in the early summer night.

"Hey, you guys see any little runts go by?"

"Yeah, I saw one go down the sewer," I said.

"The sewer?"

"Yeah, you know the place where rats like you live."

"I think you're full of shit," he said.

"Beat it, Red," Parmenti said. "Your hair is giving me a sunburn."

As the Mighty Quinn descended down the street, I heard Dominic whisper, "Thanks" from under the car.

"Anytime," I whispered back.

Parmenti looked around. "Anytime, what?" He said.

"Anytime ... huh? ... sure, anytime ... I'm willing to forget."

"All right! They shouted in unison and huddled close to each other as Parmenti dug into his pocket and pulled out a small, manilla envelope. Harris rubbed his hands and Martinelli squealed.

"I got some pot!" Parmenti said, flashing the bag near my face. "Now we can definitely pick up girls."

"That's right," Harris said. "I hear pot will make our eyes look sexy."

"And girls dig the aroma, I hear," Martinelli added.

"They smell it, and they're drawn to you, Tommy boy," said Parmenti, gleaming.

"We'll be like snake charmers," Harris said.

"Only we'll be charming girls, not snakes," Parmenti corrected him.

"We'll have them wrapped around our fingers, like snakes," Martinelli said.

"That makes absolutely no sense," Parmenti said to Martinelli.

"Where did you get the pot?" I said.

"Don't worry about where I got it," he said. "What's important is that all the lovers who hang out with girls smoke it."

"Have you ever tried it?" Harris asked me.

I knew they were going to lie about having smoked it, even though they had never seen it before. "Sure," I said, knowing it would open up the floodgates of bullshit.

"Hell, I smoked that stuff about ten times," said Martinelli.

"Ten times!" Harris spit a gob of crunched pistachios at Martinelli's feet. "I smoked it that many times when I was in the eighth grade."

"Yeah, well you guys haven't smoked this pot." The acne cream on Parmenti's face began to dissolve, leaving him with a glossy, early evening look. "This stuff will blow our brains and make us crazier than hell."

I saw myself in a mental institution for the rest of my life, side by side with the trinity without hope; Parmenti next to me forever, saying, *I'm hornier than a frog. I just wish I could meet some girls in here.*

"And if we can get some girls stoned on it," Parmenti continued, "they won't be able to tell the difference between a pig and a bluejay."

"They'll think we're movie stars," Harris added.

"Exactly," Parmenti said. "And that's when we can make our move."

"I've always wanted to be a movie star," Martinelli said.

"So, what do you say, Tommy boy?" Parmenti said.

I had told them I was willing to forget the beach episode, but the truth is I wasn't willing to let it go. I had already made a fool of myself drinking too much beer. I could only imagine the idiot I'd become stoned on pot.

"I'm feeling sick to my stomach, like I'm going to throw up," I said. "Girls don't like guys that throw up."

"Did you read that in the paper?" Martinelli said to me.

Everyone looked, incredulously, at Martinelli. No other response was needed.

"Smoke some of this pot, Tommy boy, and you'll forget you even have a stomach," Parmenti said.

"Come on, Tommy," Harris said. "One more guy will make an even number."

Critical point, Harris.

The Mister Softee ice cream truck motored down the street, blaring its pied piper jingle, coming to a stop across from where we stood. Rosemarie and Roseyanne stopped their game to get something cool and refreshing, and so did other kids playing in the street. Poor Dominic. I wanted to ask him if I could get him a cone or an ice cup. It could get lonesome lying under a parked car. There was an honor in winning, though, and that's what Dominic understood at that moment. To become a legend he had to forego all pleasure and live with discomfort, in the name of Ringalevio glory.

"Come on, Tommy boy," Parmenti said, his patience becoming tested by my silence. "The girls are out there, ripe for the taking. What do you say?"

I turned away from the ice cream truck and Dominic under the car and got right to the point, seeking to annihilate their illusions once and for all.

"I think you finally devised the perfect plan, Mario," I said, slapping him on the shoulder. "I only wish I was feeling better, so I can enjoy the rewards that are sure to follow. I'll tell you what. I'll go in and rest for a half hour or so while you and the others get the girls. Then, when you get them—and I'm sure it'll be a cinch with the pot—you can swing by and pick me up."

Parmenti, a study in disgust, bit his lip and caressed a bump along his cheek. As he glanced at Harris and Martinelli, he seemed to age a hundred years.

"We don't stand a chance, not without you, and you know it," he said.

"But you have the pot, Mario," I said. "The girls will be drawn to you like a snake to a charmer."

"Bullshit, we'll still be as ugly as sin," he said, matter of factly.

"And not very intelligent," added Martinelli.

"Other than that, we're perfect," concluded Harris.

They had come as seekers of the holy grail, the contents of their dreams bundled into a small, manilla envelope. They left as beaten, worn-weary travelers, tripping clumsily over their own feet as they wandered down the street, resigned to the reality of what lay ahead for them. There would be no girls. Not that night, and, in all likelihood, not for many years. They would smoke the pot and then eat potato chips and pretzels and maybe some pizza. That was the best they could hope for. They knew it, and I knew it.

That was the night Friday night prowls ended forever.

The metaphorical leaves turned, yet another year, and with it came divine intervention, or just good old-fashioned luck. Shortly before I turned sixteen, I made other friends around the corner, on Drew Street, the Brooklyn side, and began hanging out under fluorescent lamps in the streets, with girls who swung their long hair and shone their white teeth, and with male friends who didn't need to prowl the beach in search of girls. I had arrived the natural way.

O, brave new world!

MY GRANDMOTHER GOT ON THE TRAIN

My grandmother sat mummified like something that had been unearthed from an ancient removal and set in a chair as an artifact for display. She stared motionless at a twilight of backyard clotheslines, cradling with taut, brown-boned hands an aluminum-steel walker that obscured her pelvis and legs. Her feet, wrapped in white-woolen socks, appeared as marble relics from a world no longer seen. When she noticed my presence in her bedroom, she came to life, making first the sign of the cross, followed by a prayer she mumbled to the unmoving sky.

"Guiseppe y Maria, take me, I'm old, I'm broken, I'm no good anymore." Then, to punctuate the meaning more clearly, she crossed herself in a final *coup de grace* and said, "Take me." She spoke these words routinely, as often as anyone would listen.

She had recently returned from Jamaica Hospital, having undergone an operation and subsequent rehabilitation for a dislocated hip. Her misfortune occurred while she rode the A train, on her way to work in midtown Manhattan. Now, 82 years old, she confronted her worst nightmare, trapped at home with nothing to do.

"It wasn't an accident," she had said many times, describing her ordeal that day on the train. "I didn't slip and fall. When I got up to get off the train I had no foot to put down. It came apart like a seam in an old trouser." She knew about trousers; she had worked on them for over fifty years at B'Altman's Department Store, in midtown Manhattan, on 34th Street and 5th Avenue. Trousers she could mend. Healing an old body required a pact with powers beyond her realm.

She sat near the open window; it afforded her the best place to listen whenever the A train, two streets away, passed on the elevated tracks, into the Brooklyn tunnel, leading inevitably into Manhattan and her place of work. As she heard the sound this early evening, she leaned towards me, excited to impart her well-earned wisdom.

"Do you hear the train moving on the tracks, Thomas? (She pronounced my name TOM-ASS.) "There's no sound like it in the world. Get on that train, Thomas. Get on it while you can. Don't sit around here. Go out and work. The train's here, and then it's gone." Her excited tone vanished as the train and its sound did as well.

"I'm old, I'm tired, I'm no good anymore," she repeated, looking forlornly at the sheets—sails without wind—on the clotheslines. Her doctor, before she came home, had prescribed to her retirement; sentiments echoed by her family and co-workers, as well. After all, at 82 years old, few people, if any, worked away from home. She, however, had no intention of stopping what she had done her entire life. She was determined to rehabilitate herself and return to work.

"What am I supposed to do in retirement?" she said. "Sit home and play cards and bingo? Please, that's for senile people. Watch TV all day, sip a little soup here and eat a little cracker there and blow my nose during commercials and, if I'm fortunate enough, move my bowels once or twice a week. Is that a life, Thomas? You tell me. Or maybe I sit outside on the stoop and have my daughter, your mother, prop me up with a pillow like a doll so I say hello and goodbye and how do you do to every Tom, Dick and Harry that walks by." She crossed herself again and looked up. "Please, Guiseppe y Maria, if I can't work, then take me now, because life without work is a hell, an honest-to-goodness hell."

I wondered at her use of the word *hell*. She hadn't gone to Catholic school for twelve years, like me. She hadn't gone to any school, for that matter. After arriving from Italy as a six-year-old girl in 1905, little Assunta (her Americanized name was Susie)—an immigrant, unschooled and uneducated—walked the railroad tracks in Manhattan's lower east side, searching for loose potatoes, vegetables and fruit that fell from cargo men unloaded. She called it her first job in America, and with it came a lesson for a lifetime, her sacred creed: if you wanted to eat, you had to work. This knowledge she followed like a bright star in an otherwise dark sky; it consumed her every thought and breath. When there was no food to gather on the tracks, she picked dandelion weeds, gathering them in a bucket. She took them home and washed and plumped them up to sell on the streets. She had no time to dwell on what was hard and unfair about life. The boat ride had taught her that. She needed ingenuity to live, plain and simple.

"Time is either a blessing or a curse. When you use it to work, it's a blessing. When you sit and do nothing, it's a curse. I was blessed all my life, but right now I'm being cursed. I know what happens when a person doesn't have an objective anymore. He becomes a crazy person."

She was referencing her husband, Alfonso, who had been dead eight years. After fifty years of marriage, having borne four children, she could only recall the final image of his demise and death. He was in the kitchen of their house, stock naked, washing himself with a wet cloth. He told her he wanted to be clean when he died; therefore, she didn't stop him. What she remembered most was the moon through the window, like a torn piece of linen. (She typically saw all life and nature through the metaphoric lens of a seamstress.) He began singing, and it appeared to her that he would end his life on a note of harmony; only the singing didn't last. In its place appeared hostility. He began speaking in Italian, fighting with people who were clearly not present. Naked as an egg in the kitchen, washing himself with a washcloth near an open window, he screamed, "io mio volere soldi; mio soldi ... mio soldi ... ei un bastardo ... vai al diavolo." Even my grandmother didn't know to whom he was talking. She assumed it had something to do with gambling because he was always in debt, always owing money to mysterious unnamed associates, people capable of putting a stranglehold on him. Still, it didn't deter him from gambling further. He once hocked her wedding ring to get money to bet on a horse. The horse lost, as all his horses lost, and, in the end, he lost his mind, saving his last venomous words for his mother. "Mio madre e al puttano...puttano..."

She shuddered to think what would become of her now that she couldn't work. It wasn't dying that worried her. It was going crazy first, like her husband, Alfonso, had. She did not want to stand naked before an open window, cursing in Italian, calling her mother a whore. She much preferred to die of a heart attack, while at work, stitching a seam in a trouser. If there was a just God in the sky, that's how it would end for her.

Framed against the window, her masculine face belied her age. Her white hair, combed into a tight bun, shimmered against the sheen of her olive skin. Her nose trumpeted like an antique horn, holding itself above her brassy lips, sealed in stubbornness. The lines forming at her nostrils, snaking down to her mouth, were set deep in her flesh, as if carved by a tool. Other than those lines, her face appeared smooth as stone. It was, however, a deceptive face. Those who knew her were aware that every cell of her flesh was in conflict, her eyes the exception. Green and cool, they were the wheels that drove her will, crushing —up until the moment of her misfortune—time along the way.

"The doctor at the hospital, a young fellow he was. What audacity. He says to me, 'What were you doing going to work at your age?' I was working long before you were born I said to him. Before this hospital was built. And if you do your job correctly I'll keep working long after you're retired. He laughed. 'You deserve a medal,' he said. A medal for what? I said. For working? Keep the medal for yourself, I said. I don't work for medals. I work for self-respect. He smiled and nodded, like I was a child, and not making sense. So I said, listen, young man, people tear their pants every day, and I repair them. The next day they wear their pants again. There's no difference with my leg. It came apart and now you are the seamstress. A high-paid seamstress. Just do your job, and I'll do mine. You mend my broken leg and I'll continue to mend trousers. He didn't smile when I said that. He left the room."

She sat motionless, save for the ebb and flow of her chest, her breath flowing like water, bringing the curious face of the moon to her window. Her bedroom was as stark as her situation: a bed, dresser, night table and armchair, upon which she sat. Not much else. No embellishments, no pictures, no memories. The only feature that exuded life was the beaded garlic bulbs draped on the pillow of her bed. Part of an ancient code that had shaped her life as an immigrant, garlic was as important as anything else she brought to America on the twenty-one day journey from Naples to Ellis Island in the year 1905.

"Tell me again about the garlic," I said.

She looked away, rubbed her lips with two fingers. Finally, her hands relaxed, clasped together on her lap. Her jaw dropped, revealing hard pink lips. Her eyes drank the twilight sky, transporting her to a world long lost, like a dream.

"I ate them like candy." The words came from her mouth, bittersweet. "Every last one of them."

"You talked to them, too, didn't you?"

"I suppose I did."

"And gave them names."

"I did what kids do is what I did."

She looked at the garlic on her pillow, as if by staring at the beaded bulbs she could extract memory and strength. She told the same story every time. It never varied.

Entombed in the steerage of a boat with hundreds of others, she watched a young girl, the same age as her, cough pellets of blood into her pregnant mother's hands. The girl was dying. Even at a young age, my grandmother understood that. Women cried and old men wheezed and sighed, and the engine's noisy rotation rocked on, forward with the living. While others surrendered their stomachs to the boat's incessant rise and fall upon the sea, my grandmother held on. She refused the stale bread and watery soup and occasional bread pudding and sardines that others coughed from their intestines. Her mother and brothers succumbed to seasickness morning, noon and night. Their yellowed skin smelled sour from vomit. For twenty-one days they couldn't bathe. My grandmother had to protect herself, and the best way she knew how was by avoiding them. She realized, then and always, her survival rested in self-sufficiency. Before the trip had clocked four days, she began to drape her face within the blackness of her shawl, and there in the darkness found a burning will, an indomitable strength that would never submit to the stranglehold of life. She would not vomit like her brothers. She would not die, like the small girl near her. She would hold on, fearless, without a whimper or complaint. One day, searching among piles of luggage, she discovered an open sack of garlic. Each day she carried garlic bulbs to her *sanctum sanctorum*, the sacred spot under her shawl. She tore off individual cloves, giving them names, talking with them, laughing. At night, she ate them, like chocolates.

When the young girl died, my grandmother didn't cry like those around her. At least not in front of them she didn't. She waited until she was alone, under her shawl. She held garlic cloves in her tight-fisted hand and crushed them till their juice spilled under her small nails, and then she cried, but it would be the last time she would, as a girl or an adult woman.

The miraculous day came when the waves died down. The boat had reached New York Harbor. The hundreds of steerage passengers, including my grandmother, joined the first and second-class passengers on the deck of the boat. Together, they saw their first view of the Statue of Liberty and America.

If America was the land of freedom and equality, that notion was lost on my grandmother. She saw how differently the steerage people—her people—were treated from the first and second-class passengers. While the latter group was ushered from the boat after it docked, the former were kept in quarantine, held for inspection. After all, they were poor, and it was the poor who were more likely to have lice and other diseases, such as tuberculosis, all causes for summary rejection. From the larger boat they were transported to a smaller barge, hundreds of them, crammed like cattle. Their possessions, they were told, must be left behind, and once they passed this inspection, a longer one for the immigration clearing process awaited them at Ellis Island.

People screamed as doctors pulled their eyelids inside out with a buttonhook, checking for trachoma. She didn't scream when it was her turn. She saw no point in it. At six years old, she had already acquired a wisdom that would guide her in life. She didn't look back. She kept her head up, her eyes forward on the moving line. An official asked her the sum of two plus two. She knew to say "four," since she had heard others in line say it. When asked if she possessed money, she said no. She didn't mention the garlic in her pocket.

They were finally ushered into the waiting area. All they needed now was their sponsor, their father, Giuseppe Troisi, to show up to claim them. He had been living in New York, making money as an immigration trafficker, moving to and from America and Italy. He had finally saved enough money to bring his family to America, as he had promised on so many return trips. On that first day, however, he never showed. Nor did he appear on subsequent days. Without a sponsor to claim them, they were deported, on a boat, to Montreal. Story has it Sal, my grandmother's older brother, made money gambling on the boat, using a wooden nickel as collateral. Whatever money he won paid for their train to Boston where my grandmother's mother had a brother. They didn't know where exactly he lived. They wandered the streets until one day he found them. He contacted their father in New York City. Apparently Guiseppe didn't show up to meet them because he had another woman, and though he tried to get rid of this woman she wouldn't volunteer to leave. He was too ashamed to claim his family while he was living with another woman. His family traveled to New York, hoping to find him, but he remained evasive, invisible. His wife and children wound up in an alley on Mulberry Street, above— of all places—a garlic shop. At night, my grandmother and her brothers stole garlic, and during the day they sold it in the streets, and whatever they couldn't sell, they ate.

My grandmother never knew Guiseppe. He had never lived in the same house as his children. The few times she remembered seeing him, on a rare visit, she hid under her mother's skirt, afraid of his presence. Years later, she knew only that he had died in Italy, in his hometown, Mirabella eclano Avelinno Campagna. The Black Hand, the Neapolitan Mafioso, got hold of him, she was told upon inquiry. He was forced to sign over to them land he had owned. After he signed on the dotted line, they held his face down in water until he drowned.

Another train passed, and as it did, she stretched her neck to see beyond the yards, where white linens moved silently in the darkening sky. She had made a pledge of allegiance, to herself, to return to work, and it mattered little to her that no one understood and believed her pledge, for she knew something even God didn't know. She would do it, plain and simple.

After a demoralizing sequence of hours, days, weeks and months, walking and moving in her small room—practicing she called it—her deliverance had come. She could now spit in the face of God's master plan: the aging process, the broken bones, the rotting brain, the death of productivity. She had gone dark and empty staring down her skeletal image, and now she was ready to heave like an unbridled horse breaking from its reins. Her rehabilitation was not a miracle, she would say. Miracles were not bestowed upon people. People made their own miracles, with grit and will and determination.

I, fortunately, was there to witness the event. In truth, it was more than an event. It was epic, heroic, and likely the most courageous act I've ever seen: my grandmother, 82 years old, descending the hallway stairs, dressed and ready for work, to meet her judgment, on her own terms.

She had not trained for nothing and, yet, she knew her limitations. She stepped and stopped, conscious of each measured, calculated step she took. Watching her, it was clear to me she obeyed the indomitable laws of stubbornness and madness. Thus, she was unstoppable. To attempt to stop her would have been an act of sacrilege against the will of woman.

She descended to the bottom of the stairs, opened the front door and stood motionless on the stoop, her arms stretched and holding the wrought iron banister with each hand, appearing as a supplicant to the gods or a martyred Christian waiting for some unseen arrows or stones. Wearing a polka-dotted dress with black-heeled shoes, starched nylons and a kerchief, she stood more than a minute in a stationary lull, except for her heaving hips and rapid lungs. A shopping bag and cane looped her sleeveless arms, her left foot barely grazing the stone.

She began her descent down the stoop using the strength in her arms and the support of the banister to swing her forward. To get out of the gate she held the aluminum fencing with one hand, while with her other drove her weight into the cane, avoiding at all costs putting any stress on her left leg. From outside the gate she merely needed to walk two more blocks to the train station. I wondered if she had called her workplace. Or had she moved forward on assumption alone? Did it even matter to her? Maybe it was the process of going, of doing, that mattered only.

I watched as far as I could from the window in the door until she left my sightline. Then I stepped outside and watched her hobbling on crippled bones, waddling from side to side, shrinking to the size of a gnome as she moved down the street. I could still stop her and save her from the perilous risk of passing Mrs. Mattaglia, the siren of 75th Street, who through the sheer will of her decrepit spirit could make old people fall at her feet and later die an ignominious death in a tubular hell of hospital smells and milk of magnesia sheets.

My grandmother didn't care. She would have walked— or hobbled or crawled or slithered—into the stink of sin to get to work. I was sure she didn't even notice that her neighbor water hosed the sidewalk and moved the instrument aside to let her pass or that she mouthed a few words to her, something akin to "How do you do?" My grandmother couldn't be bothered. She didn't look up. She moved her broken machinery, dragging her left leg like an old muffler against the asphalt.

And now I began to walk and follow and pass the perilous gate of Mrs. Mattaglia. She didn't move the hose for me. She continued to water as I dodged the sidewalk and walked around the spray. When I greeted her with a "How do you do?" she opened her stingy lips and scowled.

"Your grandmother crazy?"

"Yes," I said, to appease the old woman.

My grandmother paused before the corner apartment building, adjacent to Gallo's Meat Market, and seemed to stare above its door at a blue steel fire escape. I wondered if she was thinking about the fire escape she fell from while living in an alley apartment on 98th Street and 2nd Avenue. Eight years old and tough as the dirt on a devil's back, she'd cut open her knee and fractured her wrist and ankle. A neighborhood boy, named Alphonso (yes, the same one), cruising in a wagon made of milk cartons and bicycle wheels, found her lying in the street, bloodied and bruised. He lifted her, against her will, and placed her in his wagon. He told her she needed stitches on her knee and must go to an infirmary two blocks away. He pedaled less than fifty yards, she in tow, before she rolled out and skidded face up in the gutter. "Thanks," she yelled to the surprised boy. She picked herself up and hobbled to her apartment, on one leg, where she washed and stitched her cut (perhaps the beginning of her seamstress days) and made a sling for her wrist and bruised arm.

She was eight then. Now she was eighty-two. What had really changed? Did she think of that boy even now, and had she forgiven him for trying to steal her independence at eight years old? Or was she waiting for him to come again, like he had seventy-four years earlier, to take her in his milk cart wagon, to take her to the station? Would she accept the ride this time, or would she roll out again?

The answers came crudely. She cleared phlegm and spat, continuing forward, passing the market, beginning the two-block stretch along Liberty Avenue. From that moment she remained steadfast, moving toward the station. The trees threw skeletal shadows at her feet. She crushed them with her will. Her green eyes glazed, her bulbous jaw chewing cloves of garlic, spitting their residue at the creeping bone-thin shapes moving at her feet; her eyes burned, and she smelled the taste of blood in her throat, but these were more the symptoms of desire than of malady.

An A train passed on the overhead track, crisscrossing another that appeared in the opposite direction. The steel sang and sent sparks, and for a moment I saw her raise her hands, as if saluting the train or like a wizard commanding it to stop for her. I moved and waddled behind her, imagining what it was like to walk on old bones. I imagined, as well, the taste of garlic on my tongue. I raised my left leg and used the strength of my arm against buildings to push myself forward, dragging myself along the avenue towards the station's pearly gates.

She crossed the avenue, stopping traffic, and headed for the Hudson Street station, 77th Street. The monolithic structure cast the street in shadows blue and green. She stopped at the foot of the subway stairs, perused the two dozen steps to the token entrance, and as she did she puffed and cleared phlegm and morning breath, like wisps of smoke, dreaming to herself, or perhaps waking to a dream she had clung to during her rehabilitative ordeal. A flurry of birds that nested in the station's steely beams flew overhead. She began to ascend, silently, all her energy and focus contained in the task of lifting, stepping and climbing. She moved, not on effortless wings, like the birds. Rather with arms and breath and broken legs, and a will the size of a continent. A man passed her on the stairs and appeared to ask her if she needed help. She waved him off and pulled herself up, methodically, machine-like, all muscle and madness. I went no further than the foot of the stairs and waited for her to get to the top until she disappeared beyond the token entrance. I stayed until a Manhattan bound train pulled into the station and moments later turned its irrepressible wheels forward; after which I walked back home, awake in a dream of my own:

The clouds lay islanded like painted sheep on a canvas of sun and sky, my grandmother the scarved sheperd on crippled steps made light by the wings of her will. I had followed her call to the station, and now I followed the train with my feet, running in the shade of a blue green shadow cast from the overhanging El, listening to the soft singing steel on the overhead track, feeling the fast moving heat on my skin. The A train raced towards the tunnel's mouth, my grandmother aboard, proud, stubborn, defiant. I closed my eyes to its vanishing and ran along the fading summer streets, angling away from loose-fitting dreams, rushing towards unseen worlds to come, understanding courage to be the highest form of any virtue.

My grandmother worked for another six years, repeating the routine each morning, her walk to the train station akin to climbing Mount Everest. She did it because she could. Even God couldn't do it, she'd proudly say. Only a human can do something like this because we know how to work. He never worked a day in his life. He just watches us. I don't have much respect for those who watch, whether they're God or not. Watch this, God. That's what I like to say to myself each morning, climbing the stairs, getting on the train, working till my fingers are blistered. Watch this, God. It's called work. You wouldn't know. But I know.

At 88 years old, her employer of 60 years, B'Altman's, forced her to retire. She had tried to outrace the setting sun, the circling moon, the shooting stars, the swift shadows, the spit-in-your-eye truth of life. But the truth, in the end, was faster than her It put its stranglehold around her mind and body and choked her with a realization that came with her 88 years of life: she had diabetes and high blood pressure, blood clots in her legs, failing eyesight and—worst of all for a seamstress—had developed trembling, unsteady hands. Time had to be recognized for what it was, and will always be: ruthless and unrooted. She could no longer crush it with her will.

On her last day, she was given a pin, commemorating 60 years of service, and along with it trite, conciliatory words: *no one works forever.* That's where God failed us, she thought, as she walked to the 34th Street station, to begin her journey's end, toward home, toward nothingness. We should work forever. If God were sane and just, he'd have made sure we did.

She had always had an affinity with the A train. It had always moved her forward, toward making money, toward productivity, toward the pride of being able to say, *I am one of them, the working people.* It was her lifeline, her fountain of youth. Now, on this her final train ride, it moved her backward, toward home, toward a room from which she now would never escape, a coffin-in-waiting. She saw herself, shrunken with fear, in the reflection of the train's window. Her nose began to bleed. She searched for tissue. She had none. She found instead a banana in her pocket. She pealed and ate it, then wiped her nose with the skin. She put the skin back in her pocket, where her fingers found the pin. She held it up, felt its smallness, its lightness of weight, its emptiness of words: *Commemorating 60 years of service.* She understood its meaning. It was a death sentence, given to someone when she could no longer work; when the life she lived becomes her tail, and she forevermore moves around in circles chasing after it, and the dream of life and living becomes a nightmare in the waking light. In her reflection, receding now it seemed —was it because of her failing eyesight, or a sign of life to come?—she saw what was ahead: the inevitable slow progression of idleness, and with it the demise of her spirit.

Working had helped her defer that slow progression towards what she called the nonliving. It had given her the semblance of life, made her think she was alive, with purpose. She could distract the master plan waiting for her. Now there would be no such illusion. To punctuate that point, the train went black, tunneling in the darkness of the underground, wiping out her image in a tumult of sound and fury. This is the beginning of the end, she thought. How long will it take? A year? Two? If I'm lucky, perhaps it will be sooner. In the meantime, what is there?

The lights reappeared, and with it, reality. She had no hobbies, no interests, no passions other than working. She could sit and eat and watch TV. She could have visitors, tell stories, be amusing if the mood was right, but she would never again be able to defer or deflect the inevitability of what it meant not to work. She knew the score. She was being taken to pasture, to slaughter. Her heart would weaken, her circulation would all but stop. She would eventually lose the ability to walk. She would have to be hospitalized. She had seen it in so many others. Why would it be different for her?

She got off the train. She stood on the platform, watched the train disappear around a curve. She held the sound in her ears, however, as long as she could, until that, too, became a silent whirr. Still, she didn't move. She stared down at the tracks and nearly smiled, remembering herself eighty two years earlier, walking the railway tracks in Manhattan's lower east side, in 1905, searching for food for herself and her family. Children didn't do that anymore in 1987. They went to school instead. She felt sorry for the children of the present. They have it too easy. What good is school unless it teaches you hard, lasting lessons?

She took the pin, commemorating her 60 years of service, and tossed it on the tracks. That part of her life was over. She left the platform and descended the station steps. Without the motivation of work rooted in her heart and brain, she found walking and stepping excruciatingly difficult. As she entered the street, she moved, somehow, in a mostly unconscious state. Her iron will, once the size of a continent, had shrunk. She felt small as she hobbled home.

She would get one wish. Guiseppe y Maria did, finally, take her, only not on her terms. The hospital—the metaphorical slaughterhouse—was, indeed, the final stop for her, just as she had foretold, though it had not only taken her body, which she would have gladly given. It first took her mind.

She died crazy, ignominiously, babbling and screeching, attached to tubes and machines, at age 90. Her independence taken from her, she became a caged animal. The self-respect she had nurtured her entire life turned to undignified shame. Her inner strength became an outer weakness. The last time I saw her she didn't recognize me. She called me a lazy hospital attendant who didn't know the meaning of work. As I began my exit from her room, she yelled incoherently, unintelligibly, in her native language, Italian, blistering the room with angry tones, exhausting herself with an exclamatory summation:

"Vai al diavolo, Dio!"

I had to leave. It was unbearable to see and hear my proud grandmother become little more than a mad dog.

While the hospital experience was a bad note, it was not representative of the overall composition of her life. It was a footnote, at best. I choose, therefore, this final image on her final walk from the train station to home.

She had walked mostly with her head down. Then, before she entered the house, she heard a familiar sound and turned, to look up. She saw the A train on the elevated track, snaking above the street, descending into the tunnel, leading through Brooklyn, towards Manhattan. She watched it, with her eyes and in her mind, for the last time. She smiled a knowing smile. It was to her that bright star in an otherwise dark sky. She had followed it in life, and would, I believe, as well, in death.

She opened the gate, climbed the steps to the front door, and, like the train itself, she disappeared from view, but she would never disappear from my consciousness. Her words, to this day, ring always in my ears:

Get on the train, Thomas, while you can.

I got on the train, grandma. Thank you.

HOPE BEYOND ALL HOPE

I got off the A train, left the underground station and walked along Liberty Avenue, the main artery in the East New York section of Brooklyn. The late afternoon sun crowned the Chase Manhattan Bank, as if the building owned it, as well as everything else, and loaned it to the neighborhood during the day. A strip of storefronts shouldered brown-bricked apartments, where potato-faced people appeared from windows, resting chins on sleeveless arms, their voices conveying sounds akin to the bark of dogs. Along the avenue, cars sped their engines in frenzied jerks, and high above the street the A train rumbled on the overhead track, its metal frame clanking like an oversized trash can as it descended into the tunnel which divided the boroughs of Brooklyn and Queens.

At 75th Street I turned and passed rows of two-storied flats, bricked together, lining both sides of the street. Each had aluminum, chain link fences, black wrought iron banisters and cement stoops. Only the colors of the doors and the awnings above them varied. Trees lush with newly sprung leaves made a canopy above the sidewalk. Squirrels scurried through a maze of branches, and sparrows, drunk with spring, gyrated their wings in a game of chase. Mrs. Mattaglia swept her front gate, and when she didn't sweep, she sat on her stoop, day and night, waiting for someone to throw a wrapper on the ground, or for a dog to shed a hair, to give her reason to sweep again.

A Spaldeen came bounding towards me, followed by a fair-haired, ten-year-old boy running at me, screaming, "Over here." I lifted the ball and threw it to him. I stopped and watched as Dominic Scalia and his friends stood in the street, immersed in a stickball game with the kids from 76th Street. Dominic was the pitcher, throwing the ball on a hop to the hitter, a large, bespectacled boy with red hair named Patty Quinn. Everyone called him the Mighty Quinn, but he swung the bat like a Minnie, not a Mighty, missing the ball by two feet. "Atta baby, Dominic," one of his fielders, standing on a sewer, which served as second base, yelled. "No hitter at all." I leaned against a tree, a few houses from Mrs. Mattaglia's gate. She stood like a sentry, holding her broom as a weapon, waiting for the ball to land in her front yard so she could gobble it up like a peach and cut it into a hundred slices.

Across the street, Tony Fontanino's sister (I'm not sure she was given a birth name) sat on her stoop, waving at me. She had a disability, which in 1969 would have been labeled mental retardation. Nonetheless, she had never gone to school, and for nineteen years mostly stayed inside her house, sitting near the street window or sitting on her stoop in a childish reverie, waiting for me to come home from school. She was in love with me. Out of compassion, I tried to reciprocate her love by smiling and waving back at her. I never heard her speak, though when I smiled and waved she would always laugh, covering her face with her hands, producing sounds like coughing or choking. We exchanged this communication on a regular basis. It made her day, and, in some respect, also made mine.

Adjacent to her house, I saw Sonny on his stoop, smoking a cigarette and drinking something that I'm sure was alcoholic. He was Vinny (the Rat) Palladino's uncle. He had just gotten out of jail (for manslaughter I had heard) and one of the first things he did was volunteer to be the baseball manager on our CYO baseball team, mostly made up of kids, ages 14-15, around our street. It was clear, in my neighborhood, that you didn't need sterling qualifications to lead young men. Ironically, that's the year, 1968, we won the championship, in the Tyro division, beating other schools in the Brooklyn Diocese. We didn't see much of Sonny after that. Either he went back to jail, or he married into the mob. Still, he wasn't our only coach who was associated with jail. Two doors from our house lived Sal Annunziato, in the basement of an apartment building, with his old father. Sal was a man in his thirties back then. He had never been past the fifth grade, and he wasn't smart. That alone qualified him to be our manager for two years in little league. He wasn't in jail when he was our manager. He waited a few years to get himself in some serious trouble.

A terrible incident had occurred just doors from where I lived. Sal had gotten himself so deep in the drug business that he made enemies with the wrong people, namely drug dealers. One thing about people who did and sold drugs; they had little morality and even less conscience. The drug dealers came to Sal's apartment one day and threatened to kill him. His 88-year-old father, Mr. Annunziato, tried to protect his son, using his cane to ward off the perpetrators, but the cane was no match for the guns they held. They shot and killed the old man. Sal didn't kill anyone, but he was cited for drug possession and solicitation. He lost both his father and his freedom.

I was very upset when I heard the news. I liked the old man and had fond memories of him wearing his derby low on his head, covering wisps of white hair, as he'd take his daily walk to the corner bakery, puttering down the street like a mechanical doll, his shoes squeaking along the asphalt, as if his batteries were running low. He stood no more than five feet tall, his ears small and brittle, curled like corn chips, his long nose ending in a definitive point, twitching rabbit-like whenever he laughed, which was often, mostly to himself. On his return home from the store, he'd carry loaves of Italian bread, and if he saw me, he would playfully slap my cheek and say in a heavy Italian accent, "Wheresa your girlafriend?" When I'd say I didn't have a girlfriend, he'd slap me harder and say, "Whattsa matta with you, stupido?"

The Mighty Quinn struck out, but the next hitter, a wiry little guy with curly locks, batted the ball over the outfielder's head. The ball crossed Liberty Avenue and wound up in the Sinclair gas station. By the time the outfielder retrieved the ball, the kid had circled the bases. One of the

76th Street kids yelled, "That's 7-0, and it's still top of the first."

A terrible picture came to me: Dominic and his friends huddled afterwards near the apartment building bricks, licking their wounds from an awful defeat, and someone saying, *Let's start a gang ... how about you, Dominic, you want to start a gang?* History would repeat itself. For a week or two there would be no stickball playing, just spitting and cursing and smacking innocent little kids in front of John's Pharmacy, until one of them would lose a tooth or have his face plastered with blister juice from Benny's little brother if, God forbid, he had a little brother. After that, they would hang up their tough act for the rest of their lives and return to the street games in search of lost innocence. But it wouldn't be there.

You can never get it back, Dominic, once you lose it.

I wanted to run out into the street and tell them, *Don't stop playing.* Before I could the next hitter mimicked the previous hitter's feat, hitting a line drive over the outfielder's head. This time the fielder walked after the ball, yelling past his shoulder as he did. "Damn it, Dominic, what kind of pitches are you throwing them?" I felt sorry for Dominic. When he wasn't getting clobbered in stickball games, he usually played with a Spaldeen against his stoop, until his father would come home and smack him in the head and tell him he was worthless. The game continued to get worse for him. The next batter hit a shot right back to him. The ball ricocheted off his head and rolled under a parked car. Poor Dominic had to crawl under the car to get the ball, and by the time he did the kid was crossing home plate.

Mercifully the game ended soon enough. The next batter clobbered a line drive that struck one of the parked car's rearview mirrors. The mirror fell and shattered into many pieces. Such were the perils of playing in the street, surrounded by cars and people's house windows. The kid didn't bother to run to first base. He picked up his bat and ran, along with his friends, around the corner, back to 76th Street. Mrs. Mattaglia began yelling, "I knew it ... I knew it, all you kids do is break things."

Dominic and his friends picked up their sticks and balls and walked dejectedly away. I walked further down the street, until I reached my gate, where my neighbors Rosemarie, Roseyanne and Ginny bore their knees into the asphalt street, flicking bottle caps, playing a famous New York street game called Skelly.

I saw Angela sitting on her stoop, staring forlornly, at the girls in the street. She wanted to play, I could tell. She wanted to be a normal girl, like the rest of them, but it wasn't possible, not with the father and mother she had. Her parents were real Italians. I don't mean Italian-Americans. They were from the old country, and they had old country ways of doing things. They had three daughters. The two older daughters, when they reached eighteen years old, were married to men who had been shipped over from Italy. They married these men without ever having seen them. Both of the men were similar in two ways. They each had a big nose, and they were both pizza makers. In fact, two of the pizza places on the avenue, Aldo's and Flora's, were owned by them. Angela was the youngest daughter, and also the prettiest. I had heard from my sister, who was in the same grade as her, that she didn't want to marry a big-nosed Italian who was a pizza maker. She wanted to choose her own husband. But the way she looked as she sat on her stoop, staring at the girls in the street who were free, playing Skelly, it didn't seem like she believed it would ever happen. To defy Italian family law would be the equivalent of defying God. Angela didn't have a chance, and she knew it.

Mrs. Petrone appeared out her window on the second floor, her large arms as intimidating as her shouting voice, calling to her daughter in the street below.

"Roseyanne, I need you to go to the store, on the double." Roseyanne belly-flopped on the asphalt, kicked up her feet, and told her mother that she almost had Skelly.

"Skelly can wait," her mother yelled. "I need oil to fry the chicken."

"You can wait to fry the chicken, can't you?" Roseyanne yelled back.

"No I can't wait," her mother said. "Your father wants

his chicken now."

"I'll be right there, as soon as I'm finished," Roseyanne persisted.

"Now, I said," Mrs. Petrone yelled, "or you'll be sorry." She disappeared from the window. Roseyanne hurried her game, flipping the bottle caps with precision and skill, completing all the requirements to win the game. Finally, she scooped up her prized bottle caps and went quickly inside her house.

I entered my gate quickly, ran up the steps and opened the front door. Whoever designed the turn-of-the-20th-Century building loved hallways. First came the vestibule, home of mailboxes, an umbrella can and doormat; then another door leading to the staircase to the upstairs apartment. Beyond that a narrow hallway led to the downstairs apartment where we lived. From this hallway I was able to enter the kitchen, and through this the parlor. From the opened blinds came the ghostly sails of billowed white sheets hanging in a pale blue light in the outside yard. I heard the nonstop clank of the A train and the barking of dogs from near and far. I turned to my mother, asleep in her recliner, her nylons rolled to her ankles.

A pencil-thin nerve twitched above her rosebud mouth, and though her lips were tightly drawn, I heard the mash of teeth from within them. Folded on her chest, her hands gripped a brown-beaded rosary, anointed with holy water. One finger, the index of her right hand, jerked, signaling to the others that they remained on call, ready to recite a *Hail Mary* on a moment's notice. Her finger tips, firm and rounded, were perfect for spinning beads. She made music with them, spun a continuous song. On a nearby table stood a Blessed Virgin statue, my mother's favorite icon. Anytime of the day she could look and see Mary crushing the serpent's head beneath her foot; a source of strength and inspiration to my mother who believed she could slaughter demons with her beads, giving her the much needed hope beyond all hope to which she clung. I considered waking her from the devils inhabiting her dreams, but then the pulsing nerve came to rest, and her parting lips opened to show rows of gleaming teeth.

I focused on the framed pictures along the flowered wall. Most had been recently placed, and each one featured my oldest brother, Davy. I stood facing one above the couch, the one I straightened three times a day, to no avail. The moment I turned away, it became crooked. Taken on his confirmation day, at twelve years old, his face and eyes glowed with boyish joy. None of the pictures on the wall showed him over the age of thirteen. A year earlier there had been only one picture of him; the day he graduated from marine boot camp in Parris Island, South Carolina. Now that picture was nowhere to be found.

He had been in Vietnam for over five months and hadn't written once, and it tortured my mother, knowing nothing of his whereabouts. She sometimes turned on the news hoping the grandfatherly face and trustworthy voice of Walter Cronkite would soothe her nerves. But it was never a good idea to turn on the news. As nice as old Walter Cronkite was, the news he delivered could tear a mother's heart from her chest, and it never failed to do so with my mother.

On a typical night in 1969, Mr. Cronkite soliloquized about riots in American cities, but inevitably addressed his favorite topic, that being Vietnam. He always showed film footage and fatality statistics. Most of the footage showed helicopters landing in fields, blowing the faces of soldiers below, wounded men waiting to be jettisoned from hell. My mother always made creaking, sigh-like sounds in her throat, tolerating the Vietnam news only on the miraculous hope that an image of her son would appear. Perhaps she would see him getting out of a helicopter, holding a radio, smoking a joint in a field, anything to communicate to her that he was alive. Wherever he was, he would smile directly at the camera and tell my mother everything was fine, that the marines were feeding him well.

But she never saw Davy on the nightly news. She saw only helicopters filling the sky like red-eyed, blood-filled locusts, propelling a nation of boys toward a mountain of dust and death; and news correspondents, buried in the bowels of a borrowed jungle, shouting sorry statistics in a din of despair.

At such times I would switch the channel to WOR, channel 9, where Lucille Ball, my mother's favorite, was sure to appear in all her zaniness, wearing spaghetti noodles, dripping from her head after a kitchen mishap, or peeling dried paint from her face after having a bucket of it fall on her. Moments like that my mother could understand and appreciate, and they never failed to make her laugh in full-throated ease.

My mother had written twice to a Colonel James L. Plotskey, Head of the Marine Corps Welfare and Family Assistance Section in Washington, D.C. For months she waited for a letter or telephone call, but none had come. Her only relief, other than watching Lucille Ball, was closing her eyes, with the hope that when she awaked she would look and see, in person, the same young man she saw in the pictures lining the wall. But it was clear by the way her fingers twitched and held the rosary beads that even in sleep she found no solace.

On a day previous to this one I had come home to find my mother looking dazed and confused as she sat in her recliner, her nylons rolled to her ankles. She had just opened her eyes she said, awaking from a disturbing dream. In the dream she was strolling Davy in a baby carriage along Liberty Avenue, and women on the street were stopping her and saying, "What a beautiful baby. He can win a contest." She went into Kuck's deli, leaving the baby carriage, with Davy in it, outside. When she came out of the store, she found the carriage empty. She looked frantically all around, and then she saw a marine walking towards her. It was Davy. He saluted her and kept walking past her, until he disappeared from view, as she called to him. She woke from that dream with his name on her lips.

I noticed a paper sandwiched between the arm of the chair and her elbow. Without lifting it, I could see it was the drawing Davy had done in the fifth grade. It was a drawing of a daisy growing in outer space. He had always said he wanted to be an astronaut, to explore outer space, but he became a marine instead. For years I hadn't seen the picture because my mother kept it in a closet box, but in the previous weeks it had begun to surface again, along with the photos from his childhood. I wanted to whisper into her ear, "What a beautiful baby," but I didn't. I straightened out his confirmation picture, said, "Write to her, please" and left the room.

I went into the room where I slept, the first room in a series of three, none of which were separated by doors. If my mother wanted to get to the front bedroom she had to walk through mine first, and then she'd have to walk through the middle one. We had three bedrooms in this railroad-style apartment. We were a family of eight, and to this day, I honestly don't know how or where we slept. Until the age of thirteen I slept in the same front room as my mother and father. My one sister, and my two younger brothers must have slept in the middle room. Davy, the oldest, slept in the first room. Where my second older brother, Bob, slept I have no idea; probably on the couch in the living room. When Davy left for the marines, I took over the first room, and I was thankful. I was thirteen years old and had started high school. I couldn't sleep in the same room with my parents forever. Still, privacy didn't exist for anyone, and I'm not only referring to my family. I'm referring to my neighbors as well. All the two-storied flats on the street were attached to each other. We were sandwiched between downstairs and upstairs apartments on our left and right, and we had tenants living above us. To make matters worse, each family kept their windows and blinds open at all times.

Just feet from my window, I looked in John Costelli's window. He was two years older than me. He was sitting on his bed, playing his accordion, which he had recently gotten two months earlier. I knew everything about him, as I'm sure he knew everything about me, since our rooms were adjacent to one another and so very close in proximity. I knew what time he went to sleep, what time he woke up, what he ate for breakfast, lunch and dinner, when he went to the bathroom and whether he flushed and washed his hands or not. I heard him cough, burp, and fart on a regular basis. I saw him often lying on his bed, just staring up at the ceiling, his fingers interlocked behind his head, his elbows angled like paper airplane wings. He was a junior at St. Francis Prep in East New York, Brooklyn. He had a hard time fitting in with his peers, I assumed, being that he had red hair and played an accordion.

I saw his mother come in his room and say, "Why don't you play that song Gooseberry Goose? It's my favorite." I wanted to call to him, across from me, and say, *Please, not that song again.* Only a mother could love a song like that. As much as I hated it, it had become etched in my unconscious. While most kids sang songs by the Beatles, I found myself whistling or singing "Gooseberry Goose" walking to and from the train station and even while taking a shower.

He told his mother he had to practice scales. She left his room, and as he began to practice, each erroneous note wore away tissue in my eardrums. I wished at that moment I had begun to play an instrument, so I could kill his ears as well. Then again, I'm sure living next to a family of eight gave neither him nor his sister, mother and father much peace. We had to be the loudest, most annoying family of all. But at that moment it was he and his family who were bothering me. His mother, somewhere in the kitchen, called to John's younger sister, Rosemarie, who earlier had been playing Skelly in the street.

"Rosemarie," she called, "I need you to go to Gallo's to get some chuck chop and bread for dinner."

"Wait a minute, mom," Rosemarie said, "I'm in the bathroom."

Meanwhile someone—it must have been Mrs. Ciarelli above them—was running a vacuum. It was very loud, and it shook their building as well as ours.

A few seconds later the Costelli toilet flushed, and I heard Rosemarie talking to her mother about groceries that were needed.

"How much chuck chop you want me to get?" Rosemarie said.

"Get a half pound," her mother said.

"And bread?" asked Rosemarie.

"Yes," said the mother.

"What kind?" Rosemarie wanted to know.

"Italian bread, what else?" the mother said.

Rosemarie must have been on her way, walking through

their hallway, because when her mother next spoke it was more a shout.

"And get some ketchup. We're low."

"All right," Rosemarie shouted back. I could even hear their front door slam. That's how intimate we were in proximity to one another.

I had to give John credit. He kept playing his scales with perfect concentration, unaware that I was watching him, or that toilets were flushing near him and voices were speaking loudly and a Russian tank-like vacuum cleaner was steamrolling and rumbling on the floors above his head, creating an earthquake-like situation.

The Ciarelli household above them smelled of cabbage, onions and fried liver. It was an annoying smell, but it wasn't the smells coming from their apartment that was most annoying. It was the way they talked to each other, at inappropriate times of the night. Mr. and Mrs. Ciarelli had an only son named Angelo. You might think a family of three would be quiet, but that wasn't the case. Angelo was twenty-one years old, and he didn't work. As far as I could tell, judging from the conversations coming from their window, he only watched TV, day and night, and Angelo's father didn't like it. As if on cue, every night, at one or two o'clock in the morning, Angelo's father would say, "Angelo, shut that TV, or I'll break your ass." I was certain Angelo's father woke up half the neighborhood with his eloquence. That remark by Angelo's father was usually just the beginning of a long, drawn out affair, the two of them yelling at each other from different rooms. Automatically, no matter what he was watching, Angelo would shout, "It's almost over, Dad." But I knew better. It was never over. Fifteen minutes later, Angelo's father would say, "Angelo, you son of a bitch, get your ass to bed!" Angelo offered the same rebuttal each time. "It's almost over, Dad." Twenty minutes later, I would hear Angelo's father, only this time he would be inside Angelo's room, and he would be hitting his son in the head, saying, "Do I have to break your ass to get you to stop watching that TV?" Still Angelo would be pleading that the show was almost over. Then his mother would get up and join them in the room, and she'd say, "Angelo, you should be going to bed early, so you can look for a job in the morning." To this remark, Angelo would always say, "There are no jobs." And Angelo's mother would say, "How do you know if you don't look?" Angelo would say, "I've looked." And Angelo's father would beat him again, saying, "You looked? Where did you look? You didn't look anywhere, you lazy son of a bitch." Sometimes Angelo screamed at his parents, slamming first his door before slamming the front door, on his way out. Where he went at night and in the early morning hours I always wondered. Maybe he went to a friend's house to watch TV in peace. One thing was certain. In the morning he wasn't looking for a job. And just as certain was his return home, by evening, just in time for their scene to start all over again.

On the other side we shared a wall, but not windows, with the Coppolo and Atkinson families. The Atkinsons were one of the rare Irish families on the street. They were a family of seven, three girls and two boys. The boys were the youngest, many years younger than me, and they were grungy buggers, always in the streets and gutters, picking up ants between their grubby fingers and eating them. More than once, I'd come to my gate and see them burrowing in the street. Once the older one, Howie, held out his hand, revealing a half-dozen ants and tiny bugs. He asked me if I wanted one, as if they were an assortment of chocolates he was offering me. I declined, telling him I had food inside. He didn't talk to me much after that.

The Coppolo family boasted a son, Skippy, who was awarded a purple heart for being shot in Vietnam, and a younger brother, Patsy, who was famous for being gay. I don't mean that facetiously. He became one of the first, if not the first, transgenders in New York City. A movie was made about him in 1975, starring Al Pacino, called *Dog Day Afternoon*. His life as a gay before his transformation, especially in that neighborhood, during the 1960s, long before gay pride parades and same-sex legal marriages, was a hell much more severe and degrading than any hell the nuns at St. Sylvester could have produced in their imaginations. In a neighborhood where all the boys played stickball and baseball and every manly sport possible during that time, he was more interested in dressing dolls, putting on beauty pageants and playing doctor. I didn't dress dolls or participate in beauty pageants, but I did play doctor with him numerous times as a kid. He was two years older, so he always got to be the doctor, and his younger sister, Rae Rae, and I played the patients. He was a good doctor, as far as I could recall.

Unfortunately, he wasn't as well received or appreciated by the rest of the world in Brooklyn and Queens. He got bullied and beat up repeatedly by kids from school and those in the neighborhood. One day I saw him crawl in his gate, bloodied to a pulp, needing serious medical help. Even going home, though, didn't meet his needs. His own mother, in fact, her face and arms hanging out the upstairs window, called him a faggot one day as he was leaving the house. She yelled and screamed, telling him not to come back, ever again. I don't believe he ever did come back, at least as a male. When I next saw him, in 1975 or thereabouts, he was a woman and had changed his name to Patricia. I remember asking him—this was the last conversation we ever had—"How do you like it?" He said, "I love having breasts and a vagina, if you know what I mean." I didn't know what he meant. Nonetheless, I was happy for him, even though he would be forever estranged from his family, unloved by his mother.

I knew the feeling of being unloved by a mother, though, in my case, it lasted only a few minutes. My mother laughed each time she told it, and I admit it's deserving of laughter. The first words I ever heard, upon being born— and this was according to my mother—were "I don't want him." My mother had already had two boys, and she desperately wanted a girl. Because she wanted a girl badly, everyone else involved or close to her wanted a girl, as well: my father, my grandparents, my aunts and uncles. My mother felt she had paid her dues having had two boys already, and now she wanted to be rewarded with a girl; someone with whom she could take shopping; someone she could dress in pretty clothes; someone who might care for her when she became old and sick.

After the birth, the doctor held me up and said, "Congratulations, it's a boy."

My mother didn't even look at me. "I don't want him," she said to the doctor.

"Are you sure?" the doctor said.

"Yes, I'm sure. I already have two boys," she insisted.

"Don't you, at least, want to look at him?" he asked.

"No," my mother said, assuredly, "if I look at him I'll probably want him."

Probably?

I have to forgive my mother. After all, she was drugged silly and had her hopes and dreams of having a baby girl dashed in an instant. Still, what she failed to understand at the time was that I heard every word. I wasn't exactly conscious and in a good mood at that moment, being that I was bloody, dazed and confused. Nonetheless, those words were the first I heard, and they must have stuck in my subconscious

"He's very beautiful," the nurse said. "If you don't want him, I'll take him."

I was only minutes old and already I was being passed on to someone else. I have to admit, it's been handy in my life every time something has gone wrong to refer back to this beginning, when my mother sealed my fate by saying, "I don't want him."

"You can have him," my mother said. "Besides, I don't even have a boy name picked out. That's how certain I thought I was going to have a girl."

"You'll have a girl next time," the doctor said.

"Yeah, sure," my mother said, "if I keep trying for a girl I'm sure to wind up with six children some day."

More prophetic words were never spoken.

"He's healthy and beautiful, and he's already smiling," the nurse said.

Perhaps I was smiling at the absurdity of the human condition; adrift at sea, in a world void of love, meaning or purpose. I was born an existentialist.

My mother's stubbornness finally gave way to curiosity. "Okay, let me see him," she said to the nurse.

My mother always told me it took only one look to change her mind.

"You can't have him," she said to the nurse. "He's mine, and I love him."

She took me home and lavished me with care and attention. For two and a half years I was the end all and be all of her existence. I was the Little Prince, and the words "I don't want him" began to fade from my subconscious memory, but then the unthinkable happened.

My mother gave birth to a girl, and I was suddenly cast out of Eden. The prince had become a frog. A baby girl lived in the house, and once again the words "I don't want him" haunted me, as I settled in my new role, in abandonment and exile. It was then, my mother told me, I became green with envy. She said I spent most of my third and fourth years lashing out at my sister. The female species had become my enemy.

In time, when she wasn't lavishing attention on my sister, my mother found her way back to me. I would never again be the prince, but at least I was a member of the court. But then at the age of five I contracted pneumonia (a serious illness in 1959) and was hospitalized for many days. My mother ceased to be a mother. She became a visitor, someone, like others, who had to leave at night, when the lights went out. I was truly alone in the dark, my illusion of belonging, of being loved, completely destroyed, as I realized my hospital hell. Each night when she left she whispered to me, "I'll see you tomorrow." She had no idea that between the night and tomorrow lay a world of shadows and fear, a slow drip of nightmares in a hospital room where I faced an eternity of sleeplessness. She had no idea that these nights in the hospital would shape the anxiety I would feel for the rest of my life.

The day came (the glorious day) when she rescued me. I left the hospital and went home, believing I was once again safe in the folds of motherly love and protection. But, O cruel world. No sooner had I returned to my Eden than three weeks later I was escorted, by my mother, to St. Sylvester, our parish school, once again betrayed by her. She had taken me out of the hospital, only to lead me to a worse form of exile. My mother wasn't up to date with educational theory that suggested boys should not be sent to school early; that it was better to hold them back to wait for their more developed maturity, both physical and emotional. I was only five years old, the youngest child in first grade, the only child born in 1954 instead of 1953. Children were lined up outside the school, like little penguins, waddling from side to side. Nuns walked among them. I had never seen a nun before; they appeared eerily similar to the shadowy figures I dreamed about in the hospital during one of my feverish nightmares, and there I was being led directly into their den of dark tradition. A nun calling herself Sister Mary Irene introduced herself to my mother. She said she would be my first grade teacher.

"Go with the nice nun," my mother said.

Nice nun? This was 1959. There was no such thing as a nice nun then. I clung to my mother, thinking, "Don't leave me again!" The nun wrestled my hand free from my mother's dress. My mother didn't resist or protect me. Sister Mary Irene led me to the purgatorial line where I joined the throng of other abandoned children, forced into a Catholic school system, which, in my case, would last twelve years.

By the time I was a teenager, whatever abandonment issues I possessed had long been suppressed or forgotten. I had borne that cross, climbed that hill. I knew I was loved. I always knew that. Patsy Coppolo couldn't say that. His mother may have loved him when he was a boy, but that love turned to disdain and disgust when he became—by his nature—gay and, even more so, subsequently, when he became a woman. I don't believe my mother would have ever hated me, even if I had become gay or a woman. She may have even liked the fact that she had another daughter.

I had mentioned that my family was the loudest and most annoying, and it wasn't only because we had eight people in the family. On any given day, there were more than eight people, counting the relatives that were frequent visitors. My mother's family—its roots in the poorest parts of Italy—was not exactly prestigious. While my grandmother came as an immigrant and worked for a living, her brothers didn't. Her brother Sal was homeless and often lived in our cellar or sat on our stoop all day, eating leftover food from jars and drinking cheap wine. Her brother Joey only had one leg and lived on disability. He came to the house regularly to eat food and watch baseball games. Their brother Sacco wasn't smart enough to get out of the way of a car one day. It ran over his face. He had a hard time talking after that. My grandmother's father trafficked immigrants for a living, taking people across the sea, from Italy to America. He never bothered to meet his own wife and kids when they arrived, but he made sure he helped everyone else. He met his death, like so many others, by refusing an offer by the Black Hand (the Neapolitan mafia). He had some land. They wanted it. They offered him his life in return. When he refused to surrender his land, they stuck his head in a river till he drowned, and then they took his land.

My grandfather's family was equally lacking in prestige. Some of them, like grandma "Coma sta" didn't speak English. She had come over long after every one else. She married my grandfather's father, who had divorced his first wife, my grandfather's mother. Her son Guy (short for Guido), my grandfather's half brother, would prop her up on a chair, where she'd stay for hours, smiling but not talking to anyone. I suppose she talked, once in a while, to the adults who still understood and spoke Italian, but I know the young people, like me, never had a conversation with her except to say, "Coma sta?" That's how she came to be called Coma sta.

My uncle Guy was famous for taking his nephews out to fancy restaurants. None of us knew if he even worked for a living, and yet he'd take us to eat seven-course meals in swanky places. It wasn't until years later that I learned he would walk out of these places without paying. No wonder we never went back to the same place twice. The men in my grandfather's family mostly gambled, and they had one thing in common. They all lost, all the time. My grandfather (bless his soul) couldn't be called a dignified man. He once sold my grandmother's wedding ring to pay off a bet or to make a bet. Either way it wasn't a classy thing to do.

My uncle Georgie had no interest in being a hero during World War II. He went AWOL from the Navy. He was also an adulterer and an abusive man. Nonetheless, I liked him. His name was Georgie Baldaserra. He had muscles that reminded me of Popeye. Every time I saw him he made a muscle, and I squeezed it. He liked me as well, that is until the day he took me crabbing with a couple of my cousins, Marie and Georgette. We went to Jamaica Bay when I was ten years old. When I asked him if crabbing was like fishing, he said, no, crabbing is like crabbing, and fishing is like fishing. He was a pretty straightforward guy when it came to answering questions that he didn't want to answer, and sometimes if it was a really stupid question he would just smack my head and tell me to shut up.

I spent most of my time that day watching them crab, and I was impressed. They caught dozens of crabs, though if the crab was a baby they threw it back in the bay. Otherwise, they had a large tub filled with ice, where they kept the crabs they caught. Finally, my uncle Georgie said to me, "Are you ready to do some crabbing?" I told him I was ready. He told me all I had to do was throw the net in the water and wait for the crabs to go inside it. What I didn't tell him was that I was terrified of crabs. I had watched too many Chiller Theater movies on WOR, Channel 9, where giant crabs were always attacking people. Uncle Georgie gave me a net and went back to his position, more than twenty feet from where I stood. I did what he told me. I threw the net in the water, and I waited. Ten minutes later he came over to me and said, "Where's the net?" I told him I threw it in the water, just like he told me to do.

"Did you tie it before you threw it in?" he asked.

"Tie it where?" I said.

"To the post, like everyone else tied their nets to the post," he said. "Look around you. What do you see?" I saw everyone had tied their nets to the posts.

"You told me to throw it in the water and wait," I said.

"You'll be waiting a hell of a long time, you idiot," he said. "How do you expect to get the net back? Are you going to jump in the water and swim and retrieve it?"

"I can't swim," I told him.

"Of course you can't swim, and you can't crab either," he said.

"You didn't tell me to tie it; you just told me to throw it in," I said.

"Do I have to tell you to wipe your ass?" he said. "Some things you do because it's common sense to do them. Think about it, if you throw the net in the water and you don't tie it, how do you get it back?"

"I just did what you told me to do," I said.

He slapped my head, as I expected he would. "How about if I said jump in and catch the crabs with your teeth? Are you going to do that?"

"No, because I can't swim."

"Well, the net doesn't swim either," he said, grabbing my arm and pushing me.

He walked away from me. Soon after, he drove me home, continuing to remind me how stupid I was. He never took me crabbing again, and after that I stopped touching his muscles.

Uncle Georgie was married to Aunt Viola, my mother's younger sister. They lived in South Brooklyn, on 34th Street, across from the Greenwood Cemetery, in the same house where my mother grew up. Aunt Viola was a wild card, a joker, an entertainer and very much an alcoholic, which, in the end, would kill her at the age of 50, finally succumbing to her long battle with cirrhosis of the liver. She once came with us, as our family representative—in place of my mother who suffered from agoraphobia—to St. Sylvester when my brother Bob and I got confirmed. When all the kids were lined up outside the school, ready to begin the processional to the church, she was walking around in shorts, up and down the line, high to the rafters, disrupting all the kids with her chatter and the smell of bourbon on her breath. I feel bad to this day, because I had to pretend I didn't know her. Sister Francis Edward told her she had to leave; only the children being confirmed were allowed on the line. She told the nun she was just having fun with the kids. To which the old nun replied, "They're not here to have fun; they're here to receive their confirmation." Aunt Viola said in response, "We all need to have fun, sometimes, Sister; even you." Sister Francis Edward walked away, but she wasn't done. She returned, side by side, with

Sister Superior, the most feared person on the planet. She looked like Superman, in physique, in her gown, and she could crush a child's hopes and dreams with the glance of her eyes, and if that wasn't enough she would break every bone in the child's hand with the yardstick she owned, affectionately called *Excalibur* by the student population. At that moment, Aunt Viola had my brother Bob in a headlock, and both of them were squealing with laughter, just as the processional line was about to move. Sister Superior didn't waste words like Sister Francis Edward. In fact, I never remember hearing her talk. She liked to be physical instead. It communicated more directly and to the point. She untangled Aunt Viola's grip from Bob and lifted my aunt with one arm and carried her off. In all honesty, my perception was a little off because I had my head down, hidden, I had hoped, in the luxury of obscurity. Bob was the one who told me Sister Superior lifted her and carried her off. Still, I did hear her laughter ringing in the morning sky, and her parting words.

"Good luck," she said, her voice raspy and loud, fueled by the alcohol inside her. "I'll see you at home. If the priest slaps you too hard, make sure to slap him back." She laughed. Kids on line laughed. I kept my head down. I didn't want Sister Superior to think I was an accessory to this blatant disruption of a Catholic rite of passage. Bob didn't care. He laughed the loudest. He had already been beaten by Sister Superior enough times already. What was one more time?

Uncle Guy, a bachelor for life, and his mother, Coma sta, lived down the street from Aunt Viola, and a few blocks away lived the Pinto family, my Aunt Judy (Guy's sister, my grandfather's half sister, my mother's aunt, even though she was older than Judy) and Uncle Vinny. They had two sons. They, along with my mother's brothers, Al and Bobby, each of whom had a wife and two kids, made up the main branch of the relatives who were always at the house. We had priests and nuns in the family as well. The nun was a cousin of my grandfather. She lived in Boston. She liked to drink. That's what I remember most about her. The priest was on the grandmother's side.

My grandmother's sister, Josie, had a daughter named Angie. Angie was married to Doc, once a promising minor league pitcher in the Yankees organization, until an injury cut short his career. He passed his skills on to his son Michael who was my age. At 14 years old, he had the best curveball in all of Brooklyn and Queens. Like his father, he blew out his arm, at a very young age. Angie and Doc had nine children. The oldest, Georgie (not be be confused with uncle Georgie) attended monastery school and became a priest. He had been a priest for almost ten years when it was discovered by his parish that he was having an affair, and had fallen in love, with a woman.

I was sure Georgie hadn't intended to meet this woman and fall in love, but it happened, nonetheless, and it caused a problem for Georgie since the Catholic church didn't allow—and still doesn't—its priests to be in love with women, with the exception of the Blessed Virgin, I suppose. The church made him an offer (if there's a parallel with the mafia here it's not intentional). He could remain a priest if he ended his love affair. If not, he would be discharged, excommunicated, his career over. As much as he loved the priesthood, Georgie understood that to deny the nature of love—itself a gift from God—would have been a sin greater than leaving the church. Therefore, he chose the woman.

When I re-entered the parlor, my mother was still asleep, yet her fingers, still clasping the rosary, were in a different position, as if she were subconsciously praying the whole time. As religious as my mother claimed to be, I never saw her go to mass. She was excused she told me, on account of having six children. But that wasn't the real reason. She had agoraphobia, as I already mentioned. But that doesn't even begin to tell the story of my mother's psychological and emotional life. She had just about every top ten phobia in the book: Acrophobia, Claustrophobia, Dendrophobia, Aquaphobia, Cyclophobia, Traumatophobia, Hemophobia, Necrophobia, and Nyctophobia. The real bitch is she passed these phobias on to her children, especially me. But that's not the story I wish to tell here.

Davy's confirmation picture was crooked once again. I

didn't bother to straighten it this time, but I did talk to him, as best as I could, in the way I often talked to people, in my imagination.

Write her a damn letter, will you?

I can't.

You're not dead, are you?

Of course not. If I were dead you'd know about it.

Are you MIA?

No, nothing like that.

Don't tell me you went AWOL, like uncle Georgie.

I'm not that bad.

Then what's the problem? You have pen and paper?

I have nothing to say.

How about you start with hello?

You don't understand, Tommy. It's not like when we were kids, running the streets with zip guns, pretending to be army men. We always got up after someone said, 'Got you'. Here it's different. Guys don't get up. And the reality of all the killing and dying is too much for me. That's why I can't write to her.

I can think of some terrific lies for you. I'm good at that. Tell her being in Vietnam is like going camping for a year. You roast marshmallows at night and sing campfire songs, the way John Wayne and Frank Sinatra do in the old war movies.

I don't have your imagination, Tommy boy. Just do me a favor and explain to her why I can't write, will you?

I'll do my best.

I never did explain to her why he didn't write. But I did find something one day, as I was walking in the house, escaping the suffocating New York heat outside (not that it was any better inside). As I stood in the hallway vestibule, I saw it shining white and bright, like a beacon of light. It was a letter in the mailbox, and it wasn't just any letter. I could see it was addressed to my mother. But, more importantly, I noticed the return address. It was from Colonel James L. Plotskey, in Washington, D.C.

My hands trembled as I held it. I was excited and afraid at the same time. I couldn't open it, though. Only my mother could do that. She had more invested than me.

Whether it was good or bad, she had to be the one to find out. When I went inside she was sitting agitatedly, her face directed at a fan that spun in spastic revolutions. Her sleeveless arms were soaked with sweat. A mosquito, heat-wave dumb, surveyed her temple. She swatted it away. Her breathing was very heavy, as if she were gasping for air, hoping beyond all hope for life. I didn't say anything. I approached her and held up the letter for her to see.

She stared at the letter and looked at me, blinking her eyes rapidly, as if she were confused by the dreamworld of her dreams and the actual world that lay within her grasp.

At first she didn't move. Then she heaved and gave a startled cry.

"Oh, my God."

She grabbed the letter with an appetite for knowledge I had never seen before in her. I couldn't blame her. It had been six months without a word. She had paid her dues and waited, in patience, like a Christian martyr. She deserved an answer, finally.

She read the letter aloud. Here's what it said, verbatim. I write it down with certainty because I still possess this letter, in a box stored in a closet.

Dear, Mrs. Crockett:

This is in further reply to your letter of June 23, 1969 concerning your son, Lance Corporal David J. Crockett, 228 22 46, U.S. Marine Corps. Information received at his Headquarters from overseas reveals that as of June 23, 1969, your son was well and on duty. His current mailing address is as follows:

> *Maintenance Company*
> *Service Battalion, Marine Corps Base*
> *Camp Smedley D. Butler*
> *FPO Seattle 98773*

The report further reveals that David was transferred out of Da Nang and is currently assigned duty in Nha Trang.

He has been advised to write, and I trust that you will hear from him soon. It is a pleasure to be of assistance to you.

        Sincerely,
        James L. Plotskey
        Colonel, U.S. Marine Corps Reserve
        Head, Welfare and Family Assistance
        Personal Affairs Branch

My mother's blood red eyes broke their capsules.

"He's alive and well," she whispered. "That's all I needed to know." She fell back in her chair and laughed as well as cried, harmonizing two contrary emotions, making them seem the same. She kissed her rosary beads and the icon Jesus statue, recently glued. "Thank you, Jesus," she said.

What she really meant was, *Thank you, Jesus, for suffering and dying so that my son, and all the mothers' sons in Vietnam, could live.*

Later that day, Davy's marine picture, his graduation from boot camp in Parris Island, South Carolina, went back on the wall, taking its rightful place beside St. Francis of Assisi and the other ceramic saints in the room.

That night she did something she hadn't done in a while. She wanted to sit on the stoop, as was the custom for every neighbor on a hot night. Everyone outside, on their stoops: men, women, grandmothers, grandfathers, aunts and uncles, boys and girls, cats and dogs. She sat there proudly, fanning herself, enjoying the children's street games and the buzz of the summer night, joined with her many neighbors, all along the street named 75th, in row house after row house, in a celebration of culture and tradition, knowing, in her heart there was hope beyond all hope and much life still to be lived.

THE DAWNING OF A NEW RELIGION

Miraculous events took place in 1969. I am not referring to men landing on the moon, or young people flocking to the Woodstock festival for three days of music, peace and love, or the New York Mets winning the World Series (though that, indeed, was a miracle). I am referring to the changes at Bishop Loughlin Memorial High School, when tradition gave way to cultural change; when students grew their hair long and no longer wore sports coats and ties; when lay teachers, instead of brothers, taught religion classes, replacing the agenda of fear and guilt with the evolution of the mind through higher consciousness. The Age of Aquarius had arrived, just in time to save us all.

At the forefront of this change was a man named Mr. Curtain. What struck me first about him, other than the realization that he wasn't wearing a black gown, with flapping crucifixes hanging from his waist, was his age. He wasn't, like Brother Ambrose, one hundred and sixteen years old. He was twenty-five, at most, and dressed as if he were advertising clothing for a Salvation Army Thrift Store. He wore a green, polka-dotted tie and a lime-colored sport jacket, checkered with white squares. His pants were dark green, and on his feet he wore something that looked more like a slipper than a shoe.

When he walked in holding a violin case, I assumed he played the instrument, but when he put the case down and opened it, he didn't take out a violin. He took out books, and he didn't laugh or smile when he did it. He just took out book after book, in a casual, unassuming way, as if he were unpacking groceries at home. But these were not groceries; they were books, and when he held them up, his eyes—also green to match his clothing—were soaked in sunlight. One at a time, he held high above his head each book and spoke the title: *Maps of Consciousness, The Loving Man, Meditation, Human Communication, Man and Religion.*

"Not your typical religion books, right?" he said. "You expect to read the Testaments, right? The books of Saint Francis, Saint Augustine, and Thomas Aquinas, right?" His voice, which bore a resemblance to Edward G. Robinson, especially when he emphasized the word "right," belied his curly blond locks and scattered freckles, giving him an Alfred E. Neuman boyishness. He was a far cry from the majority of brothers who looked and talked like Joe Friday on *Dragnet.*

"There's a good reason why these books aren't typical. We're not going to concern ourselves with traditional Catholicism. I'm not going to quiz you on your Catechism chapters. I assume you know, by now, who made you, and who sees and hears everything you do."

He hadn't bothered with attendance, and already his tone of voice was dripping with sarcasm about everything we had ever been taught. I sensed revolution; it was in the streets, in the music, in the clothing and the long hair; and, now, in particular, it was in my classroom that day. The students in my class now—the beginning of junior year, 1969— were much different than the kids I had started high school with two years earlier. They were looser, more confident, and many of them were stoned, on any assortment of drugs. Frankly, they didn't care about heaven and hell anymore. They just wanted to have a good time. A familiar refrain was "The world could blow up tomorrow. Live life now, while we can." Yes, those were different times, for sure. Young people today don't talk like that. They make plans, starting in preschool, for college, graduate school and beyond. I don't hear anyone say, "Let's have fun; the world could blow up tomorrow." I hear them saying instead, "I can't go out tonight; I have a test in AP Biology tomorrow."

The student most enjoying Mr. Curtain was Charlie

Eatman, across from me. I heard him say, "Right on, brother" several times. I kept my desk as far away as possible from his. It wasn't because I was prejudiced against black people. It was because of his shoes. Charlie wore the most impeccably polished shoes I had ever seen. He was a minority in more ways than one. First, he was one of a handful of black students in the school, and, second, he was from the ghetto, Bedford Stuyvesant, meaning he had a chip on his shoulder the size of New York State. And that's why his shoes were so important to him. They were a symbol, a beacon of light in a dark world. And that's the reason I kept my distance. I didn't want to accidentally step on his shoes. Not again, like I had back in freshman year.

As a freshman, Charlie's reputation was sealed during the first week. A popular white boy, a senior athlete, picked on him and challenged him to a fight. Charlie didn't back down. One day, after school, he obliged the boy. The white kid, who was not only three years older, but also several inches taller, had a large entourage, more than thirty students, with him, as they followed him to an area outside a playground, two blocks from school. Charlie walked behind them, by himself. I wasn't part of the entourage. I was just a curious onlooker. The group made a large circle, and inside were Charlie and the white kid. The fight didn't last long. Before the entourage had an opportunity to cheer and jeer, Charlie had knocked the white kid out, with one punch. I had never seen anything like it, and I was certain none of the white kid's entourage had either. Freshman year was only days old, and already Charlie was the most feared kid in the school.

The day I accidentally stepped on his shoe came shortly after the fight, and that punch he threw was fresh in my memory. The aisle where we sat was narrow. I should have been more careful. I should have walked as if I were on a tight rope over Niagara Falls. I didn't actually step on his shoe; it was more like a rub against it. But whatever it was, it was enough to produce a venomous response.

He looked at me with white eyes and said, "Dammit, mother fucker, you stepped on my shoe." I told him I was sorry, but it didn't appease his anger.

"I've killed people for doing much less," he said.

I kept thinking of that punch he threw, knocking out the white kid. I wanted to tell him I'd buy him another pair, if he deemed it necessary. I could even shine his shoes for him. I had done some shoe shining as a kid, up on Liberty Avenue, when I was eight years old.

He turned away and said, "Next time you're dead."

I would make sure there would be no next time. The brothers didn't make it easy for me, however. Charlie seemed to be in all my classes, in a seat close to mine, his shoes always shining, leaving a glare in my eyes, and a deep wound in my memory.

"The purpose of this class is this," Mr. Curtain said, as he twirled his polka-dotted tie. "We're going to lose God, in order to find him."

I had tried to lose God once, and the results weren't very good. I was six years old, in the second grade. I had just come home from school, and Catechism questions and answers still reverberated in my brain.

Who made us?

God made us.

Who is God?

God is the Supreme Being who made all things.

What do we mean when we say that God is all knowing?

When we say that God is all knowing we mean that He knows all things, past, present, and future, even our most secret thoughts, words, and actions.

What do we mean when we say that God is all present?

When we say that God is all present we mean that He is everywhere.

I had difficulty accepting this knowledge, especially when I was sitting on the toilet seat, or when I was breaking a fast during lent, only pretending to be giving up candy and cupcakes. As much as I liked God—did I have a choice?—I didn't want God to be everywhere and know everything I thought, and see everything I did. So I decided to lose Him by taking a ride on my tricycle. (I still hadn't learned to ride a two-wheeler, and would, in fact, never learn until the age of twenty-three.) I took my bike out of the gate and began pedaling fast, down the sidewalk. Surely if I rode quickly, with the wind at my back, like a young Apollo, his racing chariot dragging the sun across the sky, I would outpace God and leave him to watch over lesser mortals. I closed my eyes, felt the cool air cleanse me, felt freedom on my lips and tongue, sweet as sugar. In my reverie, I hadn't known I was crossing into the street. When I next opened my eyes it was in reaction to the sound of a car slamming on its brakes. The driver of the car was visibly upset. He got out of his car and walked towards me, only he wasn't a normal man. He wore a mask of charcoal and grease, and his ears were sharp and pointed, his teeth broken and smattered with filth. I recognized his image. Sister Mary Irene, in first grade, had showed me pictures of him, lost and misbegotten in the fires of hell.

"Be careful," he growled, flames shooting from the empty sockets of his eyes. I pedaled home as fast as I could, happy to recall the Catechism questions and answers I had learned earlier that day.

I wanted to tell Mr. Curtain that trying to lose God was an effort in vain. It could only lead to further suffering, not to mention eternal damnation. But he was not a man easily deterred. It was clear he was on a mission to seek and destroy, even if it meant he was going to take his defenseless students with him into that dark, fiery hole from whence none of us would ever escape.

He paced the room, at which point I could smell the Noxzema and perspiration coming from his skin. His green eyes were alive with electric veins, giving him the appearance of a thunderstruck scientist who spent his nights mixing and drinking chemicals. He was clearly mad; of that I was certain.

He held up the book titled, *Man and Religion,* written by Huston Smith, a favorite of his, he told us. He asked the class how many religions existed in the world. I had never heard such a blasphemous question in a Catholic school. When no one answered him, he asked another one.

"Who can name a religion other than Christianity?"

I knew there were religions other than Christianity, but I never gave them much thought because, frankly, I didn't think I was allowed to give them any thought. I knew, in particular, there was a Jewish religion not only because the Bible was full of stories about Jewish people, but, even more so, because there was a synagogue on my street where I lived. Why there was a synagogue there was hard to understand since my neighborhood was exclusively Italian and Irish, and there wasn't a Jewish person living around there for miles. The synagogue was only used on special occasions, such as a Bar Mitzvah, which I had learned was a special rite of passage for a young Jewish man, at thirteen years old. The people who walked in and out of the synagogue, wearing yarmulkes, appeared alien, and we, the kids on the street, didn't especially like them, though it had nothing to do with being prejudiced toward their religion. It had to do with territory. Their religious practices interfered with our street games, especially stickball which required us to use the entire street. The street was holy ground for us, and we didn't like having to share it with any religious creed or race.

There was another religion I knew, and this one had more significance to me on a personal level. I was aware at a young age that my father was not Catholic. He was Protestant, and, even though it came under the umbrella of Christianity, it was, nonetheless, the wrong religion. People who were Protestant didn't stand much of a chance of getting into heaven. For that reason, from the earliest age it created a rift between my father and me. It was a source of shame for me since I didn't know any other kid whose father was Protestant. I felt sorry for my father, but I also kept my distance from him. I didn't understand why my mother married a Protestant man, exposing herself and her children to the possibility of eternal damnation.

"Buddhism," Bobby Boicelli said. I was surprised, not so much by the answer, but by the person who said it. For two years I had been in Boicelli's classes and had never heard him respond to a teacher's question. A revolution was indeed in the air. The only topic he ever seemed interested in was talking about girls and his prized possession, his mustache. He told me girls really liked mustaches. Therefore, I started growing one that year. It wasn't much of a mustache, but he swore that girls would gravitate to me at a rapid speed. He said he had a dozen girlfriends at St. Michael's in East New York, Brooklyn, where most of the girls on my street and neighborhood went to school. He also had a large pointy nose, akin to Pinocchio.

After Boicelli responded, others in the class added a few other religions.

"Hinduism ... Taoism ... Judaism ... the Black religion..."

Charlie Eatman stretched his leg, his shoe coming awfully close to my desk. I shuddered in my chair.

"Is that a religion?" he wanted to know.

Mr. Curtain smiled. Many of the brothers tiptoed around Charlie. Even they had heard of his reputation. No one liked being knocked out, students or teachers.

"I'm afraid there isn't a religion called the Black religion," Mr. Curtain said.

"There should be," Charlie said, not the trace of a smile on his face.

"If it makes you feel any better," Mr. Curtain responded, "there isn't one called White, Brown or Yellow either."

Charlie nodded. "Right on, brother. I dig what you're saying."

Mr. Curtain's enthusiasm had not become derailed by Charlie's interjection. "You've already named five of the basic religions of the world," he said. "There are two more. What are they?"

"Making it with girls," Boicelli said.

Students laughed, even Charlie, who mumbled his favorite refrain, "Right on, brother." He liked Boicelli. I heard him tell him once that he reminded him of a black guy, a brother. Boicelli told Charlie he was flattered.

Even Mr. Curtain laughed, saying, "It is with great regret that I have to say that making it with girls is not one of the seven basic religions of the world."

"It is to me," Boicelli said.

Mr. Curtain took a breath to temper his laughter. "Add Confucianism and the Islamic religion to the list," he said, "and you have the seven basic religions of the world, out of which most of the hundreds of other religions have their roots. If you're going to develop an understanding of the world and the millions of people in it, then this book, *Man and Religion,* is essential."

Charlie wanted to know if Huston Smith, the writer of the book, was white. Mr. Curtain regretted to say he was.

"You honkies own everything, don't you?" he said.

No one laughed, not even Boicelli. Everyone knew it was too great a risk to laugh whenever Charlie said something seemingly humorous. No one wanted to be accused of laughing at him, instead of with him. Silence was golden in such situations.

After an appropriate pause, Frederick Massey, a straight A student, the most unlikeliest kid to be high on marijuana, and the likeliest to be voted most annoying, by students and teachers alike, said, "Why are there so many religions?"

"Genius shows itself in variety," Mr. Curtain answered. "Can you imagine if the only restaurant in the city was Beef Steak Charlie's on Atlantic Avenue? It's nice to know you have a choice. You can go to Tai Chi in Chinatown, or Caffe Cozzolino in Little Italy, or Raji's in the Village. All the foods offer our palates something in their own unique way. We wouldn't appreciate any one food if we had to eat it every day."

"You didn't mention any soul food restaurants," Charlie said.

"My apology," Mr. Curtain said. "Can you recommend me one?"

"Bella's Kitchen on Utica Avenue in Bed Stuy," Charlie said.

"Great," responded Mr. Curtain. "I'll make it a point to go there."

"You may never make it out alive, if you know what I mean."

Charlie laughed. Again, no one laughed with him, except Mr. Curtain, and that was further proof that he was mad.

"My old man eats spaghetti every day," Boicelli said. "If genius shows itself in variety, then it's not surprising that he eats the same thing every day, because he's as far from being a genius as you can get."

The class took Boicelli's cue, responding to Mr.

Curtain's genius analogy.

"Brother James eats frogs every day in science lab."

"You can't call him a genius either."

"I can eat pizza every day, no problem. It's better than the boiled cauliflower my mother makes."

"My dog's been eating Puppy Chow every day for the past eight years."

"Are we talking about food or religion?" The question exploded from Freddy. He scratched angrily at the top of his head, unleashing a snowstorm around him.

"Cool it, Freddy," Boicelli said. "We're just having a little fun."

"Right on, brother," Charlie piped.

"Sorry," said Freddy, sarcastically, "but I'd like to know what relationship food has to religion."

"Spend one night with my family and you'll understand their relationship," Boicelli snapped. "My father has a crucifixion over his bed made out of spaghetti noodles."

"Cooked or uncooked?" Mr. Curtain asked.

"Uncooked, of course," Boicelli responded. "If it was cooked, he would have eaten it by now."

Mr. Curtain laughed heartily, his teeth gleaming.

"How much longer are we going to continue this ridiculous conversation?" Freddy threw his hands up in the air.

"He's right." Mr. Curtain took off his jacket and shook it out before hanging it over his desk chair. "We have taken the food analogy to an extreme, but it was fun while it lasted."

"Can't you see I'm dying of laughter?" Freddy said.

"You'd do us all a big favor if you did die," Boicelli said, "be it from laughter or whatever."

"Oh, go trim your mustache, Boicelli, so you can speak without swallowing hairs," Freddy said.

"Why don't you change your socks, Freddy, before you get locked up for foot abuse," Boicelli countered.

Any other brother or teacher in the school would have stopped Boicelli and Freddy as they began trading insults, but not Mr. Curtain. He enjoyed the witty banter and let it play itself out before he interrupted them.

"All right," he said, "let's try to redirect our attention to the seven basic religions of the world."

"Do you mind if I ask you a question," Freddy quipped snappishly. Mr. Curtain clasped his hands and shrugged compliantly.

"Are you Catholic?" Freddy asked.

Mr. Curtain sat on his desk, twirled his tie and crossed his legs. His green eyes showed veins again. It wasn't the question that bothered him. It was the way Freddy asked it. It was clear the way Mr. Curtain bit his lower lip and looked up before addressing Freddy.

"I went to Catholic school for twelve years, during the pre-Vatican II days," he said, in a tone that was defensive, if not provocative. "Therefore, a part of me, due to circum-stances I did not consciously choose, will always be Catholic. In fact, right now, as I speak, Catholicism runs through my veins."

As he rolled up his sleeve and stared at his arm, I expected him to rip out his veins in front of the class, while cursing Catholicism for making him Catholic, when all he ever wanted was to be a hybrid of a hundred religions.

"Years ago," he continued, "I made it a point to broaden my perspective and learn about the seven basic religions of the world, not just the one that shaped and conditioned me against my will. I began searching for a spiritual life that benefited me most. If Hinduism or Buddhism or any of the others helped me, I embraced them."

"Then why are you teaching in Catholic school?" Freddy wanted to know, playing the courtroom lawyer he would one day become, I was certain.

"I'm here to see that you broaden your religious educa-tion," Mr. Curtain said, his voice becoming increasingly agitated. Freddy could do that to teachers, get under their skin, make them cringe and sound bitter, make them think to themselves, *I'd like to take this punk outside and beat him to a pulp, if only I could.*

"Shouldn't our perspectives be broadened in the religion of the Catholics?" Freddy countered. He relished the lawyer classroom role, felt it was his unalienable right to question and interrogate, to find and discover truth. "Isn't that what Catholic schools are supposed to teach?"

Mr. Curtain stood up. He was ready to risk all and do battle with Freddy, the sixteen-year-old-know-it-all. "'Catholic' is just a word," Mr. Curtain said, "just as 'Hindu' or any of the others are just words, but religion is not about words; it's about acts. If you're willing to sacrifice and help your fellow man, you're religious. If you're not willing to sacrifice and help, you're not religious, whether you call yourself a Catholic, a Hindu or a Buddhist."

"In other words, you're not really Catholic," Freddy said, drawing the ire of his classmates, including Charlie who mumbled, "That honkie mother fucker should shut his mouth." I pictured Charlie knocking out Freddy with one punch. Even that wouldn't have been enough to stop Freddy, the lawyer. He would have gotten up and sued Charlie's ass. It made no difference that Charlie was black and from the ghetto. And it also made no difference that Mr. Curtain was the teacher and Freddy was the student. The late 1960s had taught Freddy to challenge authority, just as Mr. Curtain was challenging the authority of Catholic school teaching. Neither was going to stop until something dreadful happened. I wasn't sure what that dreadful thing would be, though I was certain it would reveal itself to me soon enough.

"I am a Catholic," Mr. Curtain responded, "in a changing world."

"What does it matter if the world is status quo or changing?" Freddy demanded to know. "You're either Catholic or you're not."

"Catholicism must change with the world," was Mr. Curtain's quick reply.

"Are you saying that traditional Catholicism is obsolete?" Freddy said.

"I wouldn't say it's obsolete," Mr. Curtain said, "but I do believe we need to communicate its important messages more creatively."

"I believe you're being vague and ambiguous, Mr. Curtain."

"Okay, let me be specific and clear. Who or what is God?"

"God is omnipotent," Freddy fired back quickly. "He's

all-powerful; he's supreme."

"Meaning what?" Mr. Curtain said.

"Meaning ... "

"Meaning he's the one who holds the snake eyes," Boicelli piped in. "Meaning he runs the casino."

"I can dig that," added Charlie. "A God who likes to gamble is my kind of God."

Freddy had no response to the backseat interrupters. He was on a mission to take down Mr. Curtain, to humble his eclectic beliefs.

"Do you believe in God?" he asked directly.

"I do, indeed," Mr. Curtain responded, "only I don't believe he's a person in the sky who wears a beard and sees and hears everything we do."

Sister Carmela and the legions of nuns and brothers before and after her had all espoused God's presence in the sky, and their faith was validated on novena cards and on the stained-glass windows of the church and in the Saint Joseph Sunday Missal. God was indeed in the sky, wearing a robe white as snow, and he always had a beard.

"I believe in the God of the human heart," Mr. Curtain said emphatically.

"So, in other words," Freddy continued, "you don't have much faith in God as a supreme power."

"You're right, I don't," Mr. Curtain said, "because if the cycle of poverty and suffering is going to be broken, it's up to you and me, not a supreme power."

"The cycle of poverty and suffering will never be broken," Freddy said. "Man is too selfish."

"Like you, Freddy," Boicelli said.

"Like all of us," Freddy countered. "Therefore, the God-of-the-human-heart theory doesn't work."

"Oh yes it does," Mr. Curtain said. "I see it every day in my neighbor, Mrs. Anderson. She's eighty-eight-years old. She can't walk; she has arthritis in her legs, but she sits on her stoop all day and gives love to all who pass. She says, "How goes it, young man?' She calls anyone under the age of seventy-five a young man. One day on my way to the store she called me over and gave me a bag of bread. 'Go feed the birds for me, will you? Saint Francis isn't around anymore, so someone else has to do it.'"

"That's your example of 'God is in the human heart'? Freddy said, incredulously. "An old woman who feeds birds?"

"She does more than feed birds," Mr. Curtain said. "She sits on her stoop, loving everyone and everything. She's at peace with the poor, the sick, the hippies, the blacks, the whites, the winos. She's even at peace with the garbage men who come around early in the morning and wake her up. She can't walk, but she told me she's at peace inhaling and exhaling God as she sits on her stoop, and she does this, worships God, by sending love to all who pass her."

"She's just an old woman," said Freddy. "You're making way too much of this."

"But there's so much embodied in this old woman."

"Like what?"

"Like humanity."

"Humanity?"

"That's right. Humanity is capable of great things," Mr. Curtain said. He uncurled his limbs and started walking, circling the chairs, taking soft, even steps, the way I expected Jesus to walk if he were to visit my classroom. The sunbeams filtered from the windows followed him, and when he moved his hands streaks of light leaped through the air. At that moment, anything seemed possible. Revolution was in the air. Humanity was alive and well. Even Charlie Eatman was impressed. He said, "Right on, brother" as Mr. Curtain passed his desk.

The moment didn't last, however, because Freddy refused to accept that humanity was capable of great things. He was more attuned to humanity's destructive nature, even though, ironically he was a God-fearing Catholic. He mentioned the Vietnam War and the riots blazing across American cities, the assassinations of Robert Kennedy and Martin Luther King the previous year, and the Manson murders which had recently taken place in Los Angeles.

Mr. Curtain stopped in his tracks and let out a sigh. He thrust his chin on his chest and studied the floor. The classroom became so quiet I was able to hear clearly a bird singing as it sat perched in an outside tree. Mr. Curtain walked to the front of the room and stood facing the chalk-board. Though his face was clearly worn from battle, his eyes remained green and eager.

"All the more reason we need to find our spiritual selves," he said.

He drew a large circle, with a smaller one inside it. Inside the smaller circle he wrote the word *Humanity*. In the larger circle, he wrote the words *Ego Serpents* and made a half-dozen, worm-like drawings. When he turned to face the class, I noticed he had unbuttoned the top button on his shirt and had loosened his tie.

"Here's the future of the world in a nutshell," he said. "Humanity, an island, standing alone in a vast ocean, sur-rounded on all sides by ego serpents."

He told the class the choice was ours. We could let the ego serpents devour the island of humanity, or we could do something to save it, and if we did, we could then call our-selves religious. He himself would stand upon this island to the end and stave off the serpents. He welcomed every one of us to join him.

Boicelli wanted to know if there were girls on the island. Charlie wanted to know if black people were going to be al-lowed and accepted. Students laughed, even Freddy. Mr. Curtain, however, didn't show even the slightest trace of a smile. He had made his point and evidently no one had re-ceived it, at least seriously. I pictured ego serpents crawling into my classmates' ears, eating their lush brains, sucking their hearty blood, leaving them hollow figures of bone and dust. I listened to the bird outside. If the island was hu-manity, then the bird was its symbol of hope, perched alone on a precarious tree branch, singing to a world gone deaf. I wanted to open the window, so it could fly in the classroom and make everyone listen.

The bell rang. Students quickly left the room. I watched Mr. Curtain sit atop his desk and rub his chin. His eyes had become soft embers of diffused light. He was a forlorn man, perched alone on his island, speaking to a world gone deaf. I wanted to tell him I wasn't deaf, but I didn't. I left the room, along with everyone else.

Mr. Curtain wasn't easily deterred from his unique religious mission. In the following days and weeks, he read from his favorite books; he played songs by Simon and Garfunkel and sang along, sitting cross legged on his desk; he talked about the drug culture, including a book titled *LSD* written by Harvard professors, such as Timothy Leary; he talked about Sigmund Freud's book *The Interpretation of Dreams*. He talked about Nixon, the Vietnam War, the anti-war protesters, such as himself; he talked about the men landing on the moon, the Stonewall riots, the Woodstock festival, and whatever current event in politics, society or culture that occurred on a daily basis. In fact, he talked about everything except the Catholic religion. Gone were the days of heaven and hell and eternal damnation to sinners. He ushered in a new day, a new dawn, a new life. Revolution was in the air. We didn't have homework; we didn't have assignments. He talked mostly, and we listened.

Everyone knew it was just a matter of time before he got fired or quit, one or the other. It couldn't continue the way it was going. He and Freddy didn't get along, and every day brought new tension, and, along with it, excitement, anticipation, and the dread of what would happen next. His appearance grew worse. Each day he wore rumpled shirts that hadn't been ironed or even cleaned, for that matter. He didn't care how he looked. He started taking off his shoes, letting his bare feet hang as he sat on his desk.

The breaking point in Freddy and Mr. Curtain's tense relationship came the day Mr. Curtain decided to not only talk about Transcendental Meditation, but to show us how to do it. He told us it was the ultimate spiritual experience, better than drugs, at which point many in the class said he was full of shit. Mr. Curtain held a skinny purple bottle, shaped to hold perfume. Its opening was narrow, but still plenty wide for the incense stick which he planted inside it.

"What's that for?" Freddy asked, demandingly.

'You'll see," Mr. Curtain said, removing matches from his pants pocket.

"All right, fire it up!" Boicelli said.

Mr. Curtain struck the match and lit the tip of the stick.

Smoke raced to the ceiling. Students shuffled in their seats. Boicelli sniffed like a dog.

"You can get high on this stuff," he said.

"You won't get high on the incense," Mr. Curtain said, "but you will get high on the meditation exercise." He told us the incense wasn't even necessary. He just liked it for effect. This time he didn't sit on top of the desk. He pulled out the desk chair and sat straight-backed in it, his bare feet resting on the floor. He said he was about to close his eyes and repeat a mantra, a sound, to himself, while he breathed in and out, slowly and methodically. He couldn't tell us the name of the mantra. It was sacred, he said. The object of the exercise was to clear his head of all thoughts, images and stress, to become unified with the sensation of sound and breath.

Mr. Curtain closed his eyes and began.

Boicelli wanted to know if girls liked guys who meditated. Someone else wanted to know how something as silly as this could be better than taking drugs. Charlie was more direct and to the point.

"The honkie man has finally flipped," he said.

I closed my eyes. I imagined him on his island of humanity, his body lying limply like a rubber float, deflated upon an unconscious sea, ego serpents sucking whatever life was left inside him.

After a few minutes Mr. Curtain opened his eyes. He told us he normally did it for twenty minutes. He just wanted to give a brief example. He told us to try it at home, in a quiet room if possible. I wanted to tell him that where I lived, there was no such thing as a quiet room.

"You call that a spiritual experience?" Freddy said. "I believe, Mr. Curtain, you are confusing spiritual with physiological." That Freddy was good. I had to admit. If he were to become a lawyer, I would hire him on the spot to defend me.

Mr. Curtain agreed that it was physiological, but he said the physiological was merely a stepping stone to the spiritual. It was a tried and true exercise adopted from the Hindu religion, more than two thousand years old, helping those who practice it to experience God energy.

"God energy?" Freddy said, practically falling out of his seat. "What God are you talking about? In the Catholic religion we use prayers to receive God energy. But, then, you wouldn't know much about that, would you?"

Mr. Curtain shut his eyelids for two or three seconds, as if he were going to begin chanting his mantra again. I wouldn't have blamed him. Anything would have been better than defending his religious principles to Freddy. He opened his eyes, his hands grasping the air, like a supplicant pleading for release and salvation.

"I was in the process of explaining to you ..." he began.

Freddy cut him off. "I know what you were explaining, but it's blasphemy."

"All religions lead to the same destination," Mr. Curtain said, pointedly and unapologetically.

"Nothing but blasphemy," Freddy countered.

"Oh, stop your barking, Freddy," Boicelli said. "Your mouth is bothering me."

Freddy spun around in his seat, his pugnacious face contorted like a bulldog's. "At least I can find my mouth, Boicelli. You need to clear a path with a lawnmower to find yours."

"It's better to have mustache hairs grow on my lip than in my ears," Boicelli said.

Mr. Curtain didn't stop the combatants; he closed his eyes, arms spread, and spoke above their voices like a man having a vision.

"When the senses are stilled, when the mind is at rest, when the intellect wavers not, that's when God visits us."

Freddy turned from Boicelli to respond to Mr. Curtain's latest attempt at spirituality.

"I thought you said you weren't a Hindu."

"I'm not," Mr. Curtain responded, opening his eyes once again to the reality that as long as Freddy was around there would never be peace, no matter how much he meditated.

"But when you chant an ancient Hindu ritual you worship God you said."

"I do."

"And if you worship the same as the Hindus, that makes you a Hindu."

"There's a big difference between my practicing an ancient Hindu technique and actually being a Hindu."

"That's the way you pray and worship God. You can't contradict yourself."

"That's partially true."

"If you want to do it, you go ahead and do it, but you shouldn't tell me or anyone else to go home and try it. That's wrong. We're not here, not at this school, for that."

"You don't have to do anything you don't want. I'm just introducing you to something new. That's all."

"And you call that religious education? I call it religious blasphemy."

"You have every right to call it what you want."

"And the rest of us have a right to see it and hear it without your complaining," Boicelii interjected.

"This is Catholic school," Freddy said, raising his voice. "We should be listening to stories about Jesus and Mary Magdalene, not some Hindu kook who chants."

Mr. Curtain's response sealed the deal in regards to his fate at Bishop Loughlin. He told us Mary Magdalene, the woman who was there with Jesus at his crucifixion and his resurrection, the woman who purportedly wiped his face with a cloth after he was taken down from the cross, had been a whore, a common prostitute, before she met Jesus.

"That's blasphemy," Freddy cried.

At that moment menacing clouds gathered in the sky. I saw Freddy dressed as Pontius Pilate, leading his classmates, all wearing matching robes and sandals, across a burning desert, carrying ropes, hammers, and nails, chanting a mantra, "Crucify the blaspheme" as they whipped Mr. Curtain, thorned and bleeding, while he carried his heavy cross, soon to die upon it.

"You can't blaspheme Mary Magdalene," Freddy said. "She was canonized a saint. You're crazy; you shouldn't be teaching here."

"Okay, I admit it was stupid of me to try to introduce something new to you." Mr. Curtain said. "It's my fault. How stupid of me to think you wanted to learn."

"We want to learn, but it depends what it is. If it's atheism, no thank you."

"You haven't been listening."

"Oh yes I have."

"All I've done is praise God since I got here."

"Yes, the God in your head, that's who you've praised."

"I have news for you, Mr. Massey. That's where God begins and ends, in the head, and in the heart, of man. The main purpose of my meditating and telling you stories the last few weeks was not to make you laugh or become antagonistic. It was to point out that if we have any chance of reaching each other and making real contact we have to search our consciousnesses and—"

"And also have faith and belief in the Catholic God."

The window panes shook, as did my feet and hands. The God in heaven had come to punish Mr. Curtain for his sins, and perhaps he wouldn't stop with him. Perhaps this was the beginning of the end, starting with the shattering of glass, the collapsing of walls, the death of an unorthodox teacher; ending with God's holy angels descending into the soiled classroom, shooting arrows at those who weren't believers. I gripped the sides of my desk, hoping God would reconsider and give the world another chance, but the shaking got worse, the room darker. Still, Mr. Curtain wouldn't stop. He would never hide under his desk. He would go down shouting and fighting, like the last man on the island of humanity, or perhaps—and this was more likely—like a madman cursing the licking flames of hell.

"What do you want me to say?" He fired a bullet of spit. "Do you want me to say, 'Don't worry.' Okay, fine, don't worry." He undid his tie. "Don't worry about anything. Don't worry about the fact that insensitivity runs down the streets of New York City as if a goddamn sewer erupted." He pulled his tie from his shirt and whirled it like a weapon, then rushed to the window, to the blackening sky, and called out God. "Don't worry, it's okay, the God in the sky will awaken from his two thousand year slumber and put an end to human pain and suffering." He spun around and flung his tie against the chalkboard.

The bell signaled the end of class. Students whirled past my eyes like merry-go-round riders, a montage of color and sound. I wanted to lift myself, but couldn't. I was afraid my eyes would fall from their sockets; that my blood would spill like jelly. I saw Mr. Curtain picking up his tie, throwing it in his violin case, along with the purple incense bottle and the books he kept there. We were alone in the room; perhaps alone in thought. He mumbled to himself in broken syllables, sounds with no meaning. And to think that only minutes earlier he had chanted a mantra to receive God energy. I wanted to ask him about the burning incense sticks, the chanting mantra, the island of humanity, and the eclectic God he carried in his heart and head. Before I had a chance to ask him anything, though, he was tucking in his shirt, buckling his violin case shut, and taking long, hysterical steps out the door.

I never saw him again.

The next day, Brother Michael James appeared in his place, saying he would be taking over the class. He avoided questions about why Mr. Curtain wasn't our teacher anymore. We never did find out whether he got fired or quit; perhaps to move to India where he could meditate and live in peace and harmony with God energy. In any case, Brother James was intent on returning us to another time and place, to a Catholicism and religion, which in a few short weeks had forever changed for me. I couldn't return, and I wouldn't. Though the recollections of my experience are not always clear, what is clear are the books on my shelf, about man and religion and meditation and the maps of higher consciousness, connecting me for always with a radical teacher who changed the landscape of my mind.

EVEN JESUS DIES

Lenny's forgetful about most things that matter. The other day he went to a pre-pay gas station and paid the attendant ten dollars. Then he got in his car and left without pumping the gas. It wasn't until he ran out of gas the next day, on the Belt Parkway, that he'd realized what he'd done. His forgetfulness causes him problems. He forgets doctors' appointments; he forgets to sign his name on checks; he forgets anniversaries and birthdays; he forgets where he lives, or why he lives.

Lenny likes his forgetfulness because there's a lot he wants to forget. There's a lot I'd like to forget, too, only I'm not as forgetful as him. I remember everything. Even after all these years, I remember every detail. He doesn't want to, and, thus, he doesn't. He's willed himself into forgetfulness. That's what I believe. And he's succeeded, mostly. It's the little things he forgets—though I'm not sure they're little—that bothers me the most. He forgets to say hello and goodbye and good morning and good night. He forgets to tell me he loves me (unless, of course, he doesn't). He hasn't said it in years. It's not like I'm counting the minutes, hours and days. I'm not, believe me. It's just that when he decided to become forgetful—remember, he willed it—it included everything in his life, big and small.

I don't really believe he's forgotten everything, like he pretends he has. There's no way he could have, especially this time of the year, the Christmas holiday. There's no way he could forget this time of the year, not after what happened. It would be impossible. After all, he's not crazy. He didn't have a lobotomy. He doesn't have Alzheimer's disease. It'll be seven years this Christmas day when he discovered a hollow in his heart, and since that discovery he's never been the same. Seven years of shutting down, shutting out, and forgetting; seven years of living in the hollow of his heart, which is not like living at all.

I haven't forgotten. As bad as it was, I don't ever want to forget. That's the difference between Lenny and me. I want to remember. I'm not proud of what I remember. I don't consider it an accomplishment. I'd rather remember something good. I do, sometimes, only the good things I remember aren't as significant. Sure, I remember courting and getting married and planning a house and family. Those are good memories, and there are plenty of pictures to validate those memories, but we haven't taken the pictures out in years. The only thing Lenny takes out is his playing cards. He flips them all day when he's home; sits at the kitchen table, shuffling and flipping cards and playing solitaire, as if he were programmed to do that, and only that. No sound escapes his lips. Only the movement of his stomach, the intake and outtake of air, tells me he's alive. Playing solitaire and breathing, that's it. Little else moves him. One time I asked him—to strike up conversation—if he ever won at solitaire. He looked at me and actually spoke. "I don't play to win," he said. "I play to pass the time."

I understand that a person needs distractions from himself, from his thoughts, from his memories, especially bad ones. Even I have distractions. Every day, first thing in the morning, I make a list of things to do. There's always something to clean around the apartment, or something I need at the store to cook for lunch or dinner. You would think eating would be a distraction for him, much like playing solitaire, but it isn't. In his quest to forget, he even forgot the joy of eating food. I haven't forgotten that joy. I continue to cook; I continue to eat. In fact, I count the hours in between breakfast and lunch and lunch and dinner. I look forward to eating. I wish he would look forward to it. A man should enjoy his food, even if he hates his life.

I didn't think he could get any worse than he was seven years ago, beginning on that Christmas morning, but he's gotten a lot worse. Day after day, hour after hour, he's beginning to recede. One of these days I'm expecting him to disappear, like a puff of smoke, inconspicuously, the way he likes it, with no one around. Just disappear, evaporate, like a mist coming from a kettle, or steam coming from a pot.

In the meantime, he receives a disability check once a month. He forgets that it comes once a month. Several times a week he'll ask me, "Has the check come today?" And I'll tell him "No, it comes the first of the month." The check isn't even that much. We can pay the bills and buy groceries. That's about it. But he likes the check, nonetheless. It's money, and I know he hasn't forgotten that he once worked for a living.

Though he gives me next to nothing, I forgive him. He has known pain—the worst kind of pain—and because of that I forgive him his forgetfulness. I forgive him his negligence and his unwillingness to share his life with me, the way he once did.

I wish he would cry. He used to, especially on that Christmas morning seven years ago, and for a long time after that. But maybe that's how his heart got so hollow, from crying so much, until it became empty, like a well gone dry.

I hear a car pull up. I go to the window and look out. It's not Lenny's car. It's dark now, and the streets are icy cold, everything outside looking frozen and stuck in place. Even the train on the El track, which I can see from my window, looks like it's not moving. I want to reach out and push it, the way a child pushes a toy train forward on an electric track. I notice the tree in front of our building. It's so old and strong. The other day the winds blew furiously, testing the tree's endurance. I remember thinking it would be a heart wrenching sight to see the tree become unrooted and fall in front of my eyes, especially during the Christmas holiday. I need to know that some things, like that tree, never fall, despite the tests from nature—and maybe even God—that come its way.

I wonder what Lenny's doing out there in the icy, cold world of Brooklyn. He once knew the streets well, when he worked as a mailman. He knew the names and addresses of nearly every house, backwards and forwards. But that was in another time, in another life. He doesn't walk anymore. He only drives.

I hope he's not driving on the Verrazano Bridge. He could drive right off the bridge in a state of forgetfulness. He might even do it purposefully. I've thought of it a hundred times, and so has he, I'm sure. He hasn't done it, though. I like to believe it's a sign he wants to live. He just doesn't know how to live. I'm not great at it, either, but I do my best to live, taking my cue from the tree outside the building, holding my roots firm and steady, taking the blows from nature and God, yet keeping my balance. I'm not a hero, far from it. I'm just a woman who refuses to let pain kill her.

I've wanted to hold Lenny so many times, just hold him and say, *Let me help you through this; let me teach you how to live.* But he's become impossible to touch. He was once an affectionate man, always holding my hand. Now he's as untouchable as the stars in the heavens. I often wonder if he remembers what it's like to be held and loved. I smile at the remembrance of the man I met when we were both young. He was introduced to me, by my sister's fiancé, as Leonardo DiAgrasio. I called him Leonardo on our first date. He said he wanted to be called Lenny, and that's the name I've called him ever since.

I walk to the window and fix my eyes on the many house decorations outside. It's a Catholic neighborhood. People here decorate to celebrate the beauty and spirit of the season. I am grateful to them. I enjoy the blinking lights and candles, the many Santa faces, the reindeer, and the angels blowing trumpets to the glory that is God and heaven. I watch the lights blink: green, red, blue and yellow. I am happy, and, yet, I am nervous. I am nervous because for the first time in seven years I've decided to have and celebrate Christmas. I've been busy since the morning, since Lenny left, putting up the tree, which I bought and carried home from a nearby lot. It's a small tree, no more than four feet high and skinny, but I've made it look nice. I dug out of a closet lights and ornaments. I played Christmas music while I hung them on the tree. I also put a string of lights on the banister in the hallway and a wreath on the front door. Under the tree I placed Nativity figurines, the same ones I had had as a child. It's been seven years since I've seen them. But this year I want to see them. I want to celebrate the season. It's time again.

I'm nervous because Lenny doesn't know anything about what I've done. I didn't tell him. He would have tried to stop me. It was better to do it this way. He won't like it. He'll say it's a cruel thing to do, and maybe it is, but I'm starved for it. I want the bells, the songs, the lights. I want what other people have. I want what we used to have. I want to remember, and I want to celebrate birth.

I crouch and lift the Jesus figurine from the manger. It feels small and fragile in my hand. I want to cradle it and never let go. I want to celebrate the birth of Jesus. Like it or not, Lenny—I've been preparing to say to him when he gets home—Jesus was born on Christmas day, in a stable in Bethlehem, and people all over the world celebrate his birth, and we should as well. It's time, Lenny, I'm prepared to say. We've suffered enough, and now it's time to live again.

He won't like it, but I don't need his approval. I'm prepared to tell him that, too. I won't tell him everything. Some things I'll keep to myself, like how I went out earlier and said hello to a Santa in the store. Imagine me talking to a Santa, at my age! I'm not going to tell Lenny that. He wouldn't understand my happiness at that moment. He would call me crazy. But I will tell him that it's time to live because life is good, even to us, because it's all we have, pain and all.

I have eggnog in the refrigerator. I want to sit in the living room when Lenny comes home. I want to sip eggnog and look at the tree, and then I want to give Lenny the presents I bought, which are wrapped and lying beneath the tree. He'll refuse the presents and tell me to return them, but I'm prepared to tell him, *No, I'm not returning them. It's Christmas, and it's time to live and celebrate once again.*

The lights on the tree sparkle like fire flies. That's what

they look like when I blur my eyes and remember—long before Lenny—being a girl on summer nights with fire flies and dreams dancing in my eyes. I cry, for the joy of it. Among the lights and the tinsel and the ornaments, it's there. My memory lives.

Music from the radio plays Christmas carols. I hear *Joy to the World*. I turn the radio up louder. I want to believe there's joy in the world. I'm trying my best, Lenny, I want to say to him. Try with me.

I hear a car outside, and this time I know it's his. I know well the sound the engine makes when it shuts off. It's the same sound Lenny makes when he breathes in bed at night, or when he sits and stares at his food. I don't know if he's become like his car, or if it's the other way around, but the two of them share a kinship.

I hear the car door shut, and I laugh, because I'm nervous, and I'm also sure he did something forgetful. Either he's left the keys in the ignition or the headlights on, or if he bought something, like a tool (he's forgotten he hasn't fixed anything in years) he probably won't bring it inside. It will sit in his car for days until he sits on it by accident.

When he opens the door and shuts it, that's when I stop laughing. My blood freezes on the instant. I don't hear the music that continues to play. I only hear the stairs, beginning to creak, under the weight of Lenny's feet. A moment later I hear his voice. He begins cursing, soft at first, then increasingly louder. He's ripping the string of lights from the banister. I'm sure he's already ripped the front door wreath to pieces, branch by branch, leaf by leaf. My blood's still frozen, but I'm no longer afraid. He's expressing himself. He's remembering. He knows, with certainty, that it's Christmas. I don't do anything. I let him curse. I let him destroy the ornaments. I don't care. I'm just happy that he's alive again.

I hear him begin to ascend the stairs, his cursing, for the moment, coming to an end. The doorknob turns, but he doesn't come inside. He rushes back down the stairs and resumes his cursing. The front door slams on his way out.

Now I am afraid. I hear his car engine start, and I move to the window. The pane is frosted with the winter cold, but my hand is warm. I'm still holding the Jesus figurine. I'm grateful to be holding something.

He pulls out and drives into the darkness. I don't notice the Christmas decorations, only the darkness of the night. The world outside seems dead. The El tracks are empty, and the street is frozen in stillness. The music from the radio has left my ears for good. My idea of having and celebrating Christmas, and, in doing so, believing it would bring life and happiness to our lives, as it had for many years, seems now, at this moment, nothing more than an illusion. I stare outside and see the only truth. The streets have been dead and frozen for seven years. I can't fool myself, no matter how I try.

I take a drink. I haven't had one in two years, but I bought a bottle today. Along with the tree and the lights and the wreath, I bought a bottle of scotch, and now I'm glad I did. I know I shouldn't have. I've worked hard to rehabilitate, but I couldn't help myself. It's the Christmas holiday, I kept telling myself in the store. I want to experience like I had years ago, before the incident, when I drank moderately. There was nothing moderate about the way I drank for five years. But that's not going to happen to me again. I'm planning on having just one drink. Just one small drink, I tell myself, for the holiday. So I pour my glass. I play the music loudly again.

It takes me only one sip to realize I'm going to finish the whole bottle. One sip and it's already running through my veins like heat waves. I'm on fire; I'm burning. I know I won't stop till I'm fried to a crisp. I like it too much to stop. I like its honesty, its directness. There's no waiting for results. Already it's throwing a blanket of comfort over me. You can't stop something like that.

I'm not like Lenny. I don't forget anything, at anytime. Drunk or sober, it doesn't matter. Even now, after my second sip, I'm not forgetting anything. Not the dead world outside or Lenny's outburst in the hallway. The scotch is making it easier to remember. I'm swaying just a little now, and I'm warm, suddenly flushed in the face. I can feel the heat coming on. I can't believe my good fortune, listening to Christmas music, holding a drink in my hand. Each sip is better than the previous one. I have a friend, a companion, as if the drink is alive and knows me. We share a kinship, just like Lenny shares a kinship with his car.

Lenny's upset and he's driving around without a purpose right now, but he'll be back. I'm sure of it. The world outside is cold and dark and dead. He knows the only place where someone cares is right here. That's why he'll be back. He won't like what he sees when he comes inside, but I'm prepared to leave everything in place, right where it is, and I'm leaving the music on as well. I don't care how crazy he is or how angry he gets. I'm keeping Christmas. I deserve it, and I deserve another drink. So I have one. I'm starting to get emotional now. I feel the tears on my face. It feels good to cry. It feels good to drink and cry and sing with the radio.

O come, let us adore him, Christ, the Lord.

My heart's beating faster, and it's also bleeding faster. The sensation doesn't scare me. It makes me feel alive. I'm glad I feel; I'm glad I cry. I'm glad it's Christmas. I'm glad the tree outside is firm and steady. I can't say I'm firm and steady right now. I'm definitely swaying, but I aim to keep my balance. I won't let myself become unrooted, no matter how much I drink, and no matter how angry Lenny becomes.

I'm good and numb, like a patient anesthetized in a dentist chair, only it's not just my gums and teeth; it's my whole body. My brain though, is alive, especially with memory. I'm not dead, not yet. I'm alive, and part of being alive is remembering, even if what you're remembering is not good, even if it's the kind of memory that makes your heart bleed so much that you're hardly breathing anymore. The world may be dead, and Lenny may be dead, but I'm alive, and I have my memory and pain to prove it. I'm not proud of what I remember, but I remember it just the same. I know it does me no good, but I refuse to be like Lenny, forgetting everything, or pretending to forget, shutting down, living in the hollow of his heart.

I'm remembering the ringing bell, my hand pressing the buzzer. My hand was shaking, and my heart was beating fast, just like it is now, because a mother knows; we don't bleed for nothing. We know when the world we worked hard to create is about to be destroyed. This mother's intuition is a curse that God gives us. Why it is, I don't know, but it's a curse, I know that.

I'm remembering the footsteps on the stairs leading up to our apartment. The steps were deliberate, and there were many of them. At the same time, I heard church bells. It was Christmas morning, nine o'clock to be exact. Jesus had already been born. The bells tolled nine times, and the people on the stairs walked in time with the bells, only they weren't coming to celebrate the birth of Jesus. The priest appeared first, then the policeman. Their eyes were black with dread, their faces old and fearful. I'm not sure who spoke first. I'm not sure anyone spoke. There was no Merry Christmas or good morning or how are you. There was nothing, just silence, except for the radio playing behind me in the living room.

Silent Night, Holy Night! All is calm, all is bright.

I heard the sweetest singing voices imaginable, like God's angels, just like now as the radio plays and I drink another drink, only it's a different Christmas song, and there's no priest and policeman, and no Lenny, just me, alone, as I have been for seven years, except for this friend and companion in my hand, the liquor moving down my throat.

I sing.

O, little town of Bethlehem, how still we see thee lie.

And I keep remembering.

Maybe it was the church bells that stopped first. I believe it was. Then the priest and policeman appeared. And then there was the silence. Yes, that was it. How long it was silent is hard to say. I saw the priest open his mouth. I just didn't hear him. I went deaf. That explains the silence. I must have willed it, the way Lenny willed himself into forgetfulness. I heard inside my head. I just didn't hear outside it. As the priest was moving his mouth, I heard a voice, but it wasn't his. It was Jesus who was talking. Not the baby Jesus in the manger who had just been born. It was the grown up Jesus hanging from the priest's beads; the sad-faced Jesus with the crucified eyes and bleeding

171

temple, talking to me as only someone who knew death could talk. And I understood.

Even Jesus dies.

That's what I heard inside my ears.

And then, as if my ears suddenly became unplugged, I heard Lenny behind me, screaming, "Our baby boy, our son!"

Lenny fell to the floor, the floor from which he's never really gotten up. He rocked backwards and forwards, repeating two words over and over.

"Why God ... Why God ... Why God ... Why God ... "

I'm standing near the window again, staring at the lights blinking and moving, sipping yet another drink, and I'm thinking about Lenny. All alone, driving around, somewhere in that cold, dead world, feeling the way he's feeling. I start praying, not for myself. I never pray for myself. I know I'm like the tree. I won't become unrooted. I'm praying for Lenny. I'm wondering where he is and what he's doing, whether he's even alive. I begin reciting the *The Lord's Prayer: Our Father, who art in heaven, hallowed be thy name. Thy kingdom come, thy will be done, on earth as it is in heaven.*

Wherever he is, he's trying to forget. He doesn't understand why I put up the decorations, and he's probably circling the neighborhood, waiting for me to take everything down, to remove Christmas from the house, as if it will ever remove Christmas from our memories. But I won't do it. I'm remaining firm and steady about it. The tree outside understands. At least something understands how I feel.

Lenny, finally, comes home, more than two hours after he left. He doesn't open the door with a key. He knocks, as if he's a stranger. I hear him moaning on the other side of the door. I open it, and he falls into my arms. Like a baby, he just collapses, sobbing; the way he sobbed on Christmas morning seven years ago; the way he sobbed before he shut down, inside the hollow of his heart, and began practicing forgetfulness. He smells of scotch, as I know I do, and once again, like he did seven years ago, he's saying "Why God" over and over.

He says his name for the first time in years.

"Jimmy ... our boy ... our life ... "

He wants to know if he's ever coming home. I tell him he's not coming home; he's lost to us forever, taken from us on Christmas morning, found dead on those icy, cold streets.

"Only sixteen years old," he cries.

"Yes," I validate, "only sixteen years old."

I take Lenny in my arms and tell him it's okay to cry; tell him it's okay to feel pain and live with it and through it, as long as we do it together, side by side.

We eat food and drink coffee, and afterwards he helps me unwrap a string of white lights. Together we string them on the tree. Then we take pictures out of a box in a closet. The pictures have dust on them. We clean them and cry as we do. The pictures show the three of us, the life we shared as a family for sixteen years. I'm grateful that we had that, at least. We're not left empty-handed. Lenny's tears are everywhere, falling on his hands, on the pictures, and on the carpet. He's crying seven years worth of tears, and I'm proud of him for it.

"Jimmy ... our boy ... our life ... " he says.

"Yes, I know," I repeat his words, "our boy ... our life ... "

We listen to the radio. *Silent Night* plays. We stare at the white lights on the tree.

"Like snow falling from heaven," Lenny says.

It's midnight, and Jesus is about to be born. We know his story well. He was born in Bethlehem. We know what happens to him. He grows up into the world.

"Even Jesus dies," I tell Lenny, holding him.

And then we kiss, for the first time in years.

He closes his eyes and lays his head on my shoulder.

"Even Jesus dies," he whispers, as the white lights fall like snow from heaven.

MEETING WITH A MURDERER

The first face I recognized was Dominic Sambino's, and it stopped me dead in my tracks. He was pushing a shopping cart, while two small boys walked by his side in a supermarket parking lot. I did a double take to verify his face. I wasn't mistaken. He had acquired a midlife roundness in the waist. Otherwise, he was a handsome man, with a full head of dark hair, and altogether muscular features. He had never been a friend of mine, or even an acquaintance, for that matter, but some faces, like it or not, you remember forever, especially the face of a murderer.

I'd been walking the City Line streets for nearly thirty minutes and was beginning to wonder if I'd recognize anyone. I had no sensible reason to return. The only blood relative left was an aunt who lived with her second husband, a daffy old gaffer who claimed to be building an ark in his basement, convinced the flood was forthcoming. I had no plans to see them. The last thing I needed was Armageddon. I harbored few illusions about my life, both past and present. I did not return to connect with my childhood soul, whatever that was or is, or to awaken the sleeping leaves of summer. Let them sleep, I always said. I supposed my return was due to little more than curiosity. For what, I wasn't certain. Seeing Sambino, though, made it clearer.

I stood on the busy street while the working class moved by in disarray, each one as plain as a potato, rolling by as if someone had just loosed them from a bag. I kept my eyes on Sambino and the two small boys, whom I presumed were his children, though it didn't seem possible that this man was a father, a guiding light of young lives. If only they knew what I did: that these streets slaughtered hope in its infant cradle. Just ask your father, I could tell them. Their father, whom I never really knew, yet knew so well.

A woman walked from the supermarket, toward Sambino and the kids. At first, she appeared as any other woman in that neighborhood, a little fat and unshapely, someone who didn't have the time, energy or interest to keep up her figure. It became suddenly apparent, though, that as she walked over to Sambino and the kids, she was eyeing me. That's when I realized I knew this woman. As she drew nearer to me, I saw past what was unrecognizable and focused on her eyes. Only one woman in the world had eyes like those: Angela Girante. Her eyes were violet-blue, and if you looked into them on a clear day, you could see the Mediterranean Sea. She had been a girlfriend of mine, briefly, when she and I were eighteen years old. But, then, in those days everyone was each other's boyfriend or girlfriend, briefly, when they were eighteen years old.

She had wanted to make something of her life, move far from these Brooklyn streets, into Manhattan, and become a visual artist. Yet, seeing her standing near Sambino, it was clear she had failed. I should have left on the instant, should have fled the neighborhood and concluded it was a stupid idea to return, but I was too late.

"I can't believe it, is that you, Bobby?"

I stood immobile, smiling first at her, then at my feet, where the sidewalk sun had scorched my shadow into a thousand flakes of light.

"Nice to see you," I said. Though her body and face had understandably changed, her eyes were as beautiful as ever. Only now when I looked into them, I didn't see the Mediterranean Sea. I saw Sambino's face.

"It's been so long."

"Twenty five years, at least."

"You look great. You haven't aged one bit."

"I live in California."

"That explains it."

"Yeah."

Sambino came striding by, his kids following. I made a

conscious effort to avoid looking at Angela's eyes. I looked above, at a wispy cloud, wishing I could drift away.

"Do you remember Dominic?" she said.

I smiled through her question. I had spent years trying to forget the memory of him, and I'd done a pretty good job of it, too. California can make you do that, make you forget unwanted memories, especially those three thousand miles away in New York. The more important question was, did he remember me? We measured each other's eyes for a moment. His were brown and bloodshot, with an animal's fury. It wasn't the first time our eyes had met. Though, until this day, I had never spoken to him.

His lips locked as he looked at me, while his hands remained on the neck and shoulder of his children. I smiled sheepishly, first at him, then at her. She said something about her boys, and I said I had two kids as well. I made sure I didn't look too closely at her. She was, despite her added weight, still remarkably attractive; her eyes purple-blue and mesmerizing as ever in the afternoon light. At a different time, in a different place, I could have relished the memory of having touched her, but this was not such a time and place, not with Sambino glaring at me.

She mentioned people we'd grown up with; what they were doing, where they were. I smiled and nodded, pretended to pay attention. From the corner of my eye, I saw him squint under the sun and grip the wrist of one of his boys, who had tried to move away. He seemed momentarily distracted by the train that raced on the El tracks high above the street. The way Angela smiled and talked with such ease, it was obvious she had no idea that an episode in history connected her husband and me for always. Otherwise she wouldn't have suggested the unthinkable, asking if I wanted to stop by their house if I were going to be around for a while.

Sambino gripped his son's arm harder. "The kids are getting antsy," he said to Angela. I told her I had to visit my dying aunt. Then I added something unconsciously idiotic:

"Maybe another time."

"It was nice seeing you." She touched my arm, and as she did, I felt Sambino's breath on my skin.

"Same here," I said.

I tried to wash his memory away with a beer at a local tavern, and it almost worked. I sat at the bar, anonymously, recognizing no one, while a few older men played shuffleboard. They were red-nosed, glassy-eyed men, the smell of saw dust on their clothes, their faces pocked and marked by years of drink and apathy. I sipped my beer and tried hard not to look at them. The bartender, a whale of a man, leaned his blubbery arms against the counter and said nothing. He kept his eyes on a TV, a Mets game emitting blabbering sound. Once upon a time, I could name the players, but I'd lost touch with baseball. I had no connection to New York, and especially none to this neighborhood. I lived in California. I had for the previous twenty-five years. I had a wife and two children. That was my life, in its entirety. What happened before that was of little consequence. That's what I wanted to believe. And maybe that's why I returned: to feel nothing, so I could get on with my life; to live forever detached, in exile, from my place of birth, from unwanted memories.

I was set to leave the bar—and the neighborhood I had traveled 3,000 miles to see, even before the first nightfall—when I noticed in the mirror that Dominic Sambino stood behind me, his face softened uncharacteristically by the deflected rays of the sun from the window. Filtered light enshrouded him, as if in a halo, wrapping him in swaddling cloths, giving him a larger-than-life dimension usually attributed to holy men. The image—Saint Dominic—at another time and place, would have been laughable. But, at that moment, it chilled the skin on my back.

I had no idea how long he'd been behind me. I sipped my beer, looked absently at the TV, hoping he'd go away—in my life and dreams—forever. He sat on the stool next to me, grabbed at some peanuts, his hand larger than the bowl that held them, his knuckles strong and knobby. It was a dangerous hand; a hand that couldn't easily be dismissed, even when it was just holding peanuts. When he spoke, softly at first, he stared only at my reflection in the mirror.

"You know what I do? I run an auto glass shop owned

by my father's brother." He crunched some peanuts, as if he were punishing them. "What do you do?"

The time had come for me to pay the piper. This scene had to be played out, once and for all. I sipped my beer. Without looking up, I said, "I teach."

"No shit. What do you teach?"

"History."

"I never liked history."

His voice was sharp as a blade. I heard his hand rap the bar. He ordered a drink. J&B Scotch, straight. The bartender grunted as he poured.

"I'm not crazy about it either," I said, wondering how long we'd speak to each other in subtext.

"And yet you teach it."

"Yeah"

"And now you've come to relive it."

I lifted my eyes enough to see if he was looking directly at me, but he wasn't. He continued to stare straight ahead, at my reflection, his eyes as penetrating as if they were on top of me.

"Relive it?"

Peripherally, I saw his head snap back; saw him drink the scotch and react as if it were a bitter medicine. "My wife," he said. "Angela. You were pretty friendly with her on the street."

"We were in the same class at school."

"No shit. Did you touch each other's arms in school?"

I didn't respond. I had expected something different when he sat next to me; something that had happened twenty-five years ago on a hot August night; something that had to do with gunshots and subsequent blood and death. He couldn't have followed me to this bar to talk only about Angela.

He talked faster, more excitedly, in a higher pitch. "I'm coming from the store, I see this guy staring at me, staring at my kids, and then all of a sudden, what do you know? He knows my wife. How do you like that?"

For the first time he turned his head toward me, looking at my now empty beer. "What are you drinking? Hey, Bud, get him another one, will you?"

179

"The name's not Bud," the bartender said.

"Well, whatever it is, get my friend here a beer."

I waved my hand. "I'm good."

"Oh yeah, how good? Or should I ask my wife?" He laughed, as if we were old pals, joking with one another. The bartender brought me another beer. Sambino ordered another scotch and slid the peanuts towards me. "Try some of these. They're really good, as well."

A man and woman entered, taking the stools closest to me. She wore a skirt so short it nearly showed her ass when she sat down. The man already looked drunk. He laid his hand on one of her fat thighs. The bartender refilled Sambino's glass, and then asked the new patrons what they wanted. The woman said something obscene. The bartender didn't laugh, but the woman's partner did. Through it all, I heard Sambino swallow his liquor and smack his lips.

"What's your name?"

"Bobby."

"Yeah, I know that much. I heard my wife call you that. I mean your last name. You Italian?"

"Half."

"From the neighborhood? How come I don't know you?"

"Different crowds I guess."

"What's your last name?"

"Mullins."

"Mullins? What kind of name is that?"

"Irish."

"Irish? You look Italian.'

"My mother was Italian."

"The better half."

"Neither half was very good."

"You a St. Sylvester boy?"

"Yeah."

"What grade?"

"Sixty seven."

"I was sixty five. My wife was sixty seven."

"That's right."

"That's right? What do you mean, that's right?"

"She was in my class, I told you."

"Where else was she?"

The bartender brought the patrons next to me their drinks. The woman kept laughing at something the man was saying. I turned to them, saw the man reach under the woman's skirt. The woman leaned back, made it easier for him. Sambino, meanwhile, ordered and received another scotch, his third. I was keeping count. He finished the bowl of peanuts and asked the bartender to fill it up again.

"You're gonna have to shell them yourself," the bartender said. "I ain't got anymore of the unshelled ones."

Sambino assured the bartender he was capable of shelling his own peanuts. I took a sizeable gulp from my beer. The bartender refilled the peanut bowl. In one motion, Sambino grabbed and unshelled a peanut in one hand, nearly turning the shell to dust with his powerful grip.

"I heard you tell my wife you lived in California."

"That's right."

"Isn't that where all the fairies live?"

His speech began to slur. I wondered how many drinks would be enough for him—and where this conversation was ultimately headed? I suddenly wanted a peanut. I had an empty stomach, but I refrained. I didn't want to risk meeting his hand at the bowl.

"They live here, as well," I said.

He cracked a shell and paused before putting the nut in his mouth. "What is that supposed to mean?"

I didn't answer. The woman next to me squealed. She had spilled her drink on herself. The man wiped her blouse and the breasts neatly tucked inside it. I felt Sambino's hand brush my arm. "I said, what is that supposed to mean?"

"It's a fact," I said, turning back to him. "They live everywhere."

"You're full of shit," he said. "They don't live here, I can tell you that. And if they did, they'd be sorry for having lived here." He laughed and finished his drink. I wasn't surprised when he ordered another. "How's that drink?" he said to me, eyeing my beer. "Drink up, we're just getting started." The bartender brought him another scotch. He also poured a couple of drinks for the people next to me. The woman said she'd try to make sure this one went in her mouth.

"Like everything else," her companion said. She agreed and laughed harder than the man. The bartender stared at them, unfazed. He turned to a sudden cheer coming from the TV. I heard him say, "Fuck" as he walked away.

Sambino held his glass up, said, "Salute" and downed it in one gulp. I decided to reach for a peanut. He intercepted my hand. "You didn't say, 'Please'," he said, looking unsteady, like a man in a ring who's been punched silly before collapsing.

"That's okay," I said, releasing my hand from his grip. He cracked a shell and handed me the two peanuts inside.

"What are you doing back in the neighborhood?" he said.

I ate the peanuts. "I have an aunt who lives here. She's dying."

"We all have to die sometime, don't we?" He stared at me, his eyes blood red. He ordered another scotch. The bartender hesitated. "Is there a problem, Bud?" He said to the bartender.

"My name's not Bud," said the bartender. "It's Frank."

Sambino laughed. "I don't give a shit," he said. "I just want another drink."

The bartender turned away, disgusted. A moment later he returned with another drink, Sambino's fifth. The woman next to me grabbed my arm and said, "Excuse me, don't I know you? I know everyone around here."

"Isn't that the truth," I heard the man say.

The woman's face was freckled and flushed, her hair copper red. I had, for a brief time, known a young woman named 'Red' when I was a teenager. She was a shy, awkward girl, one of the few I remember who had a brain and used it. I didn't want to believe this woman could be her.

I smiled politely. "I don't live here," I said.

"That's too bad," she said and turned back to her friend.

I felt a peanut hit my cheek. "Why were you staring at my wife?" Sambino wanted to know.

The shuffleboard men stopped their game and stood

near the counter adjacent to Sambino. They spoke to the bartender in a language unfamiliar to my ears; something unintelligible, like gibberish. It was probably just me, having been away too long, since the bartender had no problem understanding them. He handed them a couple of drinks, and they went back to their game.

"I wasn't staring at your wife," I said.

"Why were you staring at me?"

"I wasn't staring at you, either."

Sambino held up his drink, his fifth, as if he were looking for an answer or some meaning in his life. The hand that held the glass looked suddenly small. He himself looked small as he blinked his eyes and steadied himself.

"You fucked her, didn't you?"

He almost fell off his stool. I saw him as a young man, steady and strong, a gun in his hand, the world literally within his grasp.

"We went to school together."

"That's not what I asked you." His tone became venomous. He no longer had a need for subtext. I looked at the bartender, who had been eyeing us, evidently aware of the change in tone in Sambino's voice, his unsteadiness on the stool. I had an urge to ask the woman next to me if her name was 'Red,' but she and her friend were lost in a blissful stupor.

"No, I didn't," I said.

"You didn't what?"

"I didn't do what you think I did."

"Bullshit, you fucked her. I can tell you did."

The woman next to me turned. Sambino was speaking a language she understood. The bartender came over and said, "Is there a problem? Because if there is you're going to have to take it outside."

Sambino looked surprised. I gulped the remaining beer and fished a five-dollar bill from my pocket, placing it on the counter.

"I've got to go see my aunt," I said, getting up.

Sambino grabbed my wrist. What I remember most were his nails. They were abnormally long for a man's hand. I couldn't believe I hadn't noticed them before as they held me in place with their stinging clarity.

"A man knows when someone has fucked his wife."

I looked into his bloodshot eyes and wondered if it were possible that he had no recollection of that hot, August night, twenty-five years ago. That night, not Angela, was our real shared history. He had to know that.

"She wasn't your wife then," I said, trying to pull my wrist from his clutch. He looked genuinely surprised, loosening his grip, allowing me to free myself.

"Oh, so you did fuck her? Holy shit!" He looked around, first at the indifferent bartender, then at the incomprehensible shuffleboard men, as if they were his personal confidantes, and began speaking with loud emphasis. "I'm sitting with a guy, drinking a beer that I bought for him, and he admits to fucking my wife." Only the couple next to me seemed to show any interest. They leaned towards us, amused. "This guy has some balls, I'm telling you. The size of this guy's balls! How do you like that? Right to my face. Rubs it in. Right to my face."

I could have shouted a rebuttal. I could have stood up and announced to the shuffleboard men, the bartender, and the amorous couple next to me that this person sitting next to me, Dominc Sambino, father, husband, owner of a business in the community, was, and perhaps still is, a murderer. That he once shot down two boys—Puerto Rican twin brothers from the Bronx—in cold blood, not far from this bar. But I couldn't say that. First, I could never prove it, and second—and this probably makes no sense—I suddenly felt sorry for him. He was pathetic as he sat, wobbling on his stool, looking at me through blurred, blood red eyes that now seemed to be crying, or on the brink of crying, and for all his blabbering on and on about how I fucked his wife, I was convinced his sorry state and his fixation with my return and association with his wife had little to do with the burden he carried in his soul.

Though I could never prove anything now, not after twenty-five years, I was there that night, standing on the avenue, watching the grinning face of the full moon, near the corner of 75th Street, where I lived, and I saw what happened, and I will always believe that he knows I saw what happened.

I heard yelling. I saw two boys running in my direction. Another boy followed after them. I hoped they were playing a game of tag. But I knew that thought was a pipe dream, because inside my nose I held the smell of blood. It was everywhere; in the air, and in the asphalt streets. Someone had already died, I would find out later, an Italian boy, a friend of Sambino's. He had been stabbed in the groin by one of the boys who now ran in my direction. I looked for a safe place, and I believed I had found one in the shadows of Gallo's Meat Market, under the awning. In a moment, though, I would learn that where I stood was front and center for the witnessing of cold-blooded murder.

The boy in the back caught up with the two boys. They were close enough that I could see their faces. They weren't from the neighborhood. That was clear. They were dark. Not Italian dark, but Puerto Rican dark. They were from the Bronx, a long way from home, and they would never make it home that night.

They were twenty feet from me, no more. I saw Sambino raise his gun. I heard *pop pop*, and the twin brothers fell, face first. The sidewalk quickly puddled with their blood. Sambino stood there with his raised gun. He looked at the dead boys, and then he looked at me—eyes smoking—looking at him. Time froze (and in some ways it has never unfrozen). Though it was just a moment, our eyes locked for eternity.

As sirens blared and neighbors appeared at windows, shouting along the street, Sambino ran, and his gang of friends on the next corner ran as well. I don't remember walking away. I don't remember running. I don't remember anything. I knew only that at some point I made it home. But home would never be home again after that. I would always hear sirens and screams and gunshots, and I would always smell blood and see the fallen bodies of two boys from the Bronx, twin brothers who died as they were born, clinging to one another.

The next day, and for many days afterwards, the police came around, asking questions. Their questions would never be answered. Italian neighborhoods took care of their own business. The police, especially, knew that. The smell of blood remained on the sidewalk, as did the outline, in chalk, of two bodies. The rains would eventually wash the crime away, but not in my mind. I had witnessed a murder and had to leave. That's all I thought: I had to leave.

Whatever burden I carried was minimal compared to Sambino's. That's what struck me in the bar, as he kept accusing me of fucking his wife. I never pulled a trigger. I just saw something I never should have seen, and I kept the secret to myself all these years. I did what I had to do. I ran from the neighborhood and never looked back, until this day, that is.

No, I didn't shout a rebuttal to his absurd rant. I tried, instead, to appease him. "I didn't know your wife, not like you think I did."

"Then why did you say, 'she wasn't your wife then'?"

"I don't know why I said it. It just came out of my mouth. I wasn't thinking."

"You weren't thinking? What kind of teacher are you? Teachers are supposed to think so they make the kids think. You must suck at teaching, that's what I think."

He laughed, spitting some peanuts. He signaled the bartender for another drink. The bartender glared at him.

"You better go home, Mac," said the bartender.

"My name's not Mac." Sambino retorted.

"Whatever it is, you better leave."

"I have to take a piss."

"Take a piss and leave. I don't want trouble here."

Sambino stood unsteadily and wobbled to the bathroom. I could have run away at that moment, run like I had many years ago. But for some reason—call it karma—I stayed and waited.

"You better take your friend home," the bartender said.

"He's not my friend."

"I didn't think so," the bartender said, walking away.

The redheaded woman turned to me. "So tell the truth, who fucked who?"

I laughed. She was a funny redhead, someone I could have known at eighteen years old. I kept thinking, maybe I did know her.

I stayed in the bar for one reason. I needed to know. I needed him to tell me, definitively, that we shared a moment twenty-five years ago; that we were linked forever as murderer and witness. I had no other relationship in my life where I could say that.

When he returned to his bar stool, he seemed remarkably sober, as if, in the bathroom, he had not only flushed out his urine, but all the alcohol he had consumed. The dangerous, intimidating part of him seemed gone as well. He spoke with a more chummy tone now. He put his hand over mine.

"I guess we're linked in history, aren't we?"

I was certain there was a double meaning in what he said. He would now come clean and talk openly about the incident twenty-five years ago. But what he said next nullified that hypothesis.

"We both fucked the same woman. How many people can say that?"

I almost laughed. Our roles had reversed themselves. I now felt I was the intimidator. He needed something from me, as much as I needed something from him. That was clear. So I decided to jerk the world inside his head, to see how much he needed something from me, aside from this "fucking-his-wife" nonsense.

I stood up. "Look, it was nice talking to you, really, but I do have to go."

"Sit your ass down, Buddy Mullins, or whatever the fuck your piece of Irish shit name is."

"Bobby Mullins."

"I don't give a shit if it's Mulligan stew. You're staying right where you are because this conversation is a long way from being over."

I sat back down. I never told the police anything. That's the first thing I wanted to say to him. Did I want a thank you from him? Of course not, just an acknowledgment that I wasn't dreaming all these years, that I really did see him murder two boys in the street.

"You know what really bothers me?"

I already knew what bothered him. Perhaps now I would hear it from him. Finally we would talk about the real history between us, not the jealous bullshit that was coming from his slurred mind.

But it was the bullshit that continued to consume him.

"On her deathbed you'll be there along with me. We'll be together. That's why we're having this nice chat now. On her deathbed, when she closes her eyes, and her life passes her by, you'll be one of the shit holes passing by, and I'll be there, like a chump, having been her husband, having been the father to her children, but that will mean nothing, because you'll be there as well, because you fucked her once upon a time. I'm joined to you, whether I like it or not. You see what I'm saying?"

I did not want to see what he was saying. I wanted to tell him I had better things to do than be there with him at his wife's deathbed. I planned on being three thousand miles away, and I would never again return. That was certain. This was my final visit, and it was fitting because I knew sooner or later I'd have to pay the piper and play this one out. It was fated to be this way. That night, twenty-five years ago, that summer night, decreed that this scene with him was inevitable. Only I was disappointed it spun its wheels on the periphery, rather than on the core, of truth.

"Everyone she ever kissed or loved. Every cock in the world will be there, and I'll be the husband chump. Just a piece of shit chump."

I was glad I wasn't him, that I didn't possess his skewed pathological illness.

"It's no different with your wife. Every guy she ever fucked before she met you, you and them are the same. You drank from the same well. You docked your ship in the same harbor. Think about it."

I told him I would think about it.

"Don't mock me, you piece of shit. You all ate the same forbidden fruit from the same apple tree, and when it comes time for her to recall her life on her deathbed, when everyone passes by, you'll just be one more face in the crowd. Think of that, Buddy Mulligan stew, if you haven't already thought of it. But you don't think, do you? You're a suck-ass teacher. What kind of fucking teacher doesn't think of things?"

He'd have made a great stand-up comedian, if her weren't a murderer.

"She's not really yours, when you think about it. There's no such thing. She's a shared thing. You like that? That she's a shared thing? You have her now, but someone had her before and someone will probably have her again. In fact, where do you think she is right now? She might be fucking someone right now, under your nose, you ever think of that? When they write her history, you'll be just another chump ass piece of shit. Just like I'm a chump ass piece of shit."

"Why didn't you marry a virgin?"

"Excuse me?"

"You should have married a virgin."

"Don't tell me what the fuck I should have done. Did you marry a virgin?"

"No, I didn't. It's hard to find those anymore."

"Because of fucks like you, that's why."

"I guess that's true. Fucks like me."

"I'll tell you what, when you go home, you go look in your wife's closet. You go find her old love letters. Read about the pet names she gave her former lovers. Guess what, it may have been years ago but love is love. It doesn't matter that it was years ago. Women keep that shit in their hearts; it doesn't go away. The heart remembers everything. I'm talking about women's hearts. Not my heart. My heart is cold as ice, but their hearts remember everything. All the letters, all the words, all the images."

"Love is not an emotion easily erased."

"Don't talk like a fucking teacher. Save that for your students. I'm not one of your students. I'm your enemy. Do you know that? We are adversaries, you and I. I'm sitting here having a drink with you, but I hate your fucking guts, and that's the truth."

"I'm sorry to hear that."

"And I suppose you're going to bullshit me and say it doesn't bother you that your wife has loved others?"

"If I choose to think about it."

"But you don't think. I forgot, you don't think. You piece-of-shit teacher, you."

The bartender came over to us. His face seemed aged since we'd been there. "Hey, I told you two if you had a beef to take it outside."

Before Sambino could respond, his phone rang. He took his mobile out of his pocket and stepped away, towards the bar's front entrance. His demeanor and voice changed. He straightened up. He became the professional who had a business to run, a family to support, with kids to guide so they could become good civilians.

When he put his phone away, he came back and said in a matter-of-fact manner, "I have to leave. I'm not a teacher. I have to work for a living."

He left a wad of bills on the counter. "I'll see you, Mac," he said to the bartender, without the slightest condescension.

"Parting is such sweet sorrow," the bartender said, lifting and counting the bills.

"Same to you," Sambino retorted, this time with a sting in his voice.

He extended his hand. I reached for it.

"Take your history and shove it up your ass," he said.

He squeezed my hand, hard.

"You know what I mean?"

I noticed his eyes. Only one person in the world had eyes that smoked: Dominic Sambino. They were unmistakably the same eyes I had seen twenty-five years ago, on that bloodied, moonlit night. and his point was unmistakable.

I knew exactly what he meant.

The scene now had been played out, to its completion. The Angela bullshit, was just that, bullshit. It was all subtext. I knew what he had really been talking about without actually talking about it. It was his way of doing things. His handshake, his smoking eyes, and his final words made it clear.

Yes, I knew exactly what he meant.

He walked out the door, and as he did, he seemed small and undistinguishable, just a blur, until he disappeared from my view.

I would never see him again.

I said goodbye to the redhead, to the bartender, to the shuffleboard men. I walked outside, said goodbye to the streets I had known, but from this point forward would never know again. It was over, finally.

I could go back home.

MY NIGHT WITH DORIS

I stood on the entrance ramp on the New York State Thruway; thumb out, looking to hitch a ride. The sky had turned dark, making it less likely that anyone would stop and offer me a ride. It wasn't the first time I had found myself in this situation. I had hitchhiked quite a bit, starting in the mid 1970s. Though maybe not socially acceptable, it was, nonetheless, a way of travel and life back then for many young people, including me. Today, it would be called dangerous, probably for good reason. I rarely see hitchhikers on the road anymore, and if they are out there, they're more than likely homeless. Back in my day, hitchhikers were not homeless. They were young people, most of whom, in my experience, came from proper homes and families.

I was about ready to give up for the night and try my luck in the morning. I'd seek out a place to sleep off the road, some grass, some bush or tree, perhaps a concrete slab somewhere, maybe a gas station parking lot, if I walked enough. I was twenty-two years old. I had a backpack and a sleeping bag. I could do it. In some respects I sought out hardships, called them challenges. If I faced my worst fears, I figured, somewhere down the road it would pay dividends. It was a different time, a different age. I was out to live, to find myself, to experience the world, and sometimes that involved taking risks. I don't see that in the young people today, moving through life, as if on a conveyer belt, from point A to point B to point C and so on, without detours or digressions. I'm not saying that's bad. It's just a great deal different than it was in my day. I wouldn't have known what someone meant if they had used the phrase "Stay on track." There was no track, not where I came from, not the way I grew up. There was freedom and adventure. The future embedded itself in the here and now.

I had all but given up on the possibility of getting a ride. I had been in this spot for two hours, and, as I said, it was dark. Therefore, fewer cars passed. The two-hour wait in itself was nothing. I had once been in a spot for fourteen hours, in Norway, of all places. Luckily, it was summer and it never got dark. I spent the whole night in daylight, in mostly bright sunshine. Talk about confusing. I had also once been in a California desert for twelve hours. I don't know how I got there, but it was a place where nary a car drove. The place, in fact, was void of life: no birds, no animals, no water. Even twelve to fourteen hours of waiting is nothing compared to some people's misadventures. I was once in a diner, somewhere in the god-forsaken Saskatchewan plains, where the winds blew stronger than any place I'd ever been. When I told one of the waitresses about my hitching woes, she told me the area was famous for hitchhikers getting stuck and stranded. She said one young man, years earlier, spent ten days in the area, without any luck of hitching a ride. Each day he'd go into the diner for food and strike up a conversation with one of the waitresses. It turned out that after ten futile days of trying to hitch a ride he wound up becoming engaged to the waitress and remained in Saskatchewan for much longer than he had originally bargained.

A car approached me, its headlights blinding me in a wash of illumination. The car slowed down as it passed me and pulled onto the shoulder of the road. I quickly grabbed my pack and approached the passenger side of the car. The driver was a woman, and she was alone. I'm sure that seems improbable. Why would a woman, in her right mind, stop at night to pick up a vagabond on the side of the road? You wouldn't hear of something like that today, but, like I said, this was the mid 1970s, and the truth is I had been picked up many times by women, some young and some old. This woman belonged to the latter. She looked about fifty years old. Of course when you're twenty-two you have no idea what fifty looks like. She could have been forty or sixty, for all I knew. Let's just say she was mature and motherly-looking. Yet, as I would find out, there was nothing motherly about her.

She leaned towards me and rolled down the passenger window.

"Where you headed?" she asked.

"Toronto," I said.

"Toronto sounds good to me," she nearly shouted. "Get in."

I tossed my pack in the backseat and sat next to her up front. She was a large-boned, heavyset woman, with a ruddy-red complexion, who sucked her teeth as she talked. She told me her name was Doris. I said, "Hello, Doris, nice to meet you."

I told her my name. She didn't respond.

"Are you going to fall asleep on me?" she said, before I had a chance to settle.

I looked for a smile on her face, something to indicate that she was joking, but there was no smile. I noticed how heavy and strong the arms that held the wheel were.

"No," I said, "I won't fall asleep."

The thought of falling asleep in a stranger's car was preposterous to me. In fact, the most important quality I possessed as a hitchhiker was my ability to be awake and aware. I learned this lesson on my first hitchhiking trip from a naked hitchhiker I met on a road, outside Colorado. When I inquired about his nakedness, he told me he had remembered falling asleep, in his sleeping bag, in someone's van. When he woke up, he was outside on the ground. The van was gone, and with it, his sleeping bag, his pack, his personal items and possessions, and even the clothes on his back.

I could say with certainty that I was not going to fall asleep.

"Sure, you're like all the rest," she said. "I can tell already." She turned the wheel sharply and sped back on the highway, the New York State Thruway. The radio clock glowed: 10:35 PM. "You men are always saying you won't

195

fall asleep on us, and the minute we turn around, you're fast asleep. I know what I'm talking about. Believe me, I know."

Another important quality I possessed as a hitchhiker was my ability to not overreact. I knew to expect the unexpected. There were characters driving around, especially at night, looking to get a rush out of someone. I had been there before. I had seen it. I once got a ride from a man in Germany, of all places, who said he was Jesus Christ. (Remember, this was the mid 1970s.) He said he was going to drive across the Red Sea. He wanted to know if I wanted to join him. I told him I would be perfectly happy just getting off at Munich. Another time I got a ride from a snake healer, outside Indianapolis, who played the carnival circuit. He drove with a snake wrapped around his neck. The snake slithered and snapped its tongue at me the entire ride, more than four hours, to Lexington, Kentucky.

I could go on and on about the characters I met, but it's Doris I want to write about, for reasons that will become clear.

"Let's get one thing straight," she said. "If I'm going to give you a ride, you're going to have to stay awake because I'm going to talk."

She had this way of talking. She'd say something, in a way that made it seem out of the ordinary, then pause and wait for me to react. But as I said, I had trained myself not to overreact, or even react in most cases.

"You have a problem with that?" she said.

I had absolutely no problem, and I told her that. I had had a problem several hours earlier, which was the reason I found myself stranded in the dark. Earlier in the evening, I had gotten a ride from an older man, maybe sixty. He presented himself, at first, as someone grandfatherly and trustworthy, both in tone and appearance. After driving three or four miles, however, his true nature and intention revealed themselves to me, in shocking effrontery. I should have known the minute he pulled off the freeway, taking a smaller road, saying, "This way is more scenic." I knew, with certainty, when he began speaking. He said he was curious why a good-looking young man like me was out on a road, hitchhiking, "all by his lonesome." With trembling lips, and heavy breath, he talked obsessively about the Kinsey Report. He wanted me to know, emphatically, that according to the report, nearly ninety percent of all males desired homosexual advances and contact. He placed his hand on my knee and asked if that statistic applied to me.

Situations like this one occurred more times to me than I would like to recall. Men like him had no interest in driving me anywhere. They drove the roads as predators, looking for prey. They wanted sex, plain and simple, and when they were rejected, the ride ended. Such was the case with the old man that night. The moment I rejected his advances, saying, "Sorry, I belong to the uninterested ten percent," he quickly pulled over and dropped me off, on a small road, in the middle of nowhere. He didn't even have the decency to drive me back to the freeway. I had to walk nearly three miles to get to the ramp where I mercifully encountered Doris.

No, I had no problem at all with the arrangement proposed. Though I was tired and cold, I could stay awake and listen to her talk. It was far better than what the old man had proposed.

"I really appreciate the ride," I said.

"Sure, but you don't have to kiss my ass," she said. "Not yet you don't."

She laughed a big truck driver laugh. I glanced at the speedometer: 85 MPH.

"I just want you to know that when I talk there has to be someone around to hear me, and right now, you're that person, so straighten up and smile because it's you and me, baby, and we're headed to Toronto. All the way, if you can handle me."

I laughed at her. She had a big personality, and I knew she would overwhelm me with it, but I had learned to be tolerant and never complain about a ride, unless someone —like earlier—got touchy feelie with me. I couldn't help wonder why she was out, driving alone at night, picking up young hitchhikers, and agreeing to drive to Toronto, of all places, out of the blue. As bold and ostentatious as she was, I felt I could trust her. She was a woman, after all, and women—call it social conditioning—were less likely to slash my throat or sexually assault me. She wasn't exactly the mother type, given the vibe she sent me, but she was a woman, and that relaxed me.

She wanted to know what I was searching for. I heard her clearly, but for some reason I said, "What?" She didn't like that. "Don't say 'what?'" she said. "You know what I asked you. What are you searching for?"

She mouthed the word *experience* to herself before I said it. Then she began a rant about men. She said that it didn't matter if they were twenty, forty or sixty, that men always said they were looking for experience, when, in fact, she knew from the very same experience they were seeking that what they were really looking for was to get back to the womb to become babies again, and this had everything to do with why she was driving the roads late at night. Earlier she'd walked out on her fourth husband. He wanted a mother, not a wife, and that's what she told him as she walked out the door, mimicking him as she got in her car and drove away. *Momma, are those 'taters fried well enough yet? Momma, can you get me some Pepto Bismol? Momma, can you clip my nails?* She'd had enough, she said.

"Why would a grown man call his wife Momma?" she asked me. "That makes no sense. Does it make sense to you? Well, I for one, am not anyone's momma, and I have no interest in being anyone's momma."

She had to get away, for a while, maybe a few nights, maybe more, maybe less. She just wanted to put a scare into him, and it wasn't the first time she'd done something like this. She'd made a habit of walking out of doors, had done it many times before. Most cases, she didn't return. This time she wasn't sure. She might, she might not, depending on her mood. She liked to do things on the whim: get married, get divorced, pick up strangers in the night and drive them to places like Toledo, Tarrytown and Toronto. She concluded her monologue by saying she could teach me a thing or two about experience.

I told her I had no doubt she could.

"You're not a talker, are you?" she said.

I heard her clearly, but, again, I said, "What?"

And again she didn't like my saying that.

"Listen, sweetie, if I'm going to drive you another mile, you're going to have to stop saying 'what?' I can do better than that. Believe you me. Even at 11:00 at night. I can pull over one of these here truck stops and meet someone who can do me better than that." She looked at me like she was going to crack me across the face with her strong, heavy arm. "Do we have a deal?" she said.

"You're the boss," I said.

"You don't have to flatter me. You just have to agree, that's all. I'm going to talk, that's what I do best, and I'd appreciate if you listen. Otherwise, I might as well play the radio, and if I'm going to do that, I don't really need your company, if you know what I mean. Now, I might just drive to Toronto, if that's your pleasure, but you have to stay awake and be good company."

She'd driven nearly two hours on the freeway, before picking me up, not concerned in the least where she was headed. Driving did that to her, made her carefree, nearly oblivious, toward everything but the power of motion: her ears tuned to the whirr of the wind and the engine's simple revolutions, humming to her like a chorus of bees.

"I like to drive plenty, how about you?"

"Sure."

"Sure, what?"

"I like to drive as well."

"How come you don't have your own car?"

"Don't need one."

"Of course you don't, not when you have someone like me to drive you places."

I studied her face as she drove and talked, saw the intermittent light from the highway rush across it like a spray of water, saw her eyelids move rapidly, her mouth never at rest. She was old enough to be someone's mother, maybe even grandmother. When I asked her if she had children she laughed that truck driver laugh again. She said every day she thanked the stars, the heavens, God even, for the fact that she could never conceive children.

"Can you imagine," she said, "children with the men I've known?"

She liked her life just the way it was. She had men if she wanted them, and the moment she didn't, she was out the door, free as the breeze on a summer day.

She poked at my ribs with a hard finger. "You don't want to sleep on me, trust me. The last time a guy slept on me, he paid for it."

I rubbed my ribs. She was a strong woman. I recalled the 600-pound woman who sat in the backseat while the snake healer drove to Lexington, Kentucky. I hadn't mentioned her earlier, but she was the biggest, strongest woman I had ever seen. She occupied the entire back seat while the snake, wrapped around the snake healer's neck, hissed. She didn't talk much. He did most of the talking. Mostly she made rhinoceros-like sounds the whole time. I realized at some point that those sounds were her normal breathing sounds. I had never heard such loud sounds coming from someone's mouth and nose. She did tell one story, though. She said she had married a dwarf in one of the circuses where they worked. The marriage didn't work out well, though. She said she had a habit of rolling over in bed, and each time she did she nearly crushed him to death. She said one day she woke up and he was gone. He had left town and apparently joined another circus. She ran into him a couple of years later in a circus outside of Detroit. She asked him why he left and he said, "It got to the point where I was afraid to close my eyes to sleep. I was afraid, at any moment, I'd be crushed to death." She laughed when she told the story. She had a sense of humor. I had to give her credit for that. I shouldn't have been thinking about that 600-pound woman at that moment, though. Doris was upset at me.

"I said the last time a guy slept on me he paid for it!" Again she poked my ribs. "Are you even listening to me?"

"What?" I said, moving away from her hard poke. "Yes, I'm wide awake and listening," I assured her.

She said this drive was not much fun for her; she was thinking she'd change her mind and not drive to Toronto. I just wasn't enough of a conversationalist for her. She told me I'd get married some day, and my wife would leave me. That was her prediction she said. No woman would stay married to a man who said 'what?' all the time. And no woman, especially, would stay married to a man who fell asleep on her.

I received her warning loud and clear, I told her. I would, starting that moment, change my ways and never say 'what' again. And I concurred that falling asleep on a woman was the equal of one of the seven deadly sins.

"That's right, be careful who you fall asleep on. You may wake up and find yourself in a place where you don't want to be."

Her face, half in light, half in shadow, looked suddenly as if she were wearing a Phantom of the Opera mask. Her cackling laugh came from deep inside her chest.

"I suppose that's true." The moment the words came from my mouth, I realized they were empty of meaning. I was now talking without thinking.

"You suppose it's true? It is true, sweetie."

I noticed a significant gap between her front teeth. It was the source of the sucking sound she made.

"Ask my third husband, if you don't believe me. You remind me of him"

"Who?'

"Don't say 'who' either."

"Your third husband?"

"That's right, my third husband."

She pulled a cigarette out from a pack of non-filtered Camels lying near the gear shift. She stuck it in her mouth, pushed in the lighter, and then lit up, blowing out smoke from between her gapped teeth. I shifted by body away from the smoke, but I couldn't escape it. I coughed, hoping maybe she'd take mercy on me and put it out. I couldn't tell her she couldn't smoke. She would have dismissed me. She was that type. She would have said, *Too bad, it's my car, and I'll do what I damned please.*

Discomfort was to be expected. I knew that. I had been in situations much worse. There was the time in Spain, with Diego. He had a small car, a two-seater. When he pulled over, I noticed he was driving, and his dog, a black lab, was sitting in the passenger seat. He was willing to drive me two hundred miles, with one stipulation: I hold the dog on my lap. I did, of course, because hitchhikers can't be choosey. I had already been waiting four hours on the side of the road, outside Seville. So I held the dog for two hundred miles, until we arrived in Barcelona. It foamed at the mouth, dropping its slime on me, pretty much the whole time. Diego drove without shoes and socks on his feet. To say the ride was an olfactory experience, in a negative sense, would be an understatement.

Doris knew I didn't like the smoke. It was obvious. It made her laugh callously and blow out the smoke more powerfully, in carcinogenic clouds. A frightening thought came into my head at that moment.

She hates men.

And to prove my point she rattled off a monologue full of disdain for her third husband. It wasn't without humor, though. I give her credit for that. Her delivery and timing seemed practiced. Either that or she was just a natural.

"He was a drinker." She inhaled the smoke, blew it out, sucking her teeth as she did. That was the pattern, and each time she continued the pattern I cringed.

"Come to think of it, all my husbands have been drinkers. So have I. But he was the best drinker of the lot. What was his name? Al? Or was it Pete? One of those, I'm sure. Anyway, drinking was the extent of our relationship. Touching was pretty much limited to pulling each other up off the floor, and if we talked it wasn't much more than 'hand me another,' though I have to give him credit. He did talk about leaving Maine, which was where we lived. He said Maine was the source of his problems and misery. If he left Maine and went to Florida he'd be happy. The Sunshine State: palm trees, sun and sand. If he had that, he'd be happy. But I wasn't having any of it. 'You're miserable here, and you'd be miserable there,' I'd say, 'because you're miserable with yourself, and that's who you'd be taking with you to Florida, Africa or the China Seas. If you really wanted to be happy, you'd have to be a different person, but that's not going to happen because we're stuck with ourselves, for better or for worse,' and in his case (and probably mine) it was for worse. But still the son of a bitch would fall drunk on the floor and say 'Bullshit, it's you, it's this place, that's making me miserable. My life would be different in Florida.' 'Well, what's stopping you from going to Florida?' I'd say. 'Everything's stopping me, everything.' 'Like what?' I'd say. 'Everything,' he'd repeat. 'Name one thing out of everything,' I'd say. He'd be weeping. 'One thing,' I'd keep saying. But he couldn't name one thing that was stopping him because there wasn't one thing stopping him. Just himself. Just his full-of-shit self. And then before the night was over he'd get real poetic on me, start saying, 'Fuck you, Doris. Fuck you.' So one night, after one of these episodes, after he passed out, drunk, I decided to take him to Florida. That's right, I hauled his sleepy, drunk ass into my Buick Le Sabre, in the back seat, so I wouldn't have to look at him, and I started driving. And I kept driving, through the night, through the next morning, stopping only for gas and coffee. He didn't move the whole time. He could have been dead. I wished he were, honest to God, but part of me didn't want him to be dead, because part of me wanted to see his sorry ass face when he woke up in Florida. I wanted to see how happy he'd be. I wanted to finally say to him: Al, Pete, whatever your fucking name is, here it is, here's Florida. Now you can be happy. Look around you. The Sunshine State: palm trees, sun and sand. It's all yours, you miserable son of a bitch. Now be happy. That's what I kept thinking as I was driving. I couldn't wait to see his reaction. To prove a point. And then I would leave him forever. That's what I kept thinking, flooring the gas pedal, thinking, I'm going to take him to Florida, see and hear his miserable reaction, and I'll leave his sorry ass forever. I could do better than him. I could go to the local dog pound and find something better than him.

"So the next day, late in the afternoon, I get to Florida. It looked like a shit hole to me, but I wasn't the one who wanted to be there. I headed straight for the beaches, and when I found one with everything he wanted (the palm trees, the sun, the sand) I pulled over. That's when I woke him up."

'Wake up,' I said. 'Wake up, you're in Florida.'

"I had to get out of the car, I was laughing so hard. He stumbles out of the car, squints his eyes from the glaring sunlight."

'Where the fuck are we?' he says.

'It's Florida. Palm trees, sun and sand. Look around. Be happy.'

'Fuck you, you miserable bitch. Take me the fuck home.'

"So I did. I drove back in a flash. He was in the back seat, waxing poetic the whole time. But I just closed my ears to him. I laughed as he cursed 'cause I knew I'd never see him again when we got back, and true to my word, I left that sorry sack of shit lying on the floor at home. Only this time I didn't touch him, to pick him off the ground. I left him there. As far as I know, he's still there. It wouldn't surprise me."

I complimented her on her storytelling skills.

"What storytelling?" she said. "Every word of it's true."

"I mean the way you told it," I corrected myself.

"I told it the way it happened," she said.

"It's a funny story,"

"Why is it funny?"

She acted as if I had criticized, rather than complimented, her.

"The way you told it."

"Stop saying the way I told it."

For sure she hated men, I was thinking.

"I told it because it's true," she said emphatically.

"Well, I liked the story."

"It wasn't a story, like I said. It was real life."

"That's why I liked it. It was real life, and you told it well."

I could tell she was upset. She crushed what remained of her cigarette, and quickly took another from her pack and lit up again, as if to punish me for complimenting her. A few puffs of her cigarette helped her relax for the time being.

"You have a girlfriend?" she said.

"Sort of," I said.

"Sort of? Well either you do or you don't. You don't sort of do things like that. I never sort of got married; I never sort of got divorced; I never sort of left. You need to start doing things with certainty, sweetie. If you want some experience that's what you're going to have to do. I'd be the last one to give relationship advice, but I'll say this, don't marry alcoholic men."

"I won't."

She laughed.

"And I won't marry alcoholic women, either."

"That's funny," she said. She actually smiled at me.

"Why is it funny?" I said, mimicking her earlier incorrigibility. "It's true."

"That's funny," she said again. "You have a sense of humor after all, sweetie."

I imagined what it would be like being married to her. She'd be a handful. She was as large as a truck driver, a male truck driver, and she had a mouth that could frighten the biggest and baddest of men.

"What are you? Twenty? Twenty-one? I'm guessing twenty-one. Am I right? Yeah, I'm right, you're twenty-one. That's what you are. I was twenty-one once. I know what it's like. I've been there. Around the block? Don't make me laugh. How about around the country? That's more accurate. Seen it and done it, many times over. Nothing can surprise me. Nothing. Not men, that's for sure. Not young people, not old people. Nothing human is alien to me. Someone said that. You know who said that? No, how would you? You haven't lived enough to know who said that. I've lived long, though I can't remember who said that, but someone said that. Someone always says something. That's one thing you can count on. Someone always says something. Yeah, I'm not surprised by anything. Not people, not places. Nothing."

She finally took a breath, making a loud sucking sound between her gapped teeth. I smelled her raw, stale sweat.

"You know where I'm headed?"

The question surprised me.

She was a perceptive woman. She knew what I was thinking before I said it.

"No, not Toronto. That's not what I mean. I mean, do you know where I'm really headed?"

"Is this a trick question?" I said.

"Don't be stupid."

"Then I have no idea where you're headed."

"I'm headed to hell."

She didn't laugh this time. She grunted, looked straight ahead and pressed the gas pedal harder. I saw 90 MPH on the speedometer. I thought of the previous driver, the old man obsessed with the Kinsey Report and sex with young, vulnerable men on the road. He was headed to hell, for sure. Did all roads, all drivers, lead to hell? Is that where the search leads and ends? I wondered.

"Don't worry, I'm not taking you there." She patted my knee and kept her hand there for several seconds. Uh-oh, the old hand-on-the-knee move. How many times had I experienced that in my hitchhiking travels? Too many, if truth be told. But never before from a woman big enough to crush me with her weight, if she so desired. I recalled again the 600-pound circus woman and her little friend. I didn't want to be crushed, and I also didn't want to run away to a circus. The hand on the knee wasn't a motherly move, nor was it entirely unconscious and innocent. Was this where the search inevitably led and ended? Being forced to have sex, with an old renegade women, in return for a ride to Toronto? I saw myself like Al or Pete or whatever her third husband's name was (she didn't even know). For sure, I didn't want to be gagged and tied in the backseat of her car, being drugged and driven to Florida, of all places.

She pulled her hand from my knee. I silently sighed a huge relief.

"You have to live first before you go to hell. You'll get there, just like me, but you have to earn it." She began a laugh that lasted at least ten seconds, building to a crescendo, as if rehearsed. When the laugh ended, her tone shifted to serious, as if this moment were also rehearsed. The woman had a multiple personality disorder. There was no other way to explain her behavior. I was in the hands of a crazy person. I had to stay cool, nonetheless. Let it play itself out, I told myself. She had to get tired of hearing herself sooner or later.

"I don't want to scare you with how I earned it. My first husband could tell you, if he was alive to tell you."

She purposely stopped talking. She was teasing me, wanting me to beg for the story. She knew how to create suspense and, in doing so, keep me awake.

She knew how to work men, no matter the age.

Either she has a multiple personality disorder, I thought, or she's an actor.

"He died?" I said, trying my best to sound apologetic.

"I shot the son of a bitch dead," she said, with no trace of a smile or laugh.

She grew quiet again, and for the first time on the ride, she whistled. The tune sounded familiar to me.

"For a very good reason, mind you."

She continued whistling.

If I Only Had a Brain. That's what she was whistling.

"He had a chronic problem, which became my problem. All day and night, he'd swallow, clear his throat." She imitated the sound. It was an annoying sound, I had to admit. "He didn't even know he made the sound, but he did, all the time." She made the sound again. "Can you imagine someone making a sound like that? Living with that person? Sleeping next to that person? Trying to eat breakfast next to that person? Trying to watch TV next to that person? Could you do it? Of course you couldn't. Always swallowing and clearing his throat. So I decided to clear his throat for him, clear it good. So, I shot him."

She went right back to her whistling, as if we were engaged in a casual game of *Guess that Tune.*

She may have been a good actor, but I didn't believe a word she said. I started to believe that everything she had said since the moment I entered the car had been a lie. She had a need to talk, a need to make up a life that never existed. That's what happens to people when they're 50, I assumed.

"You believe me? You better, 'cause it's true. You must think I'm an outlaw. I suppose I am, but what do you care? You're getting your ride, just the same. That's what you want, isn't it? Of course, it is. What does it matter to you whether I shot a man or not?" She poked my ribs again because I had turned away from her. It's hard to look at someone when she tells you she shot someone to death.

"But he's the only one I shot." She grabbed for another cigarette, lit it up. I let out a sigh. After she drew in the smoke, let it out and sucked her teeth, she looked straight ahead and whispered. "I poisoned the second one." She grew quiet, then let out a loud laugh. "I'm only kidding. I never poisoned anyone in my life. My second husband died without my help. I would have poisoned him, but I didn't have to. He poisoned himself, with booze. Died in his vomit, and it served him right. I used to tell him, 'You're going to drink yourself to death.' He'd laugh. Well, he's not laughing now. Then again, maybe he is. But it'd be the kind of laugh people make when they're in hell. Because that's where he is, in hell." She expelled a *Ho-Ho-Ho* type of laugh. "I guess I'll see him again, after all. That's why they call it hell. Everyone you don't want to see is there alongside you." She concentrated on her cigarette, sucking in and blowing out, in rapid succession, as if it were the last time she'd have this experience.

"You're getting tired, aren't you? Tired of me, tired of my stories. I knew you wouldn't last. You're like all the rest. I knew, in the end, you would let me down. I'll tell you what, I'm going to shut up. In fact, I'm going to pull over at this next rest stop, and do you know what I'm going to do? I'm going to get some sleep. And I'll let you do the same. Then, in the morning, we'll continue on to Toronto."

She pulled off the road at the exit and parked in the rest area. A few cars were parked, but I didn't see anyone. She told me she was going to stretch out on the front seat, and I could do the same in the back seat. As tired as I was, I wasn't sure it was safe to sleep. I didn't want to wind up in Florida or have something bad happen to me. I recalled the naked guy who had trusted someone enough to sleep in his van, only to find himself on the road, with no the possessions and no clothes. He must have been a heavy sleeper, that's for sure. I was a light sleeper, though. I could hear a pin drop before it dropped. At least we weren't sleeping on the same seat. At least I wouldn't get crushed.

These were my thoughts as I took my place in the back

seat. Doris, apparently, had no thoughts. When she talked, she talked, and when she slept, she slept. Within a minute she was snoring. I wouldn't have thought a woman like her ever shut down, but she did, and that gave me the courage to do the same.

Soon after, I opened my eyes and saw the morning light, though it was mostly grey and overcast. Doris stirred herself awake and sat up. At first, she appeared befuddled as she looked at me, as if she had awakened in a strange room, with a strange man, after a long night of drinking. I'm sure she had had that experience more than a few times. She shouldn't have been surprised to open her eyes and see a stranger. She looked different in the light; more like someone's grandmother; her face and hair more red, more flushed, more wrinkled, more freckled with liver spots and moles. She looked more like the outlaw I suspected her to be, and maybe she was an outlaw, for real, on the run from police for having shot her first husband. Anything was possible with her.

"It's Thursday," she said, rubbing her eyes and face and mouth awake. "I have to go to work."

She hadn't mentioned anything, the night before, about having to work. She had only talked about shooting her first husband, poisoning her second, and driving her third to Florida while he slept in the back seat.

It turned out she had a job and needed to get there; otherwise she'd be fired. She told me she worked at an assembly line factory in Maine, making wooden close pins. She was a long way from Maine. If she left as soon as possible she'd make it in time for her scheduled night shift.

She wouldn't be driving me to Toronto, after all. We had slept together, theoretically, in the same car, and now it appeared our relationship was over. She had wanted to teach her fourth husband a lesson—not to call her 'Momma'—and she assumed by leaving him alone for upwards of two days she indeed succeeded.

"You didn't really think I was going to drive all the way to Toronto, did you?" she said. "You're more gullible than I thought."

I supposed I was gullible, I told her.

She did drive me a few more miles north, however, leaving me on a ramp where many cars passed in the morning. "You have a fresh new day," she said when she stopped the car. "Some other crazy person like me is sure to pick you up."

I thanked her for the ride, for the evening and wished her luck on her return to Maine. I didn't mention her fourth husband. She said one last thing to me before she sped away.

"There are crazy adventures out there."

She was right about that. There were crazy adventures out there.

The ride that took me over the New York State line, into Canada, was the most unlikely of all. A camper pulled over. Inside it were a mother and father up front (the father driving) and three small girls in the back. The girls' ages were four, six and nine. It seemed improbable. Why would parents with three small girls pick up a stranger? It makes no sense, when I think about it now, but as I said in the beginning these were different times. The world was more trustworthy, people friendlier.

I sat sandwiched between the six and nine year old girls. The six year old went through my pack, taking out my clothes and possessions. She played my harmonica, slobbering all over it. Meanwhile the four year old sat behind me, squealing the whole time. It was the nine year old who was the dangerous one. She kept biting my neck, intent on giving me a hickie, I truly believed. The mother and father talked up front, and only once did the mother say anything.

"Doris, stop biting that man's neck."

Of course her name was Doris. It was only fitting.

I laughed. Yes, the world was full of crazy adventures, and even crazier people.

ABOUT THE AUTHOR

Thomas Crockett is a theater teacher and director. His books include *Teaching Drama: Fundamentals and Beyond*; two full-length plays, *The Burrow People* and *A Tyrant for all Seasons*; and a novel, *The Right Bus to Heaven*. Born and bred in New York, Mr. Crockett has lived in California for 30 years and currently resides in San Mateo, 20 miles south of San Francisco.